Praise for GEMMA TOWNLEY

FOR LEARNING CURVES

"Townley shines at creating characters who
are engaging and realistic."
—*Booklist*

"Charming."
—*Publishers Weekly*

"[The] family dynamic is fascinating. . . . Jen is an appealing
character who is sure to please readers."
—*Romantic Times*

FOR LITTLE WHITE LIES

"A fabulous book with a brilliant central idea: Don't we all
sometimes want to become someone else? *Little White Lies* is
hilarious and gripping and poignant, and I adored it."
—SOPHIE KINSELLA, author of *Can You
Keep a Secret?* and *Confessions of a Shopaholic*

"With clean prose and engaging characters, Townley has
set a classic story in a hip locale."
—*Booklist*

FOR WHEN IN ROME

"A bubbly debut."
—*New York Daily News*

"Gemma Townley's story is infectious, sweet, charming, and
hysterical. She's an author after my own heart."
—SHERRIE KRANTZ, author of
The Autobiography of Vivian and *Vivian Lives*

"As sweet and frothy as a cappuccino, this engaging *Roman
Holiday*–inspired romp reveals the importance of a 'victory
haircut' and the transformative powers of shopping at Gucci."
—MELISSA DE LA CRUZ, author of *Cat's Meow*
and *How to Become Famous in Two Weeks or Less*

"A delightful debut."
—*Shape*

Also by Gemma Townley

WHEN IN ROME
LITTLE WHITE LIES
LEARNING CURVES

THE

Hopeless
Romantic's
HANDBOOK

THE

Hopeless
Romantic's
HANDBOOK

A Novel

◆ ◆

GEMMA TOWNLEY

BALLANTINE BOOKS ▥ NEW YORK

A Ballantine Books Trade Paperback Original

Copyright © 2007 by Gemma Townley

Published in the United States by Ballantine Books,
an imprint of The Random House Publishing Group,
a division of Random House, Inc., New York.

BALLANTINE and colophon are registered
trademarks of Random House, Inc.

ISBN 978-0-345-48004-0

Library of Congress Cataloging-in-Publication Data
Townley, Gemma.
The hopeless romantic's handbook : a novel / Gemma Townley.
p. cm.
ISBN-13: 978-0-345-48004-0
ISBN-10:   0-345-48004-X
1. Chick lit.   I. Title.
PR6120.O96H67 2007
823'.92—dc22
2006048367

Printed in the United States of America

www.ballantinebooks.com

2 4 6 8 9 7 5 3 1

Text design by Julie Schroeder

For Mark, who made this hopeless romantic hopeful

The path of the righteous man is, according to the Bible and that other great morality story Pulp Fiction, *beset on all sides by the inequities of the selfish and the tyranny of evil men.*

The path of the hopeless romantic isn't exactly a bed of roses either; it's beset by equally selfish and tyrannous men who say one thing and mean another, never return your calls, and generally act like idiots. Then there are the cynics who tell you that romance is a lie, that happy endings don't exist, and that you might as well give up now and marry that guy you dated last year. The one with the odor problem whose idea of a birthday present was tickets to a football game (his favorite team's football game).

The important thing is to recognize these people for what they are. To cast them aside and continue your quest for true, unadulterated love. And if, during this quest, you realize that your love interest isn't quite the knight in shining armor you thought he was, just smile graciously, move on, and be grateful that you didn't marry the pig. Not that he'd have asked you, of course, but that isn't really the point.

—The Hopeless Romantic's Handbook

ACKNOWLEDGMENTS

There are lots of people who deserve thanks for helping me complete *The Hopeless Romantic's Handbook*. First and foremost Dorie Simmonds for her unfailing good humor, wonderful ideas, and sheer determination—I couldn't have done it without you. Sincere thanks also go to my editors, Allison Dickens and Laura Ford, along with everyone at Random House and Ballantine who have been so supportive and helpful along the way. Warmest thanks to Jommers and Caroline Douglas, whose brains I picked remorselessly on all matters pharmaceutical; to Cancer Research UK, whose website was so incredibly helpful; and, last but not least, to my husband Mark—to whom this book is dedicated—for doing his best to help me when I hurled possible endings at him and asked him to pick one (and for not being upset when I ignored his choice completely).

THE

Hopeless

Romantic's

HANDBOOK

1

Kate Hetherington sighed and put down her drink dramatically.

"I just think there has to be a better way," she said, shaking her head in disbelief. "You'd think they'd have developed some sort of radar by now."

Her friend Sal frowned. "Radar?"

"To find the perfect man. So you don't have to endure things like speed dating. Honestly, Sal, it was the worst night of my life. I hated every minute of it. I hated every man in there. And at the end, I still came out disappointed that I only got one number. I mean, it's wrong on so many levels, I don't even know where to start."

Sal shrugged. "I bet it wasn't that bad. I think it sounds like fun, actually."

Kate looked at her friend levelly. "That's because you're happily married so you know you'll never have to go. Things like speed dating always sound like fun in principle—it's the reality that's so excruciating."

"So why did you go, then?"

"Because you made me."

"I didn't *make* you! I just said you should give it a go, that's all."

Kate sighed. "I know. I think a little voice inside me really thought it might work, too. I mean, I thought I might . . . meet someone's eyes and just know. . . ."

"But it didn't work out that way?"

"No," Kate said despondently. "And the truth is, I'm kind of running out of options here. I'm going to be thirty soon, and I don't see any knights on white steeds turning up to whisk me away, do you?"

Sal shook her head. "Does the steed have to be white?" she asked, a little smile playing on her lips.

Kate grinned. "I'm willing to stretch to cream," she conceded. "If the knight is good-looking enough."

"Ah, here you are. Sorry I'm late. So, how are we all?"

Kate and Sal turned round and saw their friend Tom approaching. "Dreadful, thanks," Kate said lugubriously. "How're you?"

Tom grimaced. "In need of a drink. Can I get either of you a refill?"

Kate handed him her glass, requesting a vodka tonic, and Sal shook her head. As he disappeared off toward the bar, she frowned. "And you're sure there wasn't a single eligible man there? Not even one?"

"Not even one," Kate assured her. "They were all either creepy, letchy, or just plain weird." Sal looked at her dubiously, and Kate's hackles rose. "What?" she demanded. "Don't you believe me?"

Sal widened her eyes. "I didn't say a thing!"

"No, but you looked at me like you wanted to. You think I would have missed some gorgeous guy just waiting to sweep me off my feet?"

Sal hesitated, then blurted, "I just think that maybe your aspirations are too high. I mean, all you talk about is sweeping and knights and stuff. Instead of nice-looking, or amenable. I'm just not sure you're looking for the right . . . qualities."

"Right qualities?"

Sal put her drink down. "This is the real world, Kate, that's all. Richard Gere isn't going to turn up in a convertible car to whisk you off into the sunset."

"I don't want Richard Gere to turn up," Kate snapped. "I just want . . ."

Sal raised her eyebrows expectantly.

"Fine," Kate said with a sigh. "I admit it. My aspirations are high. I want fireworks, and I want magic. What's wrong with that? I can't help it if I'd rather chew my own feet off than endure a night of speed dating again."

"Speed dating?" Tom asked, arriving with the drinks. "So you went, did you?"

Kate nodded. "Tried it, hated it, never doing it again." Avoiding Sal's eyes, she took her drink from Tom and shuffled her chair around to make room for him.

They were sitting in the Bush Bar and Grill, a bar-cum-restaurant that was five minutes' walk from each of their homes and which hosted their weekly Sunday night drinks date. The three of them lived streets away from one another in the area of London that sat between Shepherd's Bush, West Kensington, and Hammersmith. Which particular section they chose to tell people they lived in depended on whether they were at a job interview, trying to impress someone, or hoping not to get mugged. Sal and her husband Ed lived on a road that was officially in West Kensington; Kate's zip code said W6, which meant Hammersmith, but she was really closer to Shepherd's Bush. And Tom lived on the Golborne Road, a stone's throw from the Bush Bar and Grill, and two minutes' walking distance from both of the women.

"So it was as ghastly as it sounded?" Tom said dryly.

"Worse," Kate said. "I had to meet twenty people for five minutes, which isn't long, is it?" She gave Tom a hopeful look, and he nodded firmly. "But I still ran out of things to say," she said. "I mean, they asked such stupid stuff. Like if I was an animal, which one would I be and why. What sort of a question is that?"

Tom frowned. "What animal did you say you'd be?" he asked with interest.

"I started off with a dolphin, and then someone made a joke about sperm whales and I lost the will to live. After that, I was a crocodile twice, a rottweiler, and a meerkat." She smirked a little.

"Well, no wonder you didn't meet anyone nice," Sal complained. "They probably thought you were a total Froot Loop."

"But a very sweet Froot Loop," Tom said affectionately.

"I could set you up with one of Ed's friends, if you want," Sal interjected. "I think I can safely guarantee that none of them would ask you any animal-related questions at all."

"Thanks, Sal," Kate said with a shrug. "But I'm not sure I'd have much in common with many of Ed's friends. . . ."

Sal frowned. "Because you think financiers are all pinstripe shirt–wearing bores?" she asked crossly.

"No!" Kate said. "Not at all. But come on, you and Ed are so . . . grown-up."

"Ed's only thirty-five," Sal said defensively. "It's not so old. And I'm no older than you."

"I didn't say 'old.' Grown-up is different."

"How?" Sal asked, her eyes narrowing.

Tom grinned. "Sal, darling, don't play the innocent with us. We both know that when you're at home, you and Ed talk about stocks and shares and the impact of the Budget on your pensions. Whereas I doubt Kate here even has a pension. Do you, Kate?"

Kate shifted uncomfortably in her chair. "I'm going to. You know, at some point."

"Kate!" Sal said, shocked. "You don't have a pension? That's so . . . irresponsible."

"I rest my case." Kate sighed. "None of Ed's friends would be interested in me because I don't have a stock portfolio. I don't even know how I'd go about getting one. And the truth is, I don't even care. So either I have to give up completely, or accept that I'm going to have to spend the rest of my days at nasty speed-dating events at which hideous pigs leer and stare at my breasts all night. Bloody marvelous."

"Seriously?" Tom asked. "They stared at *your* breasts?"

Kate hit him. Her lack of cleavage was a running gag with Sal and

Tom. Had been since high school when she'd been the last girl in their whole class to need a bra. "One guy stared at them for the full five minutes, actually. And then he gave me his card and said he'd love to see me again! Can you believe it? Steve, his name was. I kept his card as a reminder of everything I'm not looking for in a man."

"Nothing wrong with staring at breasts," Tom said, grinning. "I think they're a great indicator of marriage potential, as it happens."

Sal rolled her eyes. "Tom, you are incorrigible. And I don't know why you're so laid-back about the whole thing, either. When's the last time you had a serious girlfriend?"

"I pride myself on steering clear of seriousness in the girlfriend department," Tom replied with dignity. "I have enough seriousness at work, thanks."

"Being a surgeon doesn't preclude you from falling in love," Sal continued. "Don't you ever meet anyone you actually like?"

Tom blanched. "*Like* is an odd word, don't you think?" He looked down at his empty glass. "I *like* lots of things. Doesn't mean I want to move in with them, does it? Doesn't mean I want to sign my life away."

Kate pounced on the opening. To Sal, she said, "See? You say I'm hopeless, but I'm not as hopeless as Tom."

"Ah, that's where you're wrong," Tom said quickly. "You are the epitome of a hopeless romantic. Hopeless, ironically, because you do hope that the fairytale love story will come true for you. I, on the other hand, am comfortable with the fact that it doesn't. Therefore, I, unlike you, am never going to be disappointed."

"You think I'm going to be disappointed?"

Tom raised his eyebrows. "Kate, for a man to live up to your expectations, he would have to be six-foot-four, strapping but sensitive, intelligent but always willing to accept your point of view, continually sweeping you off your feet and basically dedicating his life to you. For a woman to live up to mine, she would need to be . . . well, female. And perhaps not a complete dog."

Kate scowled. "I am not a hopeless romantic. That's rubbish."

"You're not?" Tom said with an ill-concealed grin. "Do you remember how many universities you had on your shortlist?"

She looked at him curiously. "Two," she said. "No, three."

"You may have had three in the end, but only because you were forced into it. Don't you remember? You were madly in love with that guy in the year above us, Paul James. And you insisted that you had to go to Bristol because that's where he was going, and the two of you were meant to be together."

"So?" Kate knew where this was going. "I liked Bristol. It was a great university."

"Yes, but you split up with Paul at the beginning of the summer holidays! You made a major decision about your life based on some romantic notion that you were meant to be with some spotty teenager, and it could have been a disaster."

"But it wasn't, was it?" Kate said hotly. "And at least I'm open to love. At least I'm open to commitment and marriage and living happily ever after. You've become way too cynical, Tom."

"Maybe. But if I have, then I'm pleased," Tom said with a dismissive wave of his hand. "Anyway, it's not as if anyone has ever expressed any interest in marrying me. I mean, would either of you take someone like me on?"

His eyes met Kate's for a moment, and she frowned. "God, no," she said quickly. "Can't think of anything worse."

Sal sighed. "Me either," she relented, prompting Tom to pull a face of disappointment. "Fine. Well, you both enjoy your lonely existences, and drop in on me and my boring husband from time to time, won't you?"

Kate leant over and squeezed Sal's arm. "Sal, you were always ahead of the game. You had your university offers before we'd even got round to applying. You had a job before either of us had got over our end-of-university hangovers. We'll get there eventually. At least, I hope we do."

Sal smiled. "Fine, you're right. But I still think you should let me set you up," she said with another sigh.

Kate shook her head. "Thanks, but no. I'll meet my Mr. Right eventually," she said, shooting Tom a meaningful look. "At least I hope I will."

"So you're just going to wait around for Mr. Right to show up?" Sal asked. "What if he doesn't? I mean, isn't it a bit . . . risky?"

"Isn't it more risky ending up with the wrong guy because you were too scared to wait around for Mr. Right?" Kate asked defensively.

Sal frowned and Kate immediately backtracked. "I didn't mean *you*. God, I just meant, you know, that I want to be sure. . . ."

"Okay," Sal said. "Well, lovely as this has been, I think it's time to call it a night. Ed will be back from his stupid client golf weekend any minute and it would be nice to see my husband for an hour this weekend before it's time for bed."

Kate nodded. "Yeah, I guess it's getting late."

"This is a sign that we're getting old, you realize," Tom said as they pulled on their coats. "A few years ago, ten P.M. still felt early."

"Not on a Sunday, Tom," Sal said matter-of-factly. "If you're not careful, you're going to turn into one of those people who says that summers are never as long as they were when you were young."

"They're not," he protested. "And it used to snow at Christmas time, too."

The three of them left the Bush Bar and Grill and emerged onto the Goldhawk Road, shivering against the February night. "I'm going to run, I'm afraid," Sal said as soon as they'd got outside. "See you next week sometime?" She blew kisses at both of them and hurried down toward the large house that she shared with her investment analyst husband.

Tom looked at Kate and grinned. "Come on, I'll walk you home," he said, putting his arm around her. "Can't have our hopeless romantic on the streets alone at this hour."

Kate gave a plaintive sigh as they began to walk. "You don't really think I'm hopeless, do you?" she asked Tom.

"I think you're an optimist," he replied cagily. "And that's not entirely a bad thing."

"Do you really mean it, about never getting married?"

He shrugged. "I dunno. I s'pose if I meet the right woman I might."

Kate nodded. "It's not as easy, is it? I mean, it's not as easy as they make it out to be. I sometimes wonder how on earth anyone ever manages to get together and stay together. How did our parents manage it?"

"They didn't. Not all of them," Tom said with a caustic twist of the lips.

Kate reddened. "Sorry. I didn't mean *your* parents." Actually, she realized none of their parents had exactly aced the whole love and marriage thing. Tom's mother had left out of the blue when he was just seven, Sal's mother had brought her up on her own, and her own parents had spent the last thirty years arguing.

"Hey, don't worry about it. I don't consider my mother to be a parent, anyway. I mean, you have to actually parent your child to get that moniker, right? Buggering off when he's eight and ceasing all contact doesn't exactly qualify, does it?"

"Still no word then?" she asked gently. Tom almost never talked about his mother. He had barely mentioned her existence since she disappeared one day with no explanation, not even a note. But Kate knew how much it had upset him; she had seen him emerging from the bathroom at school with red eyes, fiercely denying that he was in any way bothered. That was when he had started to get so cynical. Eight was a very tender age to realize that you couldn't trust even your own mother not to let you down.

Tom shrugged again. "Dad knows where she is. Personally, I don't want to know. Got more important things to worry about."

"Like avoiding commitment?" Kate asked, smiling.

"Exactly," Tom said, grinning. "So . . . what's next in your quest to find your knight in shining armor? Have you thought about putting an ad on the Internet? 'Knight wanted to save damsel in distress. Must have own horse.' "

They had arrived outside Kate's building, so she decided to ignore that last comment. Instead, she leant up and kissed Tom on the cheek. "'Night, Tom."

Tom ignored the hint. "Maybe," he continued with enthusiasm, "you should send your picture to the four corners of the earth to four different princes who have to undergo an arduous journey and several tasks in order to win your heart. Or maybe you need to get your fairy godmother on the case? I mean, you do have one, right?"

Kate shot him a look and closed the door. Bloody Tom. Well, she'd show him. She didn't know how, but that was surely just a detail.

She decided to have a bath before going to bed—a nice hot soak to extend the weekend slightly. And she also wanted to go through her e-mail. And tidy up the kitchen, which still had the remnants of breakfast cluttering up its surfaces.

Kate sighed. Somehow there was never enough time in the day to get things done. Never enough hours to get all the boring things out of the way and still leave time for the good things, like seeing friends, watching films, going for romantic walks in the park.

Then again, she didn't have anyone to go for romantic walks *with*.

Frowning, she went to the bathroom and turned on the taps, then made her way to her cluttered sitting room, where a desk in the corner jostled for space with a large, uncovered sofa; both were heaped high with color charts, magazines, and sketches.

What was wrong with being a hopeless romantic, anyway? Why was it such a bad thing to find true love? Wasn't that what everyone really wanted, deep down?

Pushing aside a pile of papers, she turned on her computer and waited for her e-mail to pop up. Three work-related ones that would wait until tomorrow. Daily Candy telling her to "say it with cupcakes" this weekend. Amazon, telling her that her latest order had been dispatched. A Russian "attractive blonde" offering her free sex if she visited a website chat room. But nothing from the beautiful man she'd seen in a coffee shop that morning. Their eyes had met briefly and she'd accidentally-on-purpose dropped a business card as she left, hoping that he might pick it up and get in touch. That's what would happen in a film. But evidently he hadn't fallen madly in love with her, after all. Hey, it was no big deal.

She slumped a little. Tom and Sal were right—she *was* a hopeless romantic. Beyond hopeless, in fact. She was nearly thirty, she had her own flat and a proper job and was meant to be mature and savvy, but instead she honestly thought she was Meg Ryan in *Sleepless in Seattle* or *You've Got Mail*. She should just marry one of Ed's friends and be done with it, living happily ever after in a nice four-bedroom house with pension plans coming out of her ears. Except she wouldn't be happy. She'd be miserable. She wanted a romance with the love of her life, not a boring marriage to a nice man in a pinstriped suit.

Maybe it was an illness, she thought. Maybe they'd find a cure for hopeless romantics one day—a pill that would take away the need for excitement and romance and make her like Tom, hardened and self reliant. Maybe there were self-help groups she could join, with a twelve-point plan to follow. Maybe she'd meet Meg Ryan's scriptwriters there, rocking back and forth, unable to cope in a world where Brad left Jen, Meg got divorced, and however long they waited at the top of the Empire State Building, no one turned up to meet them.

Opening up her Web browser, she smiled to herself, then went to Google and typed in "hopeless romantic." To her surprise, there were more than four million pages.

HOPELESS ROMANTICS: A SEMI-ELITE CLIQUE FOR PEOPLE WHO FIND
     ROMANCE IN EVERY SITUATION
HOPELESS ROMANTIC: THE BLOG OF A GIRL LOOKING FOR LOVE
HOPELESS ROMANTIC: TAKE OUR QUIZ AND DISCOVER JUST HOW TERMINAL
     YOU ARE!

HOPELESS ROMANTIC: JOIN US NOW FOR TIPS ON ENHANCING THE ROMANCE
  IN YOUR RELATIONSHIP

Incredulously, Kate started to scroll down through the pages.

HOPELESS ROMANTIC: A WAY OF LIFE, NOT A CONDITION
HOPELESS ROMANTIC: ONE WOMAN'S STRUGGLE AGAINST ADVERSITY

There were forums, and quizzes, and diary entries—thousands and thousands of them. She was not alone! Kate grinned as she continued to scroll.

HOPELESS ROMANTIC: SICK OF BEING CALLED HOPELESS?

"Yes!" Kate said out loud. "Yes I am!" She clicked.

Buy your ladyfriend a gift she'll never forget. We guarantee she'll never call you hopeless again!

Frowning, Kate clicked back. And then her eye caught something.

HOPELESS ROMANTIC: THE HOPELESS ROMANTIC'S HANDBOOK. OUT OF PRINT
  EDITION. AUCTION ENDS IN 2 MINUTES.

It was an eBay page. Clicking it, Kate soon found herself staring at the cover of a book that seemed to date to the 1950s. On the cover was a woman with a tiny waist, a huge circle skirt, and a twinkle in her eye.

Are you a hopeless romantic? Do you long for love and passion, and feel disappointed and let down by the reality of dating? Don't despair. The Hopeless Romantic's Handbook *will save you.*

Kate rolled her eyes. A handbook for romance? How ridiculous. How desperate.

But instead of closing the page, she found herself scrolling down.

The Hopeless Romantic's Handbook *is a handbook for life. Romance is yours for the taking; you just have to find it.* The Hopeless Romantic's Handbook *won't just tell you where to look, it will help you every step of the way. This book will change your life—satisfaction is guaranteed—if you don't find true love, get your money back.*

Kate stared at the page. Get your money back? That was crazy. Who was selling this book, anyway? She scrolled to the top of the page.

C*P1D24.

C*P1D24? What kind of weird moniker was that?

But still, a money-back guarantee. You didn't see that very often on eBay.

She frowned. No one had bid for the book yet, and the starting price was just £7. It wasn't a lot of money for a book that promised to change her life.

And it closed in one minute.

Of course she didn't need a handbook. The whole idea was ridiculous. A handbook to finding love?

Then again, she wasn't doing such a great job on her own. And it *was* only £7.

Quickly she refreshed the screen. Still no bids, and just twenty seconds to go. Drumming her fingers on the edge of her desk, she sighed.

"Fine, I'll buy it," she said to no one in particular, and placed a bid for £7.01. No sooner had she submitted it than a page flashed up announcing her the winner and suggesting that she pay by Paypal. Promising herself that this purchase would remain her little secret, she began to plug in her details. Then she heard her e-mail ping. It was an e-mail from C*p1d24. Except the address was rather less opaque—it was from a Helen.Brigsenthwaite@aol.com.

Hi! Congratulations and well done. You won't regret this purchase. It's the best thing that ever happened to me. Read, enjoy, and when you're done, pass it on to bring love into someone else's life. By the way, where are you so I can work out postage costs? Thanks, Helen x

Kate stared at the e-mail. The best thing that ever happened to her? This book must be amazing. Although she wasn't sure about passing it on. If it was that good, why would she part with it?

Thanks Helen, I'm in Hammersmith, she typed back quickly. *137 Sulgrave Road. So do you mean that you read this book and found love right away? Kate x*

Really? I work just around the corner. If you pay by Paypal, will drop it in tomorrow. Am so excited for you. Lots of love, Hxx

She hadn't answered the question, Kate noticed. And it was just a book not a miracle, she reminded herself. She'd find out soon enough whether it was really worth the hype.

2

Tom Whitson whistled as he walked down the street. He loved this time of year—the time of year that everyone else hated, the time of year that saw everyone else moaning about the cold, about the long nights, about spring being just around the corner and yet so elusive. What was wrong with cold, dark nights? That's what he wanted to know. What was so horrible about a biting wind that forced you to keep your coat collar up, your head down, and your business quick? It was bracing. It was difficult. It was real life.

Not like summer. Tom hated summer. Not the half-clad-women-walking-down-the-street-everywhere-you-looked element of summer; surely no one could complain about that. But he hated the expectation, the feeling that pervaded London in the sunshine that somehow life should be bigger and better, like an American sitcom or an R&B music video full of beautiful people having a great time together.

In the winter Tom felt safe, because everyone was miserable. In the winter, you went to work, went to the pub for a quick warming drink, and then battled home through the cold. And if you managed to persuade someone to battle home with you, then so much the better. The point was, no one expected any more of you. Survival was enough.

But in the summer, everything changed. People spilled out into street cafés, talking and laughing and being so bloody happy all the time. Girls who'd been perfectly content with a regular shag over the winter suddenly wanted to go away for the weekend, to walk along the river, to *talk about stuff*. Suddenly, being a cynical, difficult bastard wasn't enough anymore. Simply put, the summer made him inadequate—in his eyes as much as anyone else's. The summer showed him up for what he really was.

Still, he thought, pulling his coat around himself, summer was a long way off yet. Plenty of miserably cold, rainy days to get through first.

His mother had left in the summer: June 24, to be precise. And two days before she left, she'd complained bitterly that she never went out anywhere anymore. That *they* never went out anywhere anymore. Tom remembered taking her jacket off the peg along with his the following morning as he got ready to go to school and asking if she'd like to come with him. At least to the school gates.

She'd just laughed at him—not kindly but scornfully, as if he'd made things worse.

And the next day, she went away for good.

At first his father had said that she'd be back. Said that the hot weather did funny things to people's heads, gave them ideas and notions, but that she'd come to her senses soon enough and until then, they'd have a fine old time, just the two of them. . . .

Tom arrived at his building and rummaged around for his keys. He didn't know why he was even thinking about all of this. It was very unlike him to allow himself to dwell on the past. He'd managed to almost completely exorcise his mother from his memory years ago, at least he'd thought he had. Why give her space in his head, he'd rationalized, when there were so many more important things to remember? Like anatomy, like the names of all the girls he'd slept with, like the best route for getting from South London to North London in the traffic. His mother was singularly unimportant in the great scheme of things.

Then he remembered what had got him thinking about her. Of course, it was Kate. Kate and her romantic notions of love and happy ever after. He worried for her, he really did. Why would someone so clever, so funny, so pretty go around with such ridiculous notions stuffed into her head? Why couldn't Kate see that all this rubbish about knights in shining armor was just going to lead to disappointment, to a broken heart?

Tom found his stomach clenching as he thought of it. He had to make her see. He had to protect her. He knew how to deal with betrayal and let-downs, but he didn't want Kate to have to endure it. He couldn't bear to stand by and watch.

The fact of the matter was that the world wasn't populated by knights in shining armor who wanted to save damsels in distress like Kate. It was populated by angry, bitter people like him who thought only of themselves and didn't want to save anyone. And even if someone like him *did* want to save someone like Kate, even if they, deep down, might love to be the kind of person who could sweep someone like Kate off her feet and proclaim their undying love for her, that didn't mean zip. Fantasies were all very well, but that's all they were. In fantasy land, his mother never left. In fantasy land, he didn't hate himself. Which just went to show what a pile of crock fantasy land really was. And, he thought to himself as he opened his front door, it was his duty, his noble mission, to make sure that Kate realized that before it was too late.

3

"For God's sake, Kate, you're late, and we've barely got time for this meeting as it is." It was Monday morning, which meant that the *Future: Perfect* weekly planning meeting was in full swing. *Future: Perfect* was a makeover show that had an afternoon slot on cable television. Kate was the interiors stylist, a job she loved and hated in equal measure. Loved, because to her each makeover represented a mini fairy tale, in which a frog was kissed and turned into a prince, or a Cinderella was plucked out of the shadows and sent to the ball; hated, because the budgets were puny and most of her colleagues were total nightmares. Magda was the show's director/producer (*Future: Perfect* couldn't afford one of each) and she had about as much interest in fairytale makeovers as she had patience for latecomers.

Kate smiled brightly and quickly found a chair.

"I assume you've got everything planned out for next week's show," Magda continued, her eyes not moving from Kate's. "You know that it's going to be all about the house, don't you? Why don't you tell us your vision for the Joneses', Kate? Tell us what you're going to do to have people riveted to their television screens."

Kate sifted through her notes quickly, flustered by Magda's outburst. The housewife, she said to herself slowly. Of course. Carefully, she took out her notepad and reviewed her scribbled notes. *Downtrodden housewife*, she read. *Domestic. Warm glow of family meals. Rein-*

vigorate marriage. Down the side of the page were some sketches Kate had drawn, presenting a visual image of the "before" and "after" of her kitchen. Each makeover had to have a theme—this one was trying to get a dowdy housewife's husband to notice her again.

Future: Perfect was known, much to Magda's annoyance, as the poor cousin of shows like *Extreme Makeover*, even though it had been there first, as she reminded anyone and everyone anytime she got a chance. The show's remit was pretty straightforward: Each week one person or couple would be made over by the team—their house, their face, and their clothes—all on camera and all leading up to the great unveiling when the person or couple, known by everyone who worked on the show as the victim or victims, would see their new look in a mirror and, hopefully, cry tears of joy. The trouble was that, with *Future: Perfect*'s miserably small budget, the victims more often than not failed to cry; in fact, they failed to do much more than peer at themselves and their houses with a look that suggested they were mildly disappointed.

Which was probably why Magda was so agitated, Kate decided. Sarah Jones, next week's victim, had been chosen carefully and Magda had made it clear to everyone that she was expecting Big Things from this episode. That she wanted people Glued to Their Screens.

"I was going to do a take on the whole Cath Kidston look," Kate said confidently. "Lots of chintz, but cool, not too country. I want to make her sexy in the kitchen—bring out the earthy sexiness of cooking, moving her out of the shadows and into the center. Maybe even slight dominatrix undertones. . . ." The dominatrix undertones hadn't been part of her plans at all, but suddenly she felt a bit reckless.

Magda was nodding furiously. "Dominatrix undertones? I love it. What else? Maybe we could convince her to leave that dolt of a husband? Set her up with a new man?"

Kate looked at her incredulously. "Or," she said, "we could reignite their marriage." She smiled, struck by inspiration. "Maybe at the end they could renew their vows! They could do it there, in the kitchen, with their children as page boys and . . ."

Magda rolled her eyes. "Don't make me puke. Anyway, breakups make much better television. Still, dominatrix undertones might do it, if we can maybe persuade her to wear some high heels. Maybe flick her husband's arse with a feather duster or something. If we get a good enough shot they might put a photograph on the television listing pages."

"Maybe Lysander could dress her in rubber," Kate said. "That ought to get the ratings up, too."

Lysander was "wardrobe," although he preferred to be called "fashion editor." He had been poached from *GQ* magazine by Magda when she'd first joined the show and had ambitions to take it onto terrestrial television within a year. This would be the making of both of them, she'd told him seriously. This was television—so much better than magazines. He'd be crazy not to take it.

That had been three years ago, and the program had not only not made it onto terrestrial, but had lost its seven P.M. slot, instead being shunted into a three P.M. daytime wilderness slot, destined to be watched by the ill, the unemployed, the retired, and exhausted mothers, none of whom interested Lysander. In the meantime his former colleagues were rising up the ranks to edit high-profile glossy magazines. They were interviewing Alexander McQueen and sitting in the front row at the runway shows in Paris, London, and New York, while he was advising overweight women on the slimming possibilities of black.

Of course, they weren't on television, he would always say, which was the one thing that he held on to, the one thing that made life tolerable. As he pointed out on a regular basis, when you told people you worked in television, they were impressed, period. So it was cable, so it was the dregs of the dregs. Television gave you kudos. Television could *lead somewhere*. That had become his mantra, repeated whenever he read about a former colleague taking over the reins at American *Vogue* or joining John Galliano's top team at Dior.

"I suppose I'm what you call a Z-list celebrity," he would joke modestly with his friends, secretly thinking that he was at least D list, if not C, and comforting himself that even D list was better than nothing.

Magda scowled at Kate. "You may not have noticed, but our ratings are dwindling to the just-above-dreadful level. And if they don't improve, there will be no more *Future: Perfect.* So let's all think of constructive ways to improve the show, shall we, instead of slating good ideas?"

Kate nodded.

"Come on then, Lysander. Give us what you've got," Magda said with a put-upon sigh.

Lysander raised an eyebrow. "I suppose I can do something to fit that . . . idea," he drawled in a way that suggested that Kate's concept was hardly worthy of the term. "So, what, we're thinking Bree Van De Kamp meets Camilla Parker Bowles? A bit country, but with simmering undertones of pent-up emotion and sexual longing. Some floral, here and there, but tamed, not allowed to . . . to . . ."

"To proliferate," Kate suggested, and Lysander shrugged.

"Camilla Parker Bowles?" Magda said with a dubious look. "That doesn't sound dominatrix. Sounds more like to the bloody manor born."

"Don't worry, Magda," Lysander said graciously. "We'll get some rubber in there, even if it's just rubber gloves."

Magda, looking unconvinced that Camilla Parker Bowles would propel them into the serious league of makeover shows, turned to Gareth, who did hair and makeup, and who was Kate's only real friend at work.

"Gareth? Anything to add?" Magda asked with another sigh.

Gareth nodded as grimly as if he'd been asked what the evacuation of the Gaza Strip meant to the peace process in the Middle East. "Well," he said after a dramatic pause, "it's a delicate balance. Sensible with a dash of sexy. Easy to do herself, but difficult enough to force her to make an effort. Different enough for her husband to notice the change, but not a shock to the system. Do you know what I'm saying?"

Kate suppressed a giggle. Gareth was the only person on the show who took the makeovers as seriously as she did—more, usually. To him, makeup and hair were life and death matters. As he told her whenever she'd had a run-in with Magda, or, worse, Penny the presenter, "This show changes lives, Kate. We carry that responsibility with us every day. It's an honor, you know. And people appreciate us so much. . . ."

"Alright," Magda said, after looking for a moment as if she wanted to ask Gareth what on earth he was talking about and then deciding against it. "Right, we've got no surgery this week, but we're getting Mr. Fitness in to design her a workout."

"Using tins from the kitchen cupboards," Gareth interjected. "Make sure he uses kitchen implements. 'A workout any woman can do at home . . .'" His eyes lit up as Lysander rolled his eyes in disgust.

"Brilliant," Magda said briskly. "Okay. Now, where the fuck is Penny?" She slanted an irritated look first at the door, then at the clock.

Penny Pennington was the presenter of *Future: Perfect*, an appointment that Kate sometimes thought had been agreed on the basis of her name's alliteration alone—well, that and her cozy relationship with the tabloid newspapers and gossip magazines whose covers she graced whenever she could muster a worthy story. Penny had been a child star in the 1980s, presenting a television show and hitting the Top Ten with a sickly-sweet single, and had never quite managed to repeat her success. The nineties had seen her releasing several songs which never hit the Top Forty, appearing in an advertising campaign for teeth-whitening toothpaste, and every so often cropping up in a celebrity magazine—once for the shock news that "one of Britain's best-loved child stars was in rehab for alcohol addiction," once for the announcement that she was getting married to a slightly better known television magician, a few times six months on, reporting that the marriage was in trouble, and eight months on, that it was over. It had been her appearance on *I'm a Celebrity—Get Me Out of Here!* that had really turned her fortunes. She'd been voted out of the reality show relatively early, but her regular spoilt-brat fits and refusal to take part in any of the Bushtucker trials had led to her being dubbed Penny Petulant, and several "exclusives" in *Hot Gossip* magazine, *Closer*, *OK!*, and *Tittle Tattle* followed.

Future: Perfect had been the only actual job offer to come out of it, however, with the promise of a salary large enough to cover the rent on a smart Chelsea apartment. But Penny viewed the show with complete disdain, as a stopgap that would kill time whilst she waited for her real celebrity career to kick back in.

On Magda's cue, the door swung open and Penny herself walked in, her eyes covered in dark glasses and her bleached blond hair hanging like straw around her face.

"So?" she said, waiting as a researcher evacuated her chair so that she could sit down. "What shit am I going to have to work with this week?"

Magda looked at her steadily. "Actually, Penny, we've got a nice little angle for the show next week. The woman in Essex, remember?"

Penny snorted. "The one who couldn't stop stuffing her face with cake?"

"We're going for country with a twist," Magda continued, ignoring Penny's little outburst. "We're focusing on wardrobe and interiors for this one—and our reference point is Camilla Parker Bowles."

Penny briefly raised her dark glasses in a dramatic gesture to give everyone a glimpse of her heavily kohled, watery blue eyes, which always shocked because they seemed so at odds with the rest of her appearance. Evidently satisfied that she'd achieved the required reaction, she placed her sunglasses back on her nose. "Even Camilla Parker Bowles doesn't warrant that kind of put-down," she sneered, then shrugged. "Fine, so Kate will be buying a couple of tea towels and Lysander'll buy her a cheap and nasty tweed jacket, I suppose.

And as usual, it'll be left to me to turn this into something that people might actually want to watch." She sighed and took out her BlackBerry, as if satisfied that nothing else of interest would come out of the meeting.

Magda took a deep breath. "Okay then," she said. "On to this week's filming. We've got the Moreleys' unveiling to get in the can—Gareth, I want you close at hand in case their nose jobs look dodgy. And Kate, have the builders finished in their house yet? We need everything ready for Wednesday, okay?"

"No problem," Kate said, crossing her fingers.

"Good." Magda handed out some pieces of paper. "Oh, and Kate, we've had a few calls from that woman—Mrs. Jacobs. From the golden oldies show we did a few weeks ago? Very upset about something from the number of times she's called."

Kate looked up, worried. "You want me to call her back?"

Magda stared at her as if she were mad. "Bloody hell, no. I'm getting the lawyers onto it."

Kate frowned. "The lawyers?"

Magda nodded. "Stop her suing for damages. Show can't afford it, Kate. You should think about that sometimes when you have some of your more extreme ideas."

"Extreme ideas?" Kate said. "Just because I like to be a bit creative . . ."

"Creating a grotto in someone's bedroom?" sighed Magda.

"That was ages ago!"

"Building a four-poster bed in a tiny semi in Birmingham?"

"They loved it. They said it was amazing."

Magda looked at her with disbelief. "Look, all I'm saying is that not everyone likes your designs all the time. I'm sure the lawyers will be able to deal with this one, but it's worth thinking about, okay?"

Kate stared right back. "Carole Jacobs said at the time that she loved her makeover," she said indignantly. "I remember her saying that she loved the way I used her wedding veil as a mini-net curtain in the bathroom."

"Well, that's worth telling the lawyers," Magda said, sighing yet again. "Don't take it so personally, Kate. She's probably only after money."

"I wasn't taking it personally until you said people didn't like my designs," Kate muttered.

"I said *some* people," Magda said irritably. "Now, can we please get on with some work? Otherwise there won't be any designs to sue us over, will there?"

4

"She *said* she liked my ideas. She approved the designs, she helped me pick out colors. . . . Why would she complain now? I mean, how can she complain when she told me how great it was?"

Kate and Gareth were sitting in the Footprint Production minibus on the way back from that afternoon's filming at a house in South London. Gareth put his hands over his ears, then sighed and turned to her. "Okay, number one, change the bleeding record. Seven hours you've been talking about this. Number two, maybe she liked it then and doesn't like it now. Or maybe a cameraman smashed one of her valuable antiques without noticing. And number three, who cares anyway, because legal is going to deal with it. Just let it go. Pretend you don't know she called up."

Kate glared at him. "But I do know she called. I bet you wouldn't be saying that if she'd called to say she was suing us because her hair looked awful."

Gareth smiled. "That's because no one ever complains about my hair or makeup. I'm a miracle worker, Kate, with enormous talents. It's a responsibility, but I like to think I use my powers wisely."

Kate rolled her eyes. After a pause she asked quietly, "Do you think my designs are over the top?"

"Finally." Gareth grinned. "This is what you've been worrying about all day, isn't it? I knew it."

"You didn't answer my question," Kate said. "Do you?"

He shook his head. "I love them. Kate, you bring sunshine and light into small terraces with dodgy plumbing. Don't listen to Magda—she wouldn't know real talent if it bit her on the arse. Why else would she have recruited Penny?"

Kate attempted a smile. "But Carole Jacobs obviously didn't like my design either."

"So what?" he said. "Do you really care what people think?"

She shrugged. "Yes, actually, I do."

"Ah," he said. "Well that's your problem, then. That's what you need to work on. Develop a thicker skin, that's my advice."

"What if I can't?" She hated the plaintive note in her voice.

Gareth smiled beatifically, put his arm around her, and looked her right in the eyes. "Then get a new job," he said. "Because if you ask me one more time whether I think Carole Jacobs liked your color scheme, I'm going to punch you, okay?"

The book was waiting for Kate when she got home an hour later. It was wrapped in brown paper and string and had been covered up by a whole heap of junk mail promising the best curry in London, first-class cleaning services, and low-cost mini cabs, but Kate saw it right away, partly because of its size, and partly because all day long in the back of her mind she'd been wondering what it was going to be like. What sort of book could change your life and bring you love—guaranteed?

She picked the parcel up and took it into the kitchen, where she poured herself a glass of water and drank it. She almost didn't want to open the package, didn't want to spoil the anticipation and expectation. Because whatever this book was, it was bound to be a let-down. No book could do what C*p1d24 had promised it would.

Could it?

Feeling her curiosity build, Kate finally picked up the parcel and began to peel off the brown paper. It was a hardback book, quite small—no more than two hundred pages—and it looked just as it had on the eBay page. Except now it was in her hands. Now it was hers.

Kate opened the book and began to read.

Dear Reader,

To the romantic at heart, the world is a place of grave beauty. And yet, to many, the romantic epitomizes an unrealistic dream—a yearning, a hope—that can never be fulfilled. To those people, I say that to be romantic is not to be hopeless. To be romantic is to have high expectations of yourself and others. To be romantic is to have dignity and coyness in equal measure; to value tradition whilst embracing all things new; to be bold and determined whilst also graceful and polite. The romantic sees the golden possibilities that so many ignore. The romantic never gives up or retreats into cynicism.

Of course, the romantic needs no handbook to guide her through life's pleasures. And yet, a helping hand is always welcome to those determined to succeed. And so, Reader, it is in this spirit that I have written The Hopeless Romantic's Handbook, *a book which I hope will be of some use to you as you glide through the adventures that lie before you, whether exotic and exciting or domestic and pleasing. I know that each of you can and will fall in love, that you can and will find the man of your dreams, and that you can and will enjoy a life of happiness, fulfillment, and, above all, romance.*

Yours humbly,

Elizabeth Stallwood

Kate read the introduction several times. Elizabeth Stallwood was so right. Kate *did* see golden possibilities that others ignored. And she didn't give up or retreat into cynicism. At last here was someone who understood, who saw the world as she did. She turned to the front and checked out the publication date. 1956. Okay, so the advice might be a little . . . *vintage*, but at least here was someone who wouldn't tease her for wanting her own fairy tale and wouldn't chide her for creating interiors that went beyond a boring color scheme.

Tom and Sal, eat your hearts out, she thought happily as she started to flick through the chapters. It was true, she didn't *need* a handbook. But she wasn't going to turn down a helping hand when it was offered.

5

Opening the Door to Opportunity

We all dream of meeting our future husband, and we know just what we will do when we do. We prepare for the day, keeping our figures trim and buying a dress in just the right flattering shape. We tell ourselves that he won't stand a chance, that we'll be witty, enticing, and alluring. We plan and practice the meals that we will cook for him and perfect our smile in the mirror in order to welcome him home after a busy day.

And yet, what preparation do we make to meet him? Just how widely do we spread our nets when we are trying to catch a mate? Do we regularly take a different route to work or visit a different gallery? Do we keep ourselves open to all possibilities?

Sadly, we do not. We hem ourselves in with routines; we say no to things or people that are unknown to us. In short, every single day we limit our possibilities for romance. The right stockings and the latest true red lipstick will be for nothing if you let the man of your dreams slip by because you are too busy following the same path that you tread every day.

And so, ladies, I propose a change. Do something different today. Take a different road to the greengrocer; buy a different cut of meat. Be bold in your choices, accept invitations that previously you may have shunned.

Perhaps this way you will meet your future husband; perhaps you won't. But either way, by bringing something fresh into your life, you will begin to *see the world differently. You will be enchanted again by things you have taken for granted. You will see that beauty is never far from your door. And you will find romance in the small things of life, which are as important as the significant ones.*

Remember that if you only stick to what you know, then what you know now is all that you will ever have. And unless your romantic dreams have already come true, what you know now is unlikely to ever be enough.

Kate munched her crunchy oat cereal as she turned the pages of *The Hopeless Romantic's Handbook* and put a bookmark in when she'd got to the end of the first chapter. Then she finished her cereal and put her bowl in the dishwasher. Do something different today, she mused. Do something different. . . .

Not that she was following the handbook word for word or anything. This was, after all, a book written for women whose daily activities were limited to going to the greengrocer and welcoming their husbands back after a day in the office. It was hopelessly out of date and really very chauvinistic.

But still, Kate thought to herself as she walked to the bathroom and started to brush her teeth, when was the last time she did something really different?

Then she frowned. Speed dating had been different. Different and awful. Different and soul destroying.

But maybe that was the wrong kind of different. Maybe Elizabeth Stallwood meant that she should walk down a new street; do something that she'd usually avoid. Like bungee jumping (Kate considered hanging from a bridge by a length of elastic to be one of the most awful and terrifying concepts, better only than a parachute jump). Or swimming (enjoyable enough, but the chlorine played havoc with her highlights). Perhaps she should investigate some local evening classes. Or take the bus to work instead of the tube. Maybe the man of her dreams was at this moment waiting at the bus stop, hoping against hope that she might walk into his life. . . .

Kate sighed as she rubbed some moisturizer into her face. Or maybe not. "Work" today meant a house in South London, which would mean a hideously long bus journey spent squished in beside some woman with her five noisy children surrounded by the vague stench of pee that always seemed to hang in the air.

Still, it would be a change from the cramped tube, where the stench was of her fellow commuters' armpits.

She stared at herself in the bathroom mirror. If her life was going to take off anytime soon, she realized, she was going to have to do something about it. Like Elizabeth Stallwood said, if she didn't change herself, her life wouldn't change either. But if she did change . . . well, who knew what might happen. Fine, she thought. Today she would do things differently. Today, she would say yes instead of no, and take the road less traveled.

Today would be the day that she stopped dreaming and started doing.

Picking up her things and putting on her coat, she left her flat and made her way purposefully toward the bus stop.

"What the hell happened to you?"

Kate scowled at Gareth. "I took the bus."

Gareth looked at her, waiting.

"It was raining," she continued, her voice brittle as she took off her coat, which was dripping with water, and hung it on a peg in the Moreleys' hallway. "And two buses went past, full of people so I couldn't get on. Then I got on one, but I didn't realize it was terminating in Clapham Junction and the driver told me I'd have to wait for another one to get down to Dulwich. So I did, but the next one was full again . . ."

"And you took the bus why?"

Kate stared dismally at her reflection in the hallway mirror. Her hair was plastered to her face, and mascara was wending its way down her cheeks.

"I thought it would make a change," she said, cursing Elizabeth Stallwood and promising herself that she wouldn't read another word of that stupid book.

"Right," Gareth said uncertainly. "Well, the bad news is Magda's looking for you. Penny wants to film the house unveiling this morning."

"This morning?" Kate looked at him in shock. "But that's impossible. We're meant to do it tomorrow. Magda said it would be tomorrow."

Gareth shrugged. "Better take it up with her nibs," he said. "In fact, speak of the devil . . ."

Kate spun around and saw Magda racing toward her.

"Kate. Got to bring forward filming to today. Don't argue, just get everything ready, will you?"

"But I can't! It's impossible!" Kate cried. "Nothing's ready. We've got to paint, to hang wallpaper—there's no way—"

"I said don't argue," Magda interrupted as she looked up from her clipboard, and Kate's heart sank. "I don't want to hear any— Bloody hell. What happened to you?"

Kate grimaced. "It's raining. I was waiting for a bus. Several buses, in fact."

"You look awful!" Magda said, goggling at her as if she were some strange, wild animal that she didn't want to get too close to.

"Yes, I do," Kate agreed.

"You can't go on camera looking like that," Magda said. "Not a chance. Oh, bloody hell. Where's Lysander? Maybe we can do the clothes today instead. Okay, Kate, we'll leave you till tomorrow. Gareth, where the hell's Lysander? Tell him I want to see him right now."

She marched off toward the kitchen and Kate felt her shoulders drop a couple of inches in relief. Saved by the bus. Or lack of one, rather.

"Someone's lucky today," Gareth said archly. "You could have been in trouble there."

"Just get me a hairbrush," she said with a little smile as she walked toward the Moreleys' sitting room. "Elizabeth Stallwood, all is forgiven," she muttered under her breath. "Here's to doing things differently."

As soon as she got to the Moreleys' sitting room, Kate knew that things were not going smoothly. It had been decided last week—three days into the project—that the unveiling would take place in the sitting room, instead of the bedroom where Kate had been focusing all her efforts. After failing in her argument for sticking to the original plan, she had begrudgingly come up with a plan B, which involved hastily stripping the wallpaper above the fireplace in the sitting room, rehanging plain wallpaper, and painting it the lovely browny pink color she'd used in the bedroom. She had carefully explained to her trusty builder, Phil, just what she wanted him to do, and he had spent the previous afternoon trying to implement the plan.

What neither of them had banked on was that when he started to strip off the wallpaper large chunks of the wall came with it.

"You're going to have to take it all down and replaster," Phil said with a sigh when Kate arrived, her hair wrapped up in one of Mrs. Moreley's towels.

Kate looked at him in shock. Magda, who had materialized beside her, just laughed.

"Replaster? Are you mad? We're filming tomorrow. Kate, tell the man. No plastering. He's going to have to cover it up."

Kate bit her lip. Magda was right—there was no time to replaster. But how could they cover up something so awful? How could she live with herself? This was why she ended up with people like Carole Jacobs threatening to sue.

Magda swept out of the room and Kate looked at Phil helplessly.

"Is there anything else we can do?" she pleaded. "Some trick of the trade you can use to save the day?"

Phil shook his head sadly, as he always did when filming had to take precedence over workmanship. It had taken a great deal of persuasion to get him to work for *Future: Perfect*—as he told Kate at the time, he was a simple bloke; he enjoyed what he did, and once he had enough money in the bank, he and the missus were going to retire to Spain, where the sun shined and the wine flowed. Working with a bunch of neurotic "TV people," as he referred to Penny, Magda, the film crew, and associated runners, and never doing anything properly was not what he enjoyed. Kate hated cutting corners, too, but she'd had too many stand-up arguments with Magda already, and they never got her anywhere. What mattered in Magda's book was what the camera saw; the rest could go hang. Or not, as the case may be.

"The paper's hanging off the wall," Phil said in a monotone. "Look at the plasterwork. Or, rather, the lack of it."

Kate followed his eyes to the wall where the Moreleys' gold and pink wallpaper was hanging desolately, large clumps of plaster clinging to it for dear life. Phil was right—he couldn't paper over that. Nor could he paint it. There was no way anyone could rectify that mess in just twenty-four hours.

"Phil, we need to do *something*." She felt sweat start to trickle down her back. "Maybe we could just film right behind the sofa, so the peeling bit won't be visible."

Phil shook his head again. "And what are we going to fix the new wallpaper to? Are we going to start it midway down the wall? Come on."

At that moment, Magda came storming back in. "Come on, come on," she said briskly. "What are you standing around for?"

Kate took a deep breath. "Magda, we're going to have to delay filming. I haven't had enough time, and we need to replaster—look at the walls. We'll have to film the unveiling on Thursday instead."

Magda laughed. "You're joking, right? You better be joking. Filming is tomorrow. Camera crew will be here tomorrow. By

Thursday we'll be on our way to Sarah Jones's to turn her into a dominatrix housewife. Understand?"

"But look at the walls!" Kate begged. "The bedroom ones are beautiful, but these . . . well, they're awful."

"So cover them. Come on, Kate. Phil, ever heard of a staple gun?"

Kate saw Phil flinch. Staple guns were worse than the devil as far as he was concerned. "If we use a staple gun, the paper will stay up for a day or two and then it'll fall down again," he said tersely.

"By which time we'll have finished filming," Magda said with a bright smile.

She swept off, leaving Kate glowering after her. How was she supposed to bring romance into people's lives when no one cared what happened when the cameras stopped rolling?

"You want me to staple gun the old wallpaper with plaster hanging off it to the wall?" Phil's expression was blank.

"We don't have an alternative," Kate said weakly, and watched as Phil mooched off.

Then she frowned. Wasn't this the day for doing things differently? There was always an alternative, wasn't there? "Phil," she said, and he turned round.

"Maybe you want me to use a bit of double-sided sticky tape an' all?" he asked.

Kate shook her head. "Underneath the plaster, do you know if it's brick?"

Phil nodded. "It is."

Kate found a smile wending its way across her face as she realized she might have a solution after all. "So let's take it back to the brick, then. Take it right back and we'll paint the bricks instead of the plaster."

"The bricks? You sure about that?"

"It'll be a feature!" Kate said with growing excitement. "It'll look great. I know it will. It'll add a warmth to the room, a bit of the history of the house exposed. The Moreleys will be able to look at it and think about all the different things that those bricks have been there through."

"And you think they're going to like it?"

Kate frowned, coming back to earth. "Of course they will. Or do you want to staple-gun wallpaper to the wall?"

"Bricks it is," Phil said, his eyes twinkling. "I tell you, things are never boring with you around." He wandered off just as Gareth reappeared.

"We're going back to the brickwork," she said. "In the sitting room."

"Isn't that a bit eighties?" Gareth asked, one eyebrow raised.

"No, it's very now. Very warehouse apartment, actually," Kate said a little defensively.

"Right. Only, we're not in a warehouse apartment are we?"

The hopeful smile slipped off her face. "I just thought it would be . . . different. You know."

"Oh, yes, I forgot. You're doing 'different' today. So, fancy a drink after work?"

Kate shook her head. "You know my rule. No socializing after work on Monday or Tuesday," she said firmly, then met Gareth's pointed stare. "Right. I see what you mean. Okay, yes. A drink sounds like a good idea. Definitely."

"You don't usually offer to lend me huge amounts of cash, either," Gareth said, grinning. "If you did that, it would be different."

Kate raised her eyebrows. "I said different, not insane," she said. "Don't push your luck."

"So," Gareth said several hours later, "you never told me how the speed dating went. Get many numbers?"

They were in a bar just around the corner from the Footprint Production offices in Acton, an area of West London once known for its sprawling housing estates, now gradually being gentrified with the overspill of professionals from Shepherd's Bush.

Kate grimaced. "I've managed to wipe it from my memory," she said. "It was awful. I tell you, never again."

Gareth raised an eyebrow. "You didn't have a good answer to the animal question, I take it?"

Kate looked up with a frown. "You know about the animal question?"

"Well, duh!" Gareth's tone was incredulous. "Everyone knows about the animal question. It's the first thing you get off pat; otherwise you're sunk."

"Thanks for warning me," Kate said crossly.

He shrugged. "So what did you say? Something cute and furry?"

"A dolphin, actually."

"Oh dear." Gareth cringed.

"It's cute!"

"It's a fish. No one wants to shag a fish," Gareth said, shaking his head.

"It's a mammal, not a fish. Anyway, it doesn't matter, because there was no one there who was remotely interesting," Kate said, keen to move the conversation on.

He nodded with faux sympathy. "No one ask for your details, did they?"

"Yes, some did," Kate said. "Well, one, anyway."

"Out of how many?"

"Twenty-four."

"Ouch. Well, I can see why you want to do things differently. One out of twenty-four's enough to make you want to skip the country. You poor thing."

"I'm not a poor thing," Kate said irritably. "Anyway, I don't want to meet someone speed dating. If it's going to happen, it'll happen."

Gareth emitted a low whistle. "You say that now, but give it a few years and you'll be going to speed dating every night of the week. I mean, things aren't looking that good, are they?" he said, shaking his head again.

"Yes they are!" Kate said, indignant. "They're looking very good.

There are millions of guys out there. And I only want one of them. Somewhere out there is my perfect guy."

"Yeah, that's where you're going wrong," Gareth said. "No such thing as perfect. You want to aim for about eighty percent. Eighty-five percent and you're onto a serious winner."

"Eighty percent? What does that even mean?"

"It means," Gareth said with studied patience, "that you have to approach it like . . . like shoe shopping. The ultimate pair simply doesn't exist, so you just have to decide where your twenty-percent compromise will be—color, quality of leather, cut, fit, shape of heel . . . you know."

"But I don't want to compromise," Kate complained. "I shouldn't have to compromise."

"Everyone compromises," Gareth said, exasperated. "Everyone!"

"No," Kate said. "No, they *don't*. Because if everyone compromises, then what's the point? If all you're ever going to get is eighty percent, then why not take seventy-five percent, or seventy? Why not just marry the first person you meet and hope for the best, and if they end up cheating on you or leaving you for someone else, then hey, no big deal. I mean, why not just forget all about love?"

Her eyes were flashing, and Gareth shrank back a little. "Fine." He held up his hands in surrender. "Whatever you say."

"Sorry." Kate shrugged. "I just . . . I want more than that, you know?"

"No, you're right." Gareth nodded sagely. "So come on then, what are you looking for? What's Mr. Right going to be like?"

Kate leaned back, thinking about it. Her lips relaxed into a little smile. "Well . . . he's got to be gorgeous, and clever and kind and . . ."

Her voice trailed off as her eyes clocked the barman and he grinned at her. She felt herself blush. He was gorgeous: tall, tanned, with short blond hair and the most amazing smile.

". . . and crazy about me," she concluded, forcing herself back to Gareth, who gave her an inquisitive look.

"And you think someone like that will just walk into your life? Well, if he does turn up, tell me will you? Because I want to go out with his brother. Now go and get us another drink."

Kate swiveled round. "A drink?" That would mean going up to the bar. Now that the barman had smiled at her, he'd think that she was going up there to talk to him. She grinned. "No problem. What do you want?"

"Lager top, please," Gareth said, handing her his glass. "And some peanuts. Or crisps. See if they've got those low-fat ones."

Kate bit her lip and walked toward the bar.

"Hey. How're you?"

She gulped. He was American. And even better looking close up. He had lovely brown eyes and long eyelashes and the squarest jaw she'd ever seen.

"I'm fine. Thank you," she said, doing her best to appear completely unfazed. "I'd like a lager top, please, and a glass of pinot grigio."

"Sure," he said. "Although, if the wine's for you, can I suggest the chardonnay instead? It's from California and it's really something."

Kate smiled. "Sure. Chardonnay sounds good, thanks."

"You're welcome." He grinned at her, and she felt herself blushing again. "You live near here?" he asked.

Kate shook her head. "Work," she said. "Although I live relatively near. Shepherd's Bush. Hammersmith. You know . . ."

The barman shrugged. "Actually, I don't. I'm new in town. Don't know anywhere. Or anyone."

"You . . . you don't?" Kate asked. "So, why are you here? I mean, what made you come to London?"

"I'm an actor," he said, putting the drinks in front of her. "From LA. Wanted to try my hand over here, you know?"

Kate gave him a nervous smile. She didn't know at all, but now was no time to admit that. "Wow," she said, "that's amazing."

"And what do you do?" he asked.

Kate shrugged self-deprecatingly. "I work in television," she said. "My production company is just up the road."

"Television? Well, that's very interesting," the barman said, his eyes lighting up. "That's five pounds, twenty pence for the drinks, by the way. And I'm Joe."

Kate fumbled in her purse for money and finally managed to dig out the right change. "Here," she said. "I'm Kate."

"Nice to meet you, Kate," Joe said, smiling.

"And you," she said, now feeling distinctly hot under the collar. Joe. Joe the actor from LA. Joe the utterly gorgeous actor from LA with a smile that would make anyone swoon at ten paces. And Gareth doubted that someone like that would walk into her life? Okay, so it had been her who had done the walking, but they were both here, weren't they?

"Maybe I'll see you again," Joe said, still smiling.

Kate nodded. "I hope so."

"Might help if you gave me your number."

She stared at him. "You . . . you want my number?"

"You don't want to give it to me?"

"No! I mean, yes. I mean . . ." Kate pulled out a business card. "My mobile's on it," she said hurriedly. "If you want to . . . Well, you can get me on that number at any time."

"Any time, huh?" Joe asked, his eyes twinkling. "Well, that sounds like quite a proposition."

Kate managed another weak smile and, clutching the drinks, made her way back to the table where Gareth was sitting.

"Took you long enough," he said. "What were you doing—chatting up the barman or something?"

She smiled enigmatically.

"You were!" Gareth yelped. "Ooh, let me take a look." He pushed Kate to one side to get a better view. Then his mouth dropped open. "Well, I can see why you took your time. Very tasty. Maybe we'll go up there later and see if we can't get his number."

"He's already got my number." She almost didn't want to say it out loud in case it jinxed things.

"You gave him your number?"

"He asked for it."

Gareth shook his head in mild disbelief. "Just like that. You go up and he . . ." He lifted his head, then broke out in a bright smile. "Well, good for you. I'm impressed. I mean, okay, he's just a barman, but still, he's a piece of art, isn't he?"

"He's an actor," Kate said. "From LA."

Gareth looked at her sharply. "He's not."

"He is!"

Gareth shook his head and lifted up his drink. "Kate Hetherington, I take it all back about the odds being stacked against you. If you can find an Adonis like that in a dive like this, then there's hope for us all. But I meant what I said."

"About what?" Kate asked with a frown.

"About wanting to go out with his brother. And you tell him, I'll be happy to fly to LA to do so."

6

Spreading Joy

Hopeless romantics see the world differently from other people. Hopeless romantics see beauty everywhere, see possibility in everything, and are eternally optimistic about the outcome of actions.

Which is why it can be extremely worrying when others who do not share your sunny disposition choose to make sharp comments or suggest that your optimism is misplaced. These people are the cynics—although they would probably call themselves "realists"—who prefer not to see beauty because it asks too much of them. Seeing the world as a place full of joy places on our shoulders the responsibility to maintain its wonder, to add to its beauty with generosity and thoughtfulness. Hopeless romantics think of others all the time, whereas cynics think only of themselves.

But it is not enough to avoid these people. That would be irresponsible and within many cynics is a hopeless romantic just waiting to escape. If we passed by all the cynics of this world, we would be lonely indeed, for they outnumber hopeless romantics by at least ten to one.

Instead, embrace them. Confront them. Challenge them. Not with bitter words and arguments but with evidence of beauty, warmth, and joyfulness. Look for the beauty in all things and point it out to others. Remind yourself of the wonder of nature and life, to ensure that you do not fall under the spell of the cynic. And if all your efforts fail, do not give up or *allow yourself to become downhearted. Simply tell yourself that they are not yet ready, and then think kindly of them. For if we are shown kindness, we learn to be kind ourselves. . . .*

Wednesday morning was filming day. Filming day was always the most manic of the week when everyone felt the pressure even if their bit was going okay, and Magda strode around barking orders at anyone and everyone. But today, Kate decided, things would be different. The painted brick wall was looking fabulous, there was no more plaster coming down anywhere, and, if anything, they were now ahead of schedule, which was pretty much unheard of. She and Phil spent the morning clearing the sitting room of all the decorating debris, and by lunchtime, Kate was reviewing their work with a big smile on her face. She was feeling the joy, she was enjoying the joy, and she fully intended to spread the joy, too. An intention that evaporated as soon as she saw Penny striding toward her.

"Kate, hi! Nice that someone's got time to stand around doing nothing! So look, it's script time. And please do not attempt to piss me off because I am just not in the mood. Understand?"

Kate nodded, doing her best to recapture her smile. She wanted to spread the joy, but showing Penny kindness just felt wrong, like being kind to a wasp that was trying to sting someone or helping a hunter harpoon a cute baby seal.

"Come on, come on," Penny said impatiently. "Let's go to the kitchen, shall we? Get some peace and quiet?"

Penny was dressed for filming, which meant tight leather jeans, a fluffy short-sleeved sweater that was the same color as her hair, and five-inch-high ankle boots. Her face was caked with makeup, and her trademark red lipstick was already beginning to creep into the lines around her mouth. On anyone else, Kate would have described them as laugh lines, but on Penny that seemed impossible.

As Penny turfed Lysander and Gareth off the kitchen table and sat down, she turned and smiled at Kate. "So, Kate, love," she said sweetly, and Kate's heart sank. Penny only used the word *love* when she was in a really filthy mood. It was like the good cop/bad cop routine except Penny played both roles. And she was never very good at the good cop bit.

Had Penny been on the show when Kate first applied for the job, Kate probably wouldn't have accepted it. Back then, Kate had been a freelance interior designer who had done the house of a friend of a friend of the chief executive of the television production company. *Future: Perfect* had just been an idea at the time, something the company was throwing ideas around for, and she had been brought in to help them develop the concept of a makeover show that covered interiors but also clothes and fitness—a life makeover for people in a rut.

It had been fun—and quite a nice change from designing for rich, difficult clients who changed their minds every five minutes and thought it was perfectly reasonable to ask her to sort out their dry cleaning when their housekeeper was off sick. Kate had been able to indulge all her romantic fantasies, making dreams come true and transforming the humdrum into the exotic and beautiful (or as exotic and beautiful as was possible for £750), and she and Gareth had both been known to cry on occasion when a makeover was particularly successful.

Of course, that was before Magda and Penny arrived, and before there were so many makeover shows on television that you couldn't switch channels without seeing someone being told what not to wear, what not to eat, or how much more exercise they should be doing. Initially *Future: Perfect* was presented by Bunny Rider, a former children's presenter, who was round and cuddly; the producers thought housewives would relate to her. But then Magda joined the team, taking on the role of producer/director, and developed *ambitions* for the show. Within a month, Bunny was out, along with most of the other staff, and Penny and Lysander were in. Kate had been kept on—she suspected because Magda knew that the chief exec had been involved in her appointment—but she knew, as everyone else knew (mainly because Magda told them at regular intervals) that Penny was the celebrity. They were dispensable; Penny wasn't.

"Let's just have a look at what we've got here, shall we?" Penny continued, pulling the script out of a counterfeit Birkin bag that she pretended was real even though the stitching was all wrong. The script, Kate couldn't help noticing, was covered in red pen as usual. "The thing is, Kate, love," she said in her patronizing tones, "I thought that with the Moreleys the idea was new beginnings. You know, putting the past behind them, that kind of thing?"

Kate nodded calmly. "That's right," she said. Kindness, she thought to herself. Spread the joy.

"Great!" said Penny with a relieved smile. "So I take it you're going to be repainting the walls? I mean, I don't mean to be funny, but they look like shit, don't they? I mean, literally, like shit. The color. Why, Kate, love, would anyone paint a wall the color of feces?"

Kate stared at her. Feces. Okay, she hadn't expected that. "I'm sorry?" she asked, her voice quivering, to her intense irritation. "What do you mean?"

"I mean, love, that the walls are the color of shit, and I'm not very comfortable with that. To be honest, I'm surprised you are." Penny's eyes were cool as she shook her head to convey just how uncomfortable she was. Kate's own eyes narrowed. Sod kindness. Didn't *The Hopeless Romantic's Handbook* say she should confront and challenge cynics, too? Now *that* she could do.

"It's not the color of shit," Kate said, attempting to keep her tone reasonable. "It's more of a latte color with a hint of rose. It's an authentic color from the nineteenth century, but brought up to date—it's very now, actually—a real color of the new millennium, and I've picked out the pinky tones in the throws on the furniture, which make the pink carpet less . . . well, less eighties." As she spoke, the defensive edge to her voice began to soften as the sheer enthusiasm she had for color, furnishings, and design awoke. "It's modern, it's restful. It moves the house on from the eighties chintz and fake Edwardian touches that were here before without losing the . . . the special feel of the place . . ." She faltered at Penny's cold expression.

"So let me get this straight," Penny said. "I'm going to have to sit on a sofa covered in a shit-colored blanket, in front of shit-colored walls and talk to Mr. and Mrs. Moreley about the exciting life they've got ahead of them? I'm sorry, but I can't see it. And what on earth is this? Tell me, what is it?"

She was pointing at the name of the paint, highlighted in the script: Dead Salmon.

"It's Farrow and Ball," Kate said in measured tones. "That's the name they gave the paint."

"Dead Salmon. Of course it is," Penny said, shaking her head. "Well, at least someone's got a sense of humor, even if they are selling rotten paint!" She laughed at her own joke for a moment, then, seeing that Kate wasn't laughing, stopped abruptly. "So, love, bottom line, what are the finishing touches you're planning to do to jazz it up a bit? Because I'm telling you now, there is no way I can deliver this script. If I were the Moreleys, I'd be suing you like that other woman you seem to have upset, but luckily for me I'd never resort to a free television makeover—I can afford proper interior designers. Not that I need them, because I also have good taste, but the point is, I don't think we've really done our best here. On the house front, I mean. You see what I'm saying?"

"Not really, Penny," Kate said, willing herself to sound strong but being betrayed by a slightly quivering voice, "The thing is, *I* am the interior design consultant. I do actually know my stuff. And I can assure you that Dead Salmon is a wonderful color that works very well in the Moreleys' living room. And Magda approved the mood boards. So perhaps you should take this up with her?"

Penny's mouth twisted into a little smile. "Funny that," she said, full of sweet poison, "I was going to suggest the same thing."

And with that, she walked off, her leather jeans swooshing as she went.

• • •

"Okay, five minutes people."

Magda appeared in the sitting room with two cameramen behind her. "You two in there—I want their faces close up when they come in. We'll be using that mirror there for the unveiling of the noses and we can get a scan shot of the room now if there's time. Where's Gareth? We're going to need him on standby in case touchups are needed."

"He's with Penny," Nick, a runner, said quickly. "She said she needed more blusher. On account of the . . . brown background."

He hesitated before saying *brown* and Kate knew what descriptor Penny had actually used.

"Well, get him down here now. Penny, too. Now, Kate . . . about this color . . ."

Kate looked up defiantly. "It's a good color," she said. "And it's too late anyway. . . ."

Magda nodded. "Look, I don't give a toss whether it's called Dead Trout or Dead Elephant. But Penny's got a bee in her bonnet and—"

Before she could finish, Penny arrived in the room, a cloud of powder and hairspray arriving with her. She was clutching two pale blue fake fur cushions and walked to the sofa triumphantly.

"There we are," she said with a satisfied smile. "Make sure these are behind my face at all times," she ordered the cameramen. "None of that shit . . . or, you know, dead fish color."

Kate's blood started to boil. "You are not putting those cushions on that sofa," she said in disbelief. "There is no way. . . ."

"Okay, and ten, nine, eight, seven, six, they're at the door. . . ."

"But . . . those cushions. They're awful. They ruin everything. . . ."

"Shhh! Forget the fucking cushions," Magda hissed. "Five, four . . ."

She signaled a silent *three, two, one* and pulled Kate out of the way just before the door opened and the Moreleys came through.

Kate forced herself to leave the room. She couldn't bear to watch her painstakingly chosen color scheme being decimated by Penny bloody Pennington.

She found Gareth and Lysander camped out in the kitchen. They waited for the dreaded call, when they would have to join Penny on the sofa for two minutes of inane conversation about why they'd chosen a particular shade of lipstick/wallpaper/shoe.

"I hate her," she muttered. "And one of these days . . ."

"Hold that thought. It's wrong to wish ill of the dead," Gareth whispered with a sympathetic smile. "God knows, even half a tub of blusher couldn't warm her face up today. Look, this'll cheer you up."

He pushed a copy of *Closer*, a weekly gossip magazine, toward Kate. There was a very unflattering picture of Penny on the center spread along with other "celebrity beach disaster" pictures.

"See? She looks like a mop. Like an upside-down mop with blond bristles!"

Kate tried to smile, but she didn't have the energy.

"Come on, Kate," Gareth said encouragingly. "You'll get over it. And no one watches the show anyway."

"Don't let Magda hear you say that," Kate muttered. "It's just . . . *pale blue*. With Dead Salmon. Of all the bloody colors she could have chosen. People will think I put them there. And they're hideous."

Gareth nodded with understanding, and turned to the monitor where Penny was attempting, unsuccessfully, to get the Moreleys to discuss their feelings about the makeover, whilst Lysander picked up a copy of *The Daily Telegraph* and pretended to look at an article about the forthcoming EU Summit although everyone knew he was checking out his former colleague's report on the latest runway shows at Paris Fashion Week.

"So, let's talk about this room, then," she heard Penny say through the monitor. Then she looked up to see Nick waving frantically at her from the corridor.

"Quick, you're on!" He bundled her out of the kitchen.

Kate walked into the living room, now filled with cameramen and hot from all the lighting.

"Ah, and now joining us on the sofa is our own interior design expert, Kate Hetherington," said Penny, fake smile flashing white teeth. "So, Kate, what *were* you thinking?"

Kate sat down with a hesitant smile. Penny was meant to have said "So, Kate, what was the thinking behind today's theme?" and she wasn't convinced by Penny's barbed little ad lib.

She smiled as brightly as she could. "Well, Penny, I wanted to warm this room up with some lovely rich coffee and chocolate colors, which bring out the richness of the carpet, whilst updating the room to give a lovely modern yet classic feel."

Her cheeks were already beginning to ache from all the smiling. *You'd think my cheek muscles would have adapted by now*, she thought. *I've been doing this for three whole years*. Her first time on television had been a nightmare. She'd been unable to focus on what Bunny was asking her, unable to think of anything except that she was being filmed, she probably looked awful, and she had no right telling anyone about design because she was hardly an expert, and everyone would realize she was a fraud and that she'd only got this far through a bit of luck. Now, however, she barely blinked at being in front of the camera, although she still cringed every time she saw herself and regularly thanked her lucky stars that no one she knew had the time or inclination to watch daytime television.

"You didn't think that brown might be just a little bit depressing?" Penny asked, her mouth turned up at the corners, her pale eyes harsh and cold.

Kate stared at her, and Penny's eyes widened slightly. What? they seemed to say. Can't take a few pertinent questions?

Kate smiled back even more brightly, as if it was now a grinning competition.

"Oh, Penny," she chirped, "I don't think *anyone* would find these lovely latte colors depressing. Soothing, perhaps, and that's just what you want in a living space, isn't it?"

"Soothing? Well, that's one way of putting it, I suppose," Penny said with a hard little laugh. "But I suppose the real question is what the stars of the show think. That's Marcia and Derek Moreley." As she spoke, the camera panned across to the Moreleys, who both looked terrified, perched on the sofa next to Penny. "So, Marcia, tell me, what do you make of the new look? Drab or dandy, that's the question," Penny asked, and Kate seethed.

The Moreleys looked around the room, apparently lost for words, and Kate's heart sank. Sod quitting the show, she was probably going to be fired after this.

"Bit much for you to take in?" Penny suggested. "Bit of a difficult color?"

Marcia Moreley shook her head. "I love it," she said softly. "Oh, I really truly love it. I can't believe it's the same room."

Penny, looking a bit put out, turned to Derek. "And what does the man of the house think? Are you happy with your new color scheme?"

Derek nodded.

"Nothing you'd like to change?" Penny persisted, her smile becoming rather forced.

"I don't like the cushions much," Marcia said thoughtfully. "But we can always move those, can't we?"

"Of course you can," Kate agreed. She tried to hide her triumphant grin, as she watched Penny's eyes narrow. "In fact, why don't we get rid of them right now? These weren't part of the scheme—they're Penny's own cushions!" With a beatific smile for Penny, she whipped the hideous cushions out from behind her and tossed them behind the sofa.

"Can I see my nose now?" Marcia asked. "And Derek's? Can we take the bandages off now?"

"Cut!" Magda rolled her eyes. "Okay, we're going to have to do this again. Marcia, darling, remember what we talked about? Try to focus on the house first. After the house, we do the bandages. Got it?"

Marcia Moreley nodded weakly. "And then we get to see our noses?"

"That's right, Marcia," Magda said with a sigh. "Now what the hell is that buzzing noise?"

Kate blanched and reached in her pocket for her phone. "Sorry." She smiled apologetically. "Forgot to turn it off."

Magda rolled her eyes again as Kate brought the phone to her ear.

"Hello?" she said. "Kate Hetherington speaking."

"Kate," said a guy with an American accent, "it's Joe. I was just calling about our date."

7

Sal put down the phone and tried to ignore the angry red light flashing on her handset, informing her that she had at least one message waiting for her. It could wait, she told herself, even though she found it nearly impossible to ignore something like that, to procrastinate even the slightest bit. Life, in her book, was a list of "to do's" waiting to be ticked off, and she prided herself on getting through her list promptly and efficiently. Husband? Tick. Nice house? Tick. Interesting and fulfilling job? Tick. Mostly, anyway.

Still, she accepted that sometimes you had to ignore the red flashing light. Sometimes she had to prove to herself that she was *capable* of ignoring it. And anyway, right now, she wanted a cup of tea.

Sal worked in the regulation department of a large pharmaceuticals firm, deciding which claims and advertising slogans the company could get away with and which ones they couldn't. "Fast, effective pain relief" was okay; "No more pain. Period" wasn't. Even though the marketing team thought it was the best slogan they'd ever come up with. She was a scientist by training but had done a stint in marketing, and her boss had told her this job would be the best of both worlds, straddling the divide between brand and science. In reality, she was more of a whipping horse for both, the focus for all their anger at the other side. She didn't mind. She could take it, after all. Sal didn't let things get to her because she was practical. Pragmatic. Ed often told her about the histrionics of his friends' girlfriends and wives—smashing plates over the smallest thing, overreacting and getting upset over nothing—and said that he was so pleased she wasn't like that. Was so lucky that "his Sal" was so down to earth and sensible.

Slowly she stood up and made her way toward the communal office-kitchen. She'd been in quite a good mood this morning—Ed had been out with clients the night before, but he'd got back before midnight, which was pretty good going. He'd even kissed her as he got up for work at five thirty A.M., remembering to close the bedroom door so that the noise from his shower didn't keep her awake.

Then, as if the God of Serendipity himself was looking favorably on her, the train had been on time; she'd even got a seat. And apart from a little dispute over the wording of a nicotine patch advert, things at work seemed to be going pretty smoothly, too. No one had called in sick and her manager hadn't appeared at her door with a pained expression on his face, which always happened when he had been bollocked by *his* manager because a decision that she had made wasn't the decision they'd wanted her to make. No, all in all, today had gone well.

So why was it that she had a niggling feeling in her stomach, she asked herself as she methodically placed a tea bag in her mug and boiled the kettle. Why was a little frown burrowing itself into her forehead and feelings of irritation—usually reserved for late nights when Ed had failed to come home at the time he'd promised—creeping into her consciousness?

There was no reason, she told herself. Which meant that she was imagining them. Which meant that if she ignored them, they would go away. Sal had no time for feelings that could not be traced to events, no time for moods that had no basis. She usually accepted that once a month her hormones, whilst not events, could result in chemical imbalances that made her feel out of sorts, but she had no truck with general malaise—in others or in herself. You made your own moods, she regularly told anyone who was willing to listen. Just as you made your own luck.

Maybe she'd slept badly, she thought. Maybe she needed a holiday. Maybe she'd call up Ed and suggest it, even though she knew he'd say he didn't have the time. Ed never had the time for holidays—he seemed to think that if he stepped out of the office for one single day, they'd realize they didn't need him after all and he'd be fired. Maybe she'd just book a day at the Sanctuary instead.

Sal jabbed at her tea bag and threw it in the bin.

The fact was that she was happy with her life. Very happy. Kate might make out that financiers were boring, and she and Tom might even think that she and Ed were boring and too grown-up, but Sal wasn't bothered in the slightest. Passion and romance were all very well, but they didn't provide for you in your old age, did they? Not everyone wanted drama and proclamations of love. Some people preferred a quieter life.

Was she one of them though? she wondered wistfully. When exactly had she and Ed got so terribly serious, anyway? They used to have fun together. Used to laugh and play silly games and spend entire weekends in bed.

But now Ed always seemed to be either at work or on some golf weekend with clients. And she seemed to spend her life either cleaning up after him or nagging him to put a shelf up, take one down, put out the rubbish, or to get home when he said he would so that her meals wouldn't be completely overcooked and ruined.

She opened the fridge to get out some milk. It probably *was* just growing up, she decided. After all, they had a mortgage to pay off now. Life was more serious—it was unavoidable.

And Kate's romantic notions of meeting Mr. Right and living a life of romantic fantasy were hardly getting *her* very far. No, pragmatism had served Sal well, and a few little blips weren't going to convince her to change course. Like she always said, you made your own luck. And she was very lucky, Sal told herself as she walked back to her desk. Very lucky indeed. In fact, she was going to call Ed right this minute, just to remind herself how happy she was.

Decisively, she picked up the phone and dialed his number.

"Hi, darling, it's me."

"Sal?" Ed sounded surprised. "What do you want?"

Sal frowned. "I just wanted to see how you are. Just, you know, to say hello to my husband."

"Right. It's just that it's quite busy here. Is everything alright?"

Sal rolled her eyes. "Yes, it's alright," she said crossly. "Do I have to be facing a crisis to call you?"

"I dunno. Look, can we discuss this later? Bit tied up here."

"Right," Sal said, her shoulders slumping just a bit. "So you'll be back for supper tonight?"

"Ah. Actually, no. Sorry. Got a thing on."

"A thing."

"Yeah. Work thing. Sorry. Probably going to be a late one, too."

"Fine. Well, I'll see you when I see you."

"You're sure everything's alright?" Ed's voice told her that he was praying things were alright. That the last thing he needed right now was for anything to be wrong, for anything of hers to demand his precious time.

"I'm fine, honestly," Sal said. "You'd better get back to work."

"Okay. See you."

He put the phone down before Sal could say good-bye, and she slowly put the receiver back before turning to stare at the pile of papers on her desk, telling herself that everything *was* fine, that Ed being busy all the time didn't mean anything, didn't suggest that anything was wrong with their marriage.

Anyway, she was busy, too, she thought, pursing her lips at the marketing blurb in front of her. How many times had she told those guys that they mustn't make claims that couldn't be backed up with evidence—yet here, yet again, was the proposed packaging for some nicotine gum with "Will stop you thinking about cigarettes forever" plastered across it.

Tutting under her breath, she crossed out the *will* and replaced it with *could*.

◆ ◆ ◆

Tom yawned and stared at the paperwork in front of him with contempt. He was a doctor, not a bloody administrator, yet he seemed to be spending more and more time these days filling out forms, writing memos, or completing time sheets. It was all such a waste of time.

"Dr. Whitson?"

He looked up to see one of the nurses hovering at his door.

"Lucy? Hi, what can I do for you?"

She was new. Quite pretty, but too many teeth. And a bit too ballsy for him, too. She looked like the sort of girl who would think nothing of taking off her top in a club and dancing on the bar. She probably holidayed in Ibiza and had a tattoo on her hip.

"I just wondered if you could look at these charts for me. Tell me if everything looks okay."

"You can't read them yourself?"

"I'd like your opinion. If that's alright?" She wasn't intimidated by him, he noticed. In fact, she was staring right at him, bold as brass.

Tom nodded and she handed him the charts. He knew them well—they were Mrs. Sandler's. He'd operated on her two months before. Nasty tumor, he recalled. Caught it quite late.

"She's back?" he asked with concern. "I thought she was on a course of chemo now."

"She was," Lucy said, "but she wasn't responding well. And now Dr. Laketin says the cancer's come back. Only she's too weak for surgery right now."

Tom stared at the charts. "Well, these look okay," he said, immediately forgetting about Lucy's teeth or possible tattoo and becoming absorbed in the lines, figures, and results that revealed so much about his patients, about the frail human condition. "It looks like she's on the right dosages. You'll need to check that this line doesn't go up—if it does, let me know right away. Is she eating alright?"

Lucy shook her head. "Keeps puking up."

"Okay, that's the problem," Tom said. "Have a word with her about it. Find out if there are any foods she particularly likes. Soup is often good."

Lucy nodded. "I think she's worried. She was telling me about her son at home. Said how she couldn't stop thinking about the fact that he's only got his dad looking after him and—"

"I'm sure she's worried, but let's focus on her treatment, shall we?" Tom interrupted. "Food. That's what she needs."

"I know, Doctor. But he's got a school play coming up, see. And she really wants to be there, but she's worried she isn't going to be better in time. . . ."

"Lucy," Tom said, "what is your job?"

Lucy looked at him uncertainly.

"What do you do?" he persisted.

"I'm a nurse, Doctor."

"Good. Well done. So, Lucy, why don't you focus on being a nurse, treating your patients, ensuring they get the right medication and care? A bit more of that and a little less chin wagging and who knows, Mrs. Sandler might actually recover enough to get to the play."

"I just thought that maybe I could have a word with her husband. You know, check that everything is okay?"

Tom's frown deepened. "And yet, here you are still talking about her personal life. Curious. Because as I think I made clear before, I am not interested, okay? Soup. Tomorrow. And watch the lines on the chart. I'll have a word with Dr. Laketin and see when he's likely to schedule her for surgery."

"Soup," Lucy said flatly.

"That's right," Tom said. "Was there anything else, Lucy?"

She held his eye for a fraction longer than was comfortable, then shook her head. "No, Doctor, that's it."

As she walked away, Tom rolled his eyes. Why did people find it so hard to remain emotionally neutral? Why did his colleagues feel the need to get personally involved with their patients? It was crazy.

A neutral doctor could make informed decisions. The right decisions. Emotion just got in the way. He'd gone into medicine to cure people, not listen to their problems.

If Mrs. Sandler refused to eat because she was worried, then Lucy simply would have to make it clear, in no uncertain terms, that she was jeopardizing her recovery. That's how you handled patients. Stick to the facts. Black and white.

In fact, he decided, he would tell her himself. Next time he saw her.

Sighing, he turned back to his paperwork.

8

The Dance of Love

Falling in love is rather like a dance. Each dancer has his or her own steps, but for the dance to work, each dancer must also understand the other's steps, and they must move together in a fluid movement, sometimes parting but always aware of the other. It is a beautiful thing to watch. And yet so many budding romances fall at the first hurdle; too many dancers spin apart from each other, or fail to bend to the other's rhythm.

The hopeless romantic understands the dance of love. The romantic knows how to achieve the delicate balance of turning heads whilst focusing her attention on one man; how to keep her suitor intrigued whilst learning everything about him.

It's an open secret that listening is an art that can prove most attractive yet that few perfect. Of course, dressing for a date is equally important— choosing eye-catching accessories to enhance your plain dress, for instance, will brighten up your date's day, choosing a perfume that is sweet but not overpowering will show that you are thoughtful, and finding the height of heel that allows you to walk elegantly whilst flattering your leg will ensure that all eyes are on you. But truly listening to a gentleman, remembering the information he imparts to you, and making thoughtful comments will do more to imprint you on his memory than any amount of powder or face cream. Learn to listen well, and romance will follow you wherever you go.

The dance of love is also a physical one. As with real dancing, the gentleman will lead this dance, but it is very important that you maintain your distance in the early stages. A chaste kiss is acceptable after one or two dates, but no more; heaven forfend that the man of your dreams should judge you to be an easy conquest. Maintain your allure by keeping a slight distance, and you can be sure that the dance will last a lifetime; move too close, and it may be over before the music has even stopped playing.

Eye-catching accessories, Kate thought uncertainly as she studied her wardrobe. Sweet perfume. It wasn't the most practical advice she'd ever been given. But, bearing in mind her successes—or lack of them—so far, she didn't really feel in a position to argue.

"Hi!"

Joe was waiting at the table when she got there, and he stood up briefly as she sat. "You look . . . lovely," he said, appraising her with a smile. "I love that . . . what is it you've got there, a brooch?"

Kate nodded, smiling. "Thanks. It's fun, isn't it?"

Joe nodded back. "It's pretty. It's so nice to see someone dressed . . . you know, elegantly. In a pretty dress. Making an effort."

Kate blushed slightly. "It's just a plain dress, really," she said.

"Well, it looks great," Joe said. "So, I hope you like the food here. It's Italian."

Kate picked up the menu and sneaked a peak over it at Joe. He was incredibly good-looking, she decided. He was wearing a simple white T-shirt that showed off his broad chest, muscled arms, and tanned skin. He looked like a Calvin Klein model. Or the gardener off *Desperate Housewives*. The kind of guy who could pick you up and toss you over his shoulder, if he felt so inclined.

"I love Italian food," Kate babbled. "You know, I went to Italy on holiday last year and there was this restaurant that did the most amazing . . ." Suddenly she stopped talking.

"What?" Joe asked. "Did the most amazing what?"

Kate bit her lip. "Scallops," she said softly. "They did amazing scallops."

"You okay?" Joe ventured, and Kate nodded. She was thinking about Elizabeth Stallwood. *Truly listening to a gentleman, remembering the information he imparts to you, and making thoughtful comments will do more to imprint you on his memory than any amount of powder or face cream. . . .*

"I'm fine," she said. "So tell me about yourself, Joe. How did an American end up working in a bar in London?"

Joe grinned. "Actually, I'm an actor," he said. "The bar work just keeps me out of trouble."

"That's right, you mentioned that at the bar," Kate said enthusiastically. "I've got a friend who went into acting. Went to Central School of Drama in Swiss Cottage—just up the road from here . . ."

Kate stopped herself again and smiled at him.

"So, tell me about your acting," she said, digging her nails into her palms to remind herself to let the guy talk this time.

"Oh, there's not much to tell," Joe said with a shrug.

Kate smiled encouragingly, clamping her mouth shut.

"Okay, then," Joe relented. "So, I've been doing a lot of stuff in LA. I was in this show, *Everything I Do*, in the second male lead role. It was kinda big in the States. But then the show comes to an end, I want something a bit different, so I come to London. Got here about a month ago, and it's cool, you know? Actually, it's freezing, but that's another story, right?"

Kate nodded, with another smile. "So what sort of stuff are you looking for?"

Joe looked pensive. "I figure a television show. I've got an agent here, he's setting me up with some auditions."

"Right," Kate said. "Of course." She nervously picked up her menu again, desperate to have something to focus on other than Joe. He was just so radiant, it felt like looking at the sun. She was convinced that every time their eyes met he could see her goofy swooning.

A few moments later, the waitress came over and they ordered their food, then Joe looked up at Kate.

"So you work in television?" he asked.

Kate shrugged. She always felt a bit awkward talking about what she did. First, she was an interior designer, not a television presenter, which made it hard to explain her role, and second, people always got so interested when she said she worked in television, an interest which died away the minute she admitted it was a little-watched daytime show.

"Oh, it's just a cable program," she said vaguely. "A makeover show."

"Cool," Joe said. "So, is it a big television company? Do they do shows? Sit-coms, that kind of thing?"

"Nope." Kate shook her head. "Just *Future: Perfect*, the cheesiest makeover show on television. I do the interiors, but to be honest I'm wondering whether it's the right thing for me. I mean, I love interior design, but we have to do everything for such a small budget and it's not like I even wanted to be on television. . . ."

"Sounds like you need rescuing," Joe said, raising his eyebrows suggestively.

Kate stared at him. Had he just said what she thought he said? Was this some kind of setup, or was he for real?

She took in his clear blue eyes and sincere expression. He didn't appear to be joking. He *was* serious, she realized with a jolt. A gorgeous, incredible man had actually walked into her life and said he wanted to rescue her.

At once she smiled sweetly. She felt like a duck, doing its best to look serene and elegant when all the time its legs were frantically paddling. She looked down at her palms, where her nails had left dark red half-moon imprints, and cleared her throat.

"Do you . . . like London?" she asked.

"I guess," Joe said after a moment. "I mean, hey, it's a great city, don't get me wrong. But it's kind of hard, too. It can be quite lonely, you know?"

"You're . . . you're lonely?" Kate swallowed.

Joe shrugged, and his eyes met hers for a moment. "I guess. God, I sound like an idiot, don't I? But yeah, I am. It's so nice to just sit here and talk, you know? It's funny, when I first saw you, I just had this feeling. . . ."

"A feeling?"

"A feeling that I'd like you."

"You like me?"

Joe laughed. "I like you a whole lot. It's kind of lucky you came into the bar, huh?"

Kate grinned, and all at once she didn't feel like her legs were paddling. Suddenly, she was gliding, or was she freefalling? Either way, she liked it.

"Very lucky," she said in a soft voice. "Very lucky indeed."

Three hours later, Joe and Kate were sitting in a cab outside Kate's flat.

"You're sure you don't want me to come up?" Joe asked softly. "I have had the most incredible evening, and I really don't want it to end."

Kate swallowed. She'd had the most amazing evening, too. She didn't know if it was the listening, or just that Joe was a wonderful guy, but she hadn't laughed so much in ages. And he'd looked at her across the table in a way that she couldn't remember anyone looking at her in ages—intently, ardently, those blue eyes of his shining at her like pools of seawater glinting in the sun. He hadn't stared at her breasts, he hadn't asked her about pension plans, and now he wanted to come up.

She wanted him to come up.

But she sensed that Elizabeth Stallwood wouldn't approve.

"Joe, I had the most wonderful time, too. And I'd love to see you again. But right now, I think I better get in," she said gently. "Don't you?"

With a reluctant nod, Joe said, "You're quite something, Kate." He sighed, then pulled her to him and kissed her lightly on the lips. "And you can be sure that you will see me again. Real soon, if I've got any say in the matter."

Feeling her heart quicken, Kate got out of the cab and made her way to the front door of her building, doing her best to walk in a straight line and not to punch the air in excitement. It was early days, but it felt rather like she might have met her Mr. Right. A Mr. Right who just happened to be a Hollywood actor. A Mr. Right who wanted to see her real soon and whose kiss had left her legs trembling.

If this was what it meant to be a hopeless romantic, then bring it on.

9

The Romantic Male

Much has been written about feminine beauty, and the ways in which women can attract a future husband and keep him happy and satisfied. But the true romantic must also choose her mate carefully. Not for her the brash, the rude, or the bore. Not for her a man who is domineering, who sees only his own ideas, and who believes that a wife is his servant, to wait upon him and respond to every whim.

For a marriage is a partnership, a meeting of minds. We bring different qualities to a marriage; a woman brings daintiness and gentleness whilst a man brings strength and financial stability. But both can bring kindness, thoughtfulness, interest, and supportiveness. Both can ask the other about their day and take an interest in the answer, even if a woman's day is not generally peppered with the excitement of the office.

And so, we must ask ourselves, what are the qualities that we must look for in our mate? How can the romantic ensure that her marriage is a happy and true one?

First, and last, and most important, we must value kindness. Kindness in spirit, which is different from generosity—itself a very worthwhile attribute and yet not as important. For kindness is a fundamental approach to life, one that holds all people dear, one that precludes meanness and cruelty, something that we can depend on when most we need it. If you find this quality in a man—if he is kind to you and to those around him, and speaks of his family and colleagues with kind words—then, Reader, hold on to him, for he will be good and true.

Of course, that is not to say that kindness is all you should look for in a man. The romantic looks for beauty in all things, and this should be no different when seeking out a future husband. A good suit, jaunty hat, and attractive smile suggest a man who cares about his appearance, and who will value your own care and attention to detail around the home. Equally, thoughtful gifts suggest a man who wishes to please and who enjoys seeing your eyes light up—a most attractive quality in a man!

A man who has hobbies and interests will be one who remains interesting over the duration of a marriage—although you should be careful of card players and lovers of horse racing. Both sports can be enjoyed by many but, sadly, for some gentlemen enjoyment may turn into obsession. If you value your housekeeping money, beware.

A gentleman's club can say a great deal about him and about the company he keeps. Consider that your future husband's friends will become your friends, and his interests your interests—we can all learn to like things if we try hard enough, but how much easier and simpler when we like them already!

Manners are, of course, terribly important, something that some people sadly fail to realize. Punctuality, holding open a door, walking on the road side of the pavement—these are such small courtesies and yet so telling of a gentleman's upbringing and values.

And finally, watch carefully when you introduce a gentleman to your own family and friends. Is he attentive and charming, or does he appear bored and preoccupied? We must make our own choices in life and not be unduly swayed by the views of our parents and friends, but a man who is disdainful of those we love will, I am afraid, eventually become disdainful of us, too.

Kate opened the door of the small restaurant/bar and made her way to a corner table. A second date, she thought nonchalantly. A second date with a gorgeous man who wanted to rescue her. A man who was attentive and charming and kind. At least she was pretty sure he was. It was as if that book was magic. Better than magic.

Taking off her coat, Kate sat down and looked around as a waitress presented her with a menu. It was a cute place, not one she'd been to before. There were wine racks full of bottles all over the walls, and the tables were wooden and rickety, with little candles on them, flickering and reflecting light onto the glass of the wine bottles.

She ordered a glass of wine and a glass of water, and some olives and bread for good measure, then she sat back and waited, listening to the conversations around her—an arguing couple, a group of friends discussing a film, two men talking in hushed tones about a financing deal.

She looked at her watch. Joe was only fifteen minutes late. That was nothing. She'd probably got here too early, she decided. Her watch was probably fast.

She took a sip of wine and looked around the room again, catching the eye of the waitress by accident and prompting her to come over. "Is everything alright?" she asked in a thick French accent. "Can I get you anything else?"

Kate shook her head. "No, no, I'm fine for now. Thanks."

Maybe she'd got the time wrong. Maybe he'd said eight thirty, not eight. Anyway, it was no big deal. He was only twenty minutes late.

Slowly Kate drained her glass of water, and then, equally slowly, she drained her glass of wine. The olives disappeared into her mouth one by one and at eight forty, she found herself mopping up the oil they'd left behind with the crusty bread.

Just as she'd swallowed the last piece, Joe appeared in front of her.

"I am so sorry," he said, sitting down and grabbing her hands. "Really I am. It has just been the most awful day. And just as I was about to leave, one of the bar staff got sick and she had to go home, so I had to stay until they could get someone else in to cover. I just couldn't let them down, you know?"

Kate smiled. Kind, she thought. "It's fine," she said immediately. "I haven't been here that long myself."

Joe looked at the empty glasses and plates in front of her, then met her sheepish smile.

"Hey, I got you something," he said, shoving his hand into his pocket and pulling out a DVD. "You said you wanted to see it, so . . ."

"*Everything I Do*. Wow, so this is your show!" Kate grinned. He was sharing his interests.

Joe shrugged. "It's from the second season, which I think was the best one. Anyway, you don't have to watch it. . . ."

"I'd love to!" Kate enthused. "Thank you. That's really thoughtful."

Joe looked at her and smiled, then he picked up the menu. "So, what do you say to more wine?"

Kate nodded and tried to remember further tips from her new relationship bible. "What was so terrible about today?" she asked, when they'd ordered a bottle of red and some food. "Did you have any auditions?"

Joe shook his head. "I was at the bar all day. Had an audition yesterday, but the part wasn't for me, you know? I thought it was going to be interesting but it turned out to be pretty average. Poor script, director didn't seem to know what he was doing. . . ." He shrugged, and Kate nodded sympathetically.

"It must be really hard," she said.

"It is!" Joe said immediately. "So hard. And there are so many jerks in this business, too. Can you believe that my agent wants me to do an ad for cream cheese? Me? It drives me crazy, I tell you."

Kate rolled her eyes. "I know. The presenter on my show's trying to get herself an advert at the moment. Seems to think it's going to raise her profile or something. It's quite tragic really."

Joe frowned. "She's doing an ad to raise her profile?"

Kate nodded. "Apparently some guy who sells car insurance in a gorilla suit got higher billing in a celebrity magazine so she's up in arms."

"A gorilla suit?"

"I know," Kate said on a laugh. "It's ridiculous, isn't it? But Penny is obsessed with her celebrity rating. I guess it's all she's got."

Joe nodded seriously. "She famous, then? Your presenter?"

"Her name's Penny Pennington. One-hit wonder, and placed on this earth to make sure I remain miserable."

"One-hit wonder?" Joe frowned.

"Fly me high, fly me to the sky, give me wings, and never say good-bye," Kate sang. "Remember that song?" Joe shook his head and Kate shrugged. "Maybe it was only big in the UK. Anyway, it was number one for a few weeks in the late eighties, and somehow she's managed to claw a career out of it."

"Huh." There was a pause as Joe digested this information.

"So," Kate said, taking another sip of wine, "what are your interests? I mean, outside of acting. What do you do in your spare time?"

Joe's face broke out in a slow, seductive smile. "I'd like to hang out with you more in my spare time."

Kate grinned. "Good answer," she said, reddening slightly.

"So when you've finished that wine, how about you and me go back to your place?" Joe asked softly, moving his hand onto hers. "I could maybe check out your interior design skills."

Kate blanched. "Oh, God, my flat really isn't a very good advert for my designs, actually," she sputtered. "I mean it's a bit of a mess, far too much stuff. . . ." She caught Joe giving her a strange look, and her nerves danced. "You don't want to see my flat to assess my design skills, do you?"

Joe shook his head. "Not so much." A little smile was playing on his lips, and Kate felt a shiver of excitement go down her back.

But she had to wait. The book said wait, and so far it hadn't let her down.

She bit her lip. "It's still a bit early," she said quietly. "For me, I mean. I really like you, but . . . well . . ."

Joe held her gaze for a few seconds, then nodded. His gaze was intent. "No problem," he said. "I can wait. I respect that."

Then he grinned. "I'd prefer not to wait, of course. There's something about you, Kate. Something special. But hey, let's just enjoy the evening, huh?"

Kate smiled in relief and wondered what Elizabeth Stallwood would make of Joe. Full marks, she suspected. With or without a jaunty hat.

10

Overcoming Obstacles

We often feel that life is full of difficulties, and that events conspire against us. How often have we broken a heel before an important date or discovered that our soufflé has failed to rise just as our guests are arriving? How frustrating when a special evening is ruined because of an argument or because your friend is late. How irritating when your companions are dull and your life appears to be drab and so unlike the dreams and aspirations you have for it.

But also consider those days when everything seems to go in our favor. The springlike morning when you stroll along the street happily watching elegant men and women walk by; that enjoyable afternoon when you meet friends for a gossip over coffee; those magical evenings spent among the theater crowds in the glittering lights of the West End.

Was it the sun which made that morning so special? Was the conversation with your friends so much better on that afternoon than on any other? Was the play really the best you have ever seen?

Perhaps. Or perhaps, on those wonderful days, it was you who brought the sunshine, the interesting conversation, and the joie de vivre. Did you wake up on those days full of life and enthusiasm for what lay ahead?

Now recall the morning of a day of difficulties. Did you wake feeling rested and happy? Or did a dark cloud loom over the day from the moment *you opened your eyes? Did you expect things to go awry, and might you have perhaps contributed to the argument that ruined your evening? Did the heel break purely accidentally, or had you put off having your shoe mended for weeks, convincing yourself that it would last another wear?*

You may consider me unfair. It may be that you are indeed unlucky and that events conspire against you from time to time. But the true romantic does not let problems get in the way of her enjoyment of life. The romantic knows just how to pep up a dull dinner party with sparkling conversation and with generous and flattering comments. The hopeless romantic avoids arguments because she nips them in the bud before they have a chance to flower—using her listening skill and understanding to calm her companion's nerves.

In short, the hopeless romantic knows that she is the owner of her destiny, that she can choose either to enjoy each and every day or to feel put upon. The romantic sees an obstacle as something to test her mettle, an exciting challenge for which she will need to use her intelligence, her charm, and her optimism. The romantic knows that by focusing on all that is good and pleasing in her life, she will always keep her spirits high and her lips smiling.

And because the romantic spreads joy wherever she goes, she finds that dark clouds and broken heels not only fail to dampen her spirits, but that they become less and less frequent, for she knows she can overcome any obstacle and render obstacles themselves obsolete.

Kate frowned. Here it was, Saturday night, and instead of being out with Joe-the-Perfect-Man, she was on her couch in sweatpants, whilst he worked in the bar, no doubt surrounded by a gaggle of gorgeous women. It was fine to say that the hopeless romantic was in charge of her own destiny, but it patently wasn't true in her case. And in what way was a Saturday night in front of the television an exciting challenge that would test her mettle?

Still, she wasn't worried. Not after their last date. They'd talked for hours, and as for that kiss outside the restaurant . . . She sighed as she remembered it. No, she was pretty sure Joe wouldn't be looking at any other women. And she hadn't invited him up, either. It had taken all her mental strength and she'd nearly buckled several times, but she'd come home alone for a second time, which, she hoped, would mean that Joe would be desperate to see her again.

Not that this helped her right now, though, home alone with nothing to do.

She shut the book with a thump, but the words replayed before her eyes. *The romantic knows that by focusing on all that is good and pleasing in her life, she will always keep her spirits high and her lips smiling.*

Fine, she thought. Things that were good and pleasing in her life:

1. Joe. Enough said.
2. Her friends. Tom and Sal had been around forever. They lived around the corner. And Sal always had a fridge full of food.
3. Her job. Except for that woman who might be going to sue her, of course. And Penny, who pretty much seemed to spend her life making Kate's a misery.
4. Her flat. It was a tip, but it was hers. Well, hers and the mortgage company's. But mostly hers.

She studied the list. Was that really it? Then she frowned, looked around the room, and thought of a few more good and pleasing things.

5. *Sleepless in Seattle.*
6. Galaxy chocolate bars.
7. Takeout pizza.

Satisfied, she smiled broadly and picked up her purse to go in search of all three. Who was she kidding? Her life was great.

◆ ◆ ◆

The next evening, Kate and Tom got to the Bush Bar and Grill at exactly the same time.

"And how is my favorite hopeless romantic?" he asked with a smile, kissing her on the cheek and heading for the bar.

"Pretty well," Kate said happily. "And how's my favorite grumpy doctor?"

Tom raised an eyebrow. "Not grumpy, just battered and bruised by the world conspiring against him," he said. "Now, can I get you a drink?"

Kate declined. "Actually, I was going to buy a bottle of champagne."

Tom stared at her. "Champagne? Are we celebrating? If so, shouldn't I know what it is first?"

Kate shrugged. "Well, I've got an announcement to make. I am no longer a *hopeless* romantic, at least not in your interpretation, because I may just have a boyfriend. Plus, since I'm in such a good mood, I thought that we should celebrate our friendship."

"Our friendship?" Tom asked incredulously.

"Yes," Kate said. "You realize we've all know each other for more than twenty years now? I think that's worth celebrating."

"You're completely mad," Tom said with a shrug. "But if you wish to squander your money on champagne, please don't let me stop you. And did you just say you've got a boyfriend?"

"That's right." Kate grinned. "At least, you know, we haven't discussed it yet or anything, but I've got a good feeling about it. A very good feeling."

"You've got a boyfriend? That was a bit sudden, wasn't it?" Sal said breathlessly, appearing beside them. "Sorry I'm late. Argument with Ed. Don't ask. So, boyfriend?"

"He's American," Kate said with enthusiasm. "*And* he's an actor."

"An actor in work or an actor working as a waiter?" Tom asked.

Kate frowned. "How do you know he works in a bar?"

Tom grinned. "I didn't. It was a lucky guess. Isn't LA meant to be full of actors working in bars?"

Kate rolled her eyes. "Okay, so right now he's working in a bar. But he was in this show called *Everything I Do* which was really big in the States."

"It must have been big to achieve the career trajectory of waiting tables in London," Tom said dryly.

Kate glared at him. "Stop being so bloody cynical. He's gorgeous and he's going to be hugely successful and I don't care what you think."

Tom was still grinning. "But I thought you wanted to celebrate our friendship with champagne? Surely you must value my opinion?"

"Champagne?" Sal asked. "Why are you and Tom celebrating? I don't understand."

Kate sighed. "The *three* of us," she said, annoyed. "I wanted the three of us to celebrate our friendship. You know, to think how lucky we are and everything."

"Lucky?" Sal asked. "In what way are we lucky?"

"In all ways," Kate said, exasperated. "We've got jobs, we've got each other, you've got Ed, for goodness' sake. How lucky is that?"

Sal shrugged. "Let me see: I'm lucky to be married to someone who'd rather play golf than see his wife, and to be mortgaged up to the hilt so we can't afford a holiday, am I?"

Kate looked at her helplessly. "I just thought . . ."

"Kate, you're on a high because you've finally had sex after a drought, that's all," Tom said. "Whereas we're the same miserable buggers we were last week. Ignore us."

"Actually, we . . ." Kate started to say, then decided that Tom didn't need to know about her sex life or lack of it. "I thought you shagged a different girl every week," she said instead. "Shouldn't you be on a constant high?"

"I suppose the novelty wears off after a while," Tom said with a thin smile. "So, are we going to get drinks or are we just going to stand here all evening?"

"Fine," Kate said crossly, wondering whether putting her friends near the top of her list of things to be happy about might not have been a little premature. "No champagne, then. Do you think the two of you could see your way to drinking some wine instead?"

They bought a bottle of Australian red and found their usual table.

"So," Sal said when they'd all sat down. "Tell us about your new boyfriend. Where did you meet him?"

Kate grinned. "In a bar. His bar, actually. The one where he works. I was with Gareth. Anyway, we went out to dinner and then went out again a few nights ago, and he's really nice."

"Nice?" Tom said. "I thought girls didn't want to go out with 'nice' boys."

Kate rolled her eyes at him. " 'Nice' as in gorgeous and funny and sweet," she said irritably.

"And did your eyes meet across the bar? Did you know at once that he was the one?" Tom asked, a little smile playing on his lips.

"Oh bugger off," Kate said. "Why do you always have to be so cynical about everything?"

"Yes, shut up, Tom," Sal agreed. "So d'you think it's serious, Kate?"

"Maybe." Kate smiled. "I mean, I think so. I hope so. You know we were talking last week about speed dating and stuff? Well, I started thinking that maybe you were right, that I should just go out with someone—anyone—and stop worrying about whether he's the one, or whatever. And then I met Joe and it feels really right, you know? And I'm just so pleased that I didn't. Settle, I mean. He said I was really special."

"Special?" Tom said. "Pass the sick bag. Next he'll be sending Hallmark cards to his 'special someone.' "

Kate glared at him. "Just because you've never been special to anyone in your life, or, God forbid, let anyone become special to you, you don't have to knock my new relationship," she snapped. "You're just jealous, that's all."

Tom frowned. "I'm only interested in someone calling me special if it is in the middle of or just after the coital act. And only in reference to my performance. I'm serious—if either of you ever call me special, our friendship is over. Terminated. No second chances."

"Like that's going to happen," Kate muttered, and took a swig of wine.

Sal smiled thinly. "Tom, being special to someone is not a death sentence, you know. I mean, there is life after marriage and commitment."

"I'm sure there is," Tom said. "Just not for me."

"What, because it's boring? Because being married makes you somehow unable to have fun?" Sal demanded.

"Can I just say for the record that Joe and I are not getting married," Kate put in. "I mean, you know, it's been two dates. . . ."

"Great. So you think marriage is boring, too," Sal said crossly.

"I don't!" Kate said, indignant. "I just don't want you thinking that someone calling me special means I'm about to walk up the aisle with him. I mean, I might, one day. But not quite yet . . ."

Tom scowled. "You actually think you might marry this guy and you've known him for less than a week? Are you mad?"

"No!" squealed Kate. "I'm not bloody marrying him. I just said that . . . Oh, forget it. This is ridiculous."

"Fine," Sal said, folding her arms defensively. "So you all just have fun, and I'll stay at home being married and boring, shall I?"

Tom turned to Sal with concern. "Sal," he said gently, "believe me that Kate and I are having no fun at all. Well, Kate might be, but it will probably be short-lived and then she'll be as depressed as she usually is and you will again reign supreme as the only one of us mature enough to sustain a proper adult relationship."

Kate raised her eyebrows at him. "It *won't* be short-lived," she said. "At least, I hope it won't. But Sal, he's right—you're not the boring married one. You're the lucky married one."

"You say that," Sal said with a shrug, "but I bet the two of you haven't spent the weekend at home alone—well, until four o'clock this afternoon, anyway. I bet this drink isn't the only exciting thing that's happened to you all weekend."

Tom grinned and raised his glass to her. "I've been at work all weekend, so actually it is."

"And I watched *Sleepless in Seattle* on my own last night," Kate added, with a little smile.

Sal looked at them sheepishly. "Did you two think that it was going to be like this? I mean, when I left university, I thought things were going to be so brilliant."

"And they are," Kate said. "You just have to focus on what's good and pleasing in your life, and then you'll always keep your spirits high."

Tom and Sal stopped and stared at her.

"Kate," Tom said, "that is the most ridiculous thing you've said all night. You are obviously suffering from a rush of endorphins brought about by the erroneous notion that you are in love with this American chap. If things don't improve, I might have to write you a prescription."

Kate's eyes narrowed. "I might well be in love with Joe, and it's more than a chemical reaction," she said levelly. "But that's not the point. The point is that I've met a great guy, who's good and kind and strong and noble, and I really like him, okay? Plus, I have two great friends. . . ." She looked meaningfully at Tom. "Sorry, *one* great friend and one pretty great but also quite annoying one, and I also have a job that pays my bills and that I quite enjoy sometimes. So feel free to rain on your own parade if you want to, but leave mine alone, okay? I'm happy, and if you don't like it, then frankly I don't care."

Tom gave her a quizzical look, then shrugged. "Well then," he said, "let's hope your Mr. Right lives up to your expectations, shall we?"

11

Drawing a Romantic Line

A few years ago, the idea of a gentleman expecting more than to be offered a hand to kiss was quite beyond the pale. Indeed, those were simpler times, when affection between courting couples was limited to words and glances, which were in their own way really very powerful.

Today's hopeless romantic, however, must navigate difficult and choppy waters where expectations are very different and decisions so much harder. A kiss may just be a kiss, but it can lead very quickly to a great deal more. How many young girls have given away too much, too soon, only to be left heartbroken as their "suitor" moves on to his next conquest.

Of course the true romantic will choose her suitor carefully, as discussed previously, and this vetting process will reduce the likelihood of misunderstandings and broken promises. But however strong a man's word, remember that the flesh can be weak and that what is exposed can no longer be hidden.

However much you admire and trust your gentleman caller, then, I advise the following guidelines. A demure kiss is always an acceptable way to finish a date. Any man who expects more in the early stages is unlikely to have honorable intentions.

As a relationship flourishes, you may be tempted to go further, and modern medical advances mean that it is now quite possible for girls to do so.

But do not do so unadvisedly, because a broken heart is so very difficult to mend.

Before you embrace the modern world and say yes to a man who is keen for your attentions, be sure to satisfy yourself on the following: Is this man the man of your dreams? Are you the woman of his? Do you talk regularly about the future? Is he keen to gain acceptance by your family, and does he implore you to spend more time with his? When he looks at you, is it with love or simply desire? Would this man be a good role model and father to your children, or do you sense that he would shirk his responsibilities?

The true romantic will know the answers to these questions and will know accordingly whether she wishes to give more of herself than might be traditionally proper. Love affairs do not always last forever, nor should they; but for the duration of the affair, both parties should long for a lifetime together though events may deny them their dream. Affairs without love, on the other hand, are different entirely and will provide no beautiful memories or teach you no lessons. For, in truth, if you give to the undeserving, it only makes you poorer.

Sarah Jones, the rather overweight woman who was sitting in front of Kate, was playing nervously with the hem of her dress and every so often brushed beads of sweat from her nose and upper lip.

"So," Kate said, picking up her notes. "As you know, with *Future: Perfect*, we're looking for an image makeover that's going to suit you. I'm Kate Hetherington, and I'll be making over your house. Now, I've been looking at your notes and your video, which, by the way, was great!" She flicked a quick look at Mrs. Jones to see if this comment had had the desired effect of calming her a bit, maybe even getting her to smile, but it was no good. She looked terrified.

"Anyway," Kate continued, "we all agreed that what we'd like to do is create an ambience in your home that enables you to live your busy family life but that reinforces the feeling of sanctuary, if you know what I mean?"

Sarah Jones looked at her blankly.

"A special place where you can feel comfortable and cosseted," Kate said with an encouraging smile. "Somewhere that reinforces the wonderful feeling of domesticity—that celebrates the fact that you are in fact a domestic goddess!"

Sarah Jones's face was still impenetrable, but Kate jotted down her own words. Lines like that were perfect for her piece on camera.

She was doing her best to be enthusiastic, but she had to admit she was struggling. Joe had called her late last night, when she'd just got back from the Bush Bar and Grill, telling her that his shift had finished, that he'd been thinking about her all day and that he wanted to come over.

And she'd said no.

Naturally, she'd regretted it at once, and she'd been unable to sleep all night, worrying that he'd get tired of her turning him down and that she was crazy for following a stupid code aimed at women in the 1950s. Now she was seriously cranky.

"So," Kate went on, her forced smile beginning to strain the muscles in her cheeks, "I've got some lovely fabrics for you to have a look at, and some great paint colors—lots of bold patterns, and bold but faded colors, if you see what I mean? Kind of lived in . . ."

She handed a large mood board to Sarah, on which she had painstakingly painted some warm blue and green wall colors, matched against some IKEA fabrics that looked as bright as anything you might find in a Cath Kidston shop.

Sarah didn't appear to be enticed by the swatches, however, her face remaining tense.

"This is just the board for the kitchen, but we're doing the sitting room, too," Kate hurried on. "Along the same lines, but toned down a bit . . ."

Please say something, she begged silently. Please just say one thing. All she needed was a smile or a nod and a "that one looks nice" and she could get to work. Or rather, Phil could, directed by her.

Sarah cleared her throat and looked up.

Kate gave her the most cheerful smile and an encouraging nod.

"I want a leather couch. Like that Linda Barker one in that advert."

A leather sofa? Kate frowned. How did that fit with the *Desperate Housewives*-meets-Camilla-Parker-Bowles theme? The only kind of leather sofa that could work would be a large, old slouchy one, and that would absorb the budget for not one show but three.

"Well," she said, knowing that it was important never to say no but instead to offer alternatives, "I'm not sure which sofa you mean, but don't you think that with these wonderful colors it might be an idea to cover your existing sofa instead? Think of all the family memories of that lovely sofa—and now you'll be able to keep it, whilst also updating it to fit the new color scheme!"

"Black leather and chrome, it was," Sarah stated. "My neighbor's got one just the same. Leather and chrome, that's what I want."

Kate took a deep breath. "The thing is, Mrs. Jones—Sarah, I mean—the concept we designed for you doesn't really include a leather sofa. And you'll probably be aware that our budgets are really very tight, so a sofa would absorb almost the whole lot."

Sarah Jones stared at her, unflinching. Then she leant in close and grabbed Kate's hand. "Look," she whispered desperately, "I don't care about your concepts. You're young and pretty, so you won't be able to understand, but I've been married for sixteen years. Had three children and look like it, too. For the past ten years, my husband's been sleeping with a woman lives across the road and hasn't so much as kissed me on the cheek. No amount of makeup or concepts are going to change the fact that I haven't had sex for years. So what I want is a leather sofa. One that's better than what she's got. And he's not going to be allowed to plant one buttock on it, not if I've got anything to say about it. Do you understand?"

Kate thought for a moment, then nodded. She did understand. More than she wanted to. She closed her eyes briefly, remembering the noise of her parents screaming at each other when she was eight, remembering how she listened to every word from her vantage point on the stairs. Remembering the words *that woman* being used meaningfully in conversations as though Kate wouldn't know what it meant. Remembering telling herself that she would never have a marriage like theirs, a marriage that felt as if it was secured with Sellotape instead of superglue.

She also knew all about pent-up frustration and not having had sex for so long she could barely remember how it worked; knew about waiting so long for perfection that she was in danger of missing out completely. But she also knew that a leather sofa was not at all what she had in mind for Sarah Jones's house. "Let's talk about this later, shall we?" she said in a soft voice, and stood up. Then she walked to the hallway and took out her phone.

"Joe?" she said when she got through. "It's me. How does seven P.M. at mine sound?"

He arrived at 6:45 P.M., holding a bottle of wine. A bottle of wine that didn't get opened until two hours later.

Kate had been right about him being the kind of guy who could carry someone over his shoulder. No sooner had they started kissing than he whisked her into his arms and carried her silently, strongly, into the bedroom where he slowly but carefully peeled off her clothes.

"You're beautiful," he said as he kissed her. "So hot. So sexy."

And Kate didn't even blush. Didn't worry about pulling in her stomach or turning off the lights as Joe moved on top of her, exploring every inch of her body. She felt beautiful. And hot. Dammit, she was a sexy woman with the man of her dreams between her legs, and nothing, nothing was going to make her feel anything else.

And if, by chance, *The Hopeless Romantic's Handbook* ended up covered by her jacket so that it couldn't see quite what was going on, it didn't mean anything. Kate was just doing her own little dance of love. And hers was definitely physical.

12

Joe was woken up by the phone ringing, and found himself in an empty bed. A bed that still smelled deliciously of sex. He looked at the number flashing on his phone, and grinned.

"Bob!" he said cheerfully as he brought the phone to his ear. "How's it going? You got some good news for me?"

"Joe, hi," said his UK agent. "Listen, I'm afraid it's not what you were hoping for."

Joe frowned. Not what he was hoping for? Was the money not good enough? What?

It had been his best audition yet. He'd had a good feeling about it from the start, had a sense that things were about to start going right for him. *Over Here, Over There* might as well have been written for him, it was so perfect.

Sure, the casting director had said something about his playing the "dumb little brother" in *Everything I Do*, a description he'd abhorred ever since he'd been hounded by press articles talking about how he wasn't the brightest button. Like people couldn't tell the difference between an actor and a part. He wasn't dumb. He got a sports scholarship to a great college. But no one ever mentioned that, did they?

Still, this had been his part. An American guy having a relationship with an English girl. As he'd pointed out to the casting director, he even had an English girlfriend of his own, pretty much. He'd barely have to act at all.

"Okay," he said, a little uncertain. "What's the problem?"

"They loved you," Bob said, "but . . . they've decided to go with someone else. With an English actor."

Joe shook his head in disbelief. It was impossible. That was his part. Everyone could see, *it was his part.*

"They gave it to an *English* guy? You're serious? Why the fuck would they do that? Why would they not give it to me?"

Joe's heart was racing angrily in his chest. He could have played the part with his eyes closed. He barely needed a script, for God's sake. And they chose a fucking English guy?

"Joe, listen, try to understand. You were great. They said you were really impressive. But he's a name, this guy. He's in the press all the time. They're just nervous about using an unknown. They said—"

"An unknown? I'm an unknown? Did they not listen to me? I was the second male lead in *Everything I Do.* It's a huge show."

"The thing is, Joe, that show finished a while back now. And there hasn't really been anything since. . . ."

Joe felt the white anger rising up inside him, the anger that had begun to develop shortly after *Everything I Do* got dropped. Those studio bastards. They promised him they'd have another part. Kept telling him how important he was to them. And then, as soon as the final show was in the can, that was it. No one returned his calls. No one made him a single offer.

No, that wasn't quite true. He'd had one offer. An offer to play an idiot in some new sitcom, which was a "pastiche" of *Everything I Do,* whatever the hell that was. Joe was asked to reprise his role, but according to his agent, this time he wouldn't be making the jokes; he'd *be* the joke.

He told them to go to hell, of course. And then, when nothing else had come through, he said he'd think about it after all, and they said, "Don't worry about it, we've found another pretty face." Bastards. Well, he was going to show them. He had to show them. He was going to go back to LA having made it in London. He was going to be a hot property.

"I've done stuff," Joe said petulantly.

"Thing is, Joe, opening a car show or two doesn't really count for a lot here."

"I am a well-known actor," Joe said, undeterred by Bob's car show comment. Hell, everyone had to do what they could to make a buck or two sometimes, didn't they? "Fact is, they could have had an LA actor with major studio experience, and they're calling me an unknown? Who is this guy? What's he been in?"

Bob cleared his throat. "He was in an advert for car insurance. Dressed as a gorilla."

Joe was silent for a moment. The word *gorilla* was ringing some bells, but he couldn't remember why. "A gorilla?"

"It captured the public's imagination. He does celebrity appearances. And he was on *Celebrity Dance Academy.*"

"Sorry, what? What the fuck are you talking about? Is that a show?" Joe was doing his best to keep his voice level, but he couldn't hide his outrage. He needed that part. They should have been begging to have him, and instead they'd offered the part to a frigging gorilla.

"It's very popular. Celebrities have to learn to dance and they get voted off by the public. He did it dressed in his gorilla costume. . . ."

"You want me to dress up as a gorilla?" Joe asked tersely. "Is that what you want? Or what about a kangaroo? You think that might get these assholes to take me seriously? I mean, tell me, really, what the hell is going on here?"

Bob sighed. "I've got some other auditions here. Joe, just be patient, these things take time."

"Sure they do," Joe said, trying to calm himself down. Now was not the time to shout at his agent. "I know that. I just had a good feeling about that show, you know?"

"I know. I did, too. Look, there's other stuff. Not quite as high profile, but you got a callback for that cream cheese commercial."

Joe frowned. "Cream cheese? Bob, I told you, I'm not doing that crap. I'm Joe Rogers."

"Sure. But it's good money. Just whilst you're waiting for the right part?"

"Not a chance. I've got my image to think about, Bob. And I'd appreciate it if you'd think about it, too."

Joe slammed down the receiver, then sighed. He wouldn't let this get him down. Wouldn't let it dent his confidence. He was Joe Rogers, a successful actor, and he was better than a talking gorilla any day of the week.

He sank slowly back under Kate's sheets and cursed the fact that she'd gone to work already. He needed some sympathy here. Needed her to look at him with those doe eyes and remind him that he was talented and sexy.

Restlessly, he sat up again, then picked up his cell phone. Kate might be at work, but there was always later, wasn't there?

"I cannot bloody well believe that they put the gorilla ahead of me again."

Kate looked up from her phone, smiling. It was lunchtime on the *Future: Perfect* set and she had a text message from Joe suggesting a drink that evening.

"The gorilla?" she asked vaguely.

"Yes, this bloody man in his gorilla suit. They put his interview before mine—page fourteen, would you believe, shoving me back to page twenty-six, and he gets a photo flash on the cover, whereas I just get a little line at the bottom."

"I wouldn't say your bottom line is particularly small," Gareth said with a little glint in his eye, and Penny glared at him.

"I'm going to call my agent," she snarled, standing up. "I've had enough of this shit."

Before she could leave, Magda stormed over. "Have you seen this interview?" she asked, holding up a second copy of the magazine Penny had been brandishing.

"I *know*," Penny intoned. "Page twenty-six. Can you believe it?"

Magda glared at her. "No bloody mention of *Future: Perfect* is what I was wondering about," she said angrily. "We had a deal, Penny, and the deal was that we overpay you and in return you get your grubby little interviews in celebrity magazines and you talk about nothing but the show."

Penny rolled her eyes. "Magda, don't be so naïve. Like anyone would interview me about the show for an hour."

"Well, if you're not careful, they won't be able to," Magda said, her eyes flashing. "You're going to find yourself out of a job, if the show doesn't fold first." She threw the magazine down on the Joneses' table and stomped out of the kitchen, leaving Gareth and Kate shooting silent looks at each other.

"Bloody drama queen," Penny muttered under her breath. She picked up the magazine and pulled out her mobile phone, wandering out to the garden.

Gareth sighed with relief; then he turned to Kate conspiratorially. "You know this show's going under," he said. "I mean, if Magda and Penny don't implode first. Apparently the sponsor's thinking of pulling out."

"Really?" Kate asked, worried. It was all very well to bitch about her job, but she was still grateful that she had one.

"It didn't come from me," Gareth said, looking around to check that no one was listening, "but I wouldn't be surprised if they bin the show after this series. That's why Magda's got perpetual PMT at the moment."

Kate frowned as Penny came striding back in. "And they put the gorilla first!" she was shouting. "Has it had any hit singles? Does it have its own reality makeover show? No, it bloody well doesn't. I want you to ring them up, and I want you to tell them that I am unhappy. Very unhappy . . . Yes, I know. Yes, I do understand that. . . .

No, I know the advert is very popular and is on network television, but . . . Fine. Well, get me an advert too then. . . . Yes, I know I said that, but I've changed my mind. It has to be national, though."

She snapped her phone shut and looked at Kate, then Gareth. "And you can stop staring, thank you very much," she said, tossing her hair—or at least trying; her hair was so stiff with products that it wouldn't play ball. "As soon as I'm starring in my own national advertising campaign I won't have to work with dross like you anymore."

As she walked off, Gareth rolled his eyes. "What the hell's she going to advertise?" he asked archly. "Only way she could make anyone money is by people paying to keep her out of their living rooms."

As he spoke, Magda swept back in. "Kate, a word?"

Kate looked up expectantly.

"Your stalker's called again," Magda said. "Wouldn't say what the problem was, just that she wanted to talk to you. It's a bad sign, Kate, not leaving a message. Legal haven't spoken to her yet but they want to know what you did. Any problems, shortcuts, that sort of thing. So they can prepare."

"Prepare?" Kate echoed. That sounded bad.

"So they know what to expect," Magda said. "And so they know who's culpable—the show or you."

"Culpable for *what*?" Kate asked.

Magda shook her head vaguely. "I don't know. Ask legal. I'm just passing on the message."

She wandered off, and Kate put her head on the table and covered it with her hands.

"Don't stress," Gareth counseled her. "Just deny all knowledge of anything that went wrong. They can't touch you for it if they can't prove it."

"But I don't know what I'm supposed to have done!" she said indignantly. "Why can't I just talk to her? Why does legal have to get involved, anyway? She was really nice on the show. I don't understand."

"You've got her number, haven't you?" Gareth said. "Call her if you really want to."

Kate stared at him. Of course. She had everyone's numbers in her files.

"What if Magda's right and she records the conversation?"

"Just don't say anything incriminating. At least you'll know what the problem is."

"You're a star, Gareth." Kate beamed. "Yes. I'm going to bloody well call her."

"Atta girl," Gareth said. "Now, do you mind telling me why Sarah Jones keeps going on about getting a leather sofa?"

13

The Art of Compromise

If only all our interactions and conversations were sweet, fulfilling, and trouble free. But sadly, all too often our friendships are peppered with squabbles and disagreements; even lovers' tiffs can sometimes be unavoidable. One of us wants to go to the theater; the other wishes to stay at home. One of us enjoys country pursuits on the weekend; the other enjoys the convenience of the town.

The hopeless romantic, however, knows that disagreements need not lead to sadness and distress. Handled well, a disagreement can be turned into a wonderful opportunity to show that you are willing to compromise, to prove to the other that you can put their feelings first. And when we do this, all too often, our lover or friend will realize that they are capable of putting our feelings first, too. And so, from cross words come kind ones. From hopelessness comes hope.

Romance, you see, is not a trip to the theater or a small but expensive gift. Romance is a way of life, a generosity of spirit, and the generous soul will always have everything that it needs. . . .

As soon as Kate got home that evening, she dug out Carole Jacobs's phone number from her files and made her way to the kitchen. She picked up the phone, started to dial, and put it down again. Then she sat back on her chair, drumming her fingers on her kitchen table.

The trouble was, she thought nervously, that it was all very well for Elizabeth Stallwood to talk about compromising and putting other people's feelings first, but she'd probably never had anyone threatening to sue her. How could Kate show Carole Jacobs that she was willing to put her feelings first when she didn't even know what her feelings were?

Actually, she suspected that she did know what her feelings were. She'd gone back through her notes to find out what could have upset Carole Jacobs and she figured it must have been one of two things. There was the staple-gunning—curtains this time, because there hadn't been time to fit a double curtain rail. And then there was the fact that they'd sanded the floor, but only around the furniture and not under, at Magda's express instructions, again because of a lack of time. Which meant that Carole wouldn't be able to move even a chair without their cheap shortcut becoming very evident.

Maybe she was angry about both. Maybe there was something completely different. But did she really have to sue Kate because of it? What kind of crazy overreaction was that?

Slowly, her hand inched back toward the phone as she stared at the crib sheet in front of her on which she'd written down as many arguments as she could think of as to why it wasn't her fault that Carole Jacobs was so unhappy with her makeover.

The lawyers at *Future: Perfect* had told her once that the important thing was never to say *sorry* about anything because then you were admitting culpability and people could sue. Instead she should use words like *regret* and *it's a shame*, which sounded either incredibly pompous or utterly patronizing, but still. She didn't make the rules, she told herself staunchly.

"I regret that you are unhappy with your makeover.

"It's a shame that the show didn't deliver what you'd hoped.

"I regret having ruined your home and created in you a mortal enemy who won't leave me alone. . . ."

Kate grimaced. She could do this. She knew she could.

Taking a deep breath, she picked up the phone and dialed, then listened to it ringing, hoping against hope that Carole wouldn't be in, that she'd moved, that she'd gone to stay with a relative in Outer Mongolia for a few months.

"Hello?"

"Carole Jacobs?"

"Yes, dear? And to whom do I have the pleasure of speaking?"

Kate startled. Mrs. Jacobs sounded nice, just like she remembered. Which was bad, because now she felt guilty instead of indignant.

"It's Kate. Kate Hetherington from *Future: Perfect*," she found herself saying. "I'm just calling to say that I'm sorry. Whatever it is you're upset about, or annoyed about, or whatever I did to your house that was so awful, I'm really sorry. It's all my fault and I'll fix it if I can. Okay?"

Carole Jacobs didn't say anything, and Kate bit her lip anxiously. "Um, hello? Are you there?" she asked tentatively.

"Yes. Yes I am. I'm sorry, I thought you were a prank caller. What do you mean 'upset about'? I'm not upset about anything."

Kate frowned. "I'm sorry. You called the show. You called up to complain, and they don't let us . . . I mean, they like to handle things like that in a different department. But look, I'd just like us to discuss it like reasonable people, if that's okay. I mean, there's no need to involve anyone else, is there?"

"I don't know, dear. Is there?"

Kate's frown deepened, and she looked back at *The Hopeless Romantic's Handbook*.

Handled well, a disagreement can be turned into a wonderful opportunity to show that you are willing to compromise, to prove to the other that you can put their feelings first.

"Why don't you tell me what you didn't like about the makeover," she said in her gentlest tones. "And then we'll see what we can do.

Obviously, your feelings are the most important ones here. So, I mean, what I'm trying to say is that hopefully we can reach a compromise."

There was another pause. "What I didn't like?" Carole asked.

"That's right. Anything at all."

"The lipstick," Carole said at last. "I know that cerise is frightfully old-fashioned, but it's so jolly. That nice young man was only trying to be helpful but I didn't like that browny color he put me in. So drab, you know. If I'm going to bother with lipstick, I like it to be bright and cheerful."

"The lipstick," Kate repeated, nonplussed. "Okay, well, I'll definitely talk to Gareth about that. So what about the house? I mean, what didn't you like about the house?"

"But that's just the point," Carole said. "I did like it. I liked it very much. And I thought it was very clever, too. Why spend money needlessly sanding a floor that no one sees? Tell me, do you really do the whole makeover for under seven hundred fifty pounds?"

Kate's eyes narrowed. Carole had to be double bluffing—maybe she was saying all this to get Kate to admit that she had cut corners, and then there would be a lawsuit wending its way to her before she knew it.

"We do have to stick to a budget," she said, feeling her way. "So we do focus on the areas that will get maximum benefit. . . ."

"But you wouldn't know from looking, would you? I mean, none of my friends know about the bits under the furniture. At least they didn't until I showed them. No one else will do that, you see. They don't like cutting corners. They don't understand that every penny matters."

Kate took a deep breath. She was thoroughly confused by this conversation. Either she was being hoodwinked by a very sharp operator, or . . .

"Mrs. Jacobs, why did you call *Future: Perfect*?" she asked.

"Oh, to ask you to help," Carole said at once. "You brightened up my life, dear, and I thought, well, if you can brighten up my life for less than seven hundred fifty pounds, then you might be able to brighten up the hospice, too. I work there, you see. Next to the hospital. And it's ever such a dull place—really not conducive to recuperation. So I thought I'd call. But you're ever so busy, dear. Terribly hard to get hold of."

Kate stared at the phone.

"You don't want to sue me?" she asked.

Carole gasped. "Sue you? Why on earth would I do that? Oh, dear, you're not in any trouble, are you? Oh, I am sorry."

"Right. I mean, no, I'm not," Kate said awkwardly. "Sorry, did you say you wanted to talk to me about a hospice?"

"That's right, dear."

"What kind of hospice?" Kate asked. She had no idea if there even were different kinds. She wasn't even sure that she knew what a hospice was.

"Cancer patients, mostly. They have treatment at the hospital, and then they come to us. Like a halfway house between hospital and home. It can be ghastly, you know, cancer. People don't always want to go home. Others need constant medical care but don't want to be in hospital any longer than absolutely necessary. Now, we don't have a great deal of money, but we've been raising funds for a while now, and I thought, If anyone can make our money go a long way, it's that nice girl from the television with all the wonderful colors she uses. Oh, it is good of you to call, you know. I know that you people do have very busy lives. My niece is the same—always rushing about, never time to stop for a cup of tea, let alone a visit."

"You want to renovate it?" Kate asked, her interest piqued.

"Oh yes. It would make such a difference, you see. To so many people."

"How . . . how big is the hospice?"

"Oh, let me see, we've got thirty people at the moment. Some of them share, of course. But I would think there must be about twenty-five rooms. And the television room, too. And the dining hall, although people do tend to eat on trays in the television room these days. I'm not sure I really approve of it, but there we are."

Kate gulped. "So we're talking twenty-seven rooms?"

"Or thereabouts, yes. It's a lot, I know. But just the smallest changes would make such a big difference."

Kate frowned, but already she was getting excited. In her mind she was imagining a sweep of the paintbrush bringing joy to all those poor cancer patients, beautiful window treatments giving them hope and optimism for the future. But then again, she'd been reading too much Elizabeth Stallwood lately. "It sounds amazing!" she said cautiously. "I'm honored. You know, that you want my help."

"Perhaps you'd like to take a look at the place," Carole Jacobs suggested. "See what can be done?"

"I'd love to," Kate said. "I mean, obviously I've got a full-time job, so I'd only be able to help out a bit, you know, weekends and stuff. But I'd be really happy to get involved. So, what's the budget?"

"Fifteen hundred pounds."

Kate stared at the phone. "Sorry, I don't think I heard you correctly. I thought you said fifteen hundred pounds."

"That's right," Carole said brightly. "I know it's not much, but what do you think you could do with that?"

Kate swallowed. "That might . . . buy the paint," she said. "You're serious? That's your entire budget?"

"I'm afraid so," Carole said, cheerfulness unabated. "But I'm sure everyone will pitch in and help."

Kate bit her lip. She didn't know what to say.

"Come and see us," Carole said into the silence. "Just come and see the hospice and you can give me your honest appraisal. Everyone will be so excited. We've never had a real celebrity visit before."

"I'm really not a . . ." Kate started to say, then shrugged. She didn't suppose it mattered if thirty hospice residents considered her a celebrity. And didn't true hopeless romantics say yes to new things, after all? "Fine," she said. "I'll come tomorrow."

Putting the phone down, she couldn't work out whether she was more relieved or terrified by her conversation with Carole. Just what was she getting herself into?

But before she could delve too deeply into the answer, the door-bell rang.

14

Sal wished she could stop thinking about Kate having sex with her new boyfriend. Not that she was actually thinking about them; it was more the idea of it. Of Kate having the excitement of sex with a new boyfriend. Sal could barely remember the frisson of the first shag with someone. Those intense glances, the brushing of skin on skin, the *exploration* . . .

The trouble was, however much you told yourself that sex improved as a relationship developed, nothing could ever replace the fever with which you jumped on someone for the first time. The way you needed them, right then, that instant.

Married sex had loads going for it—comfort, confidence to try new things (that only happened in the first few weeks, of course), the in-depth knowledge of how to achieve mutual orgasm as quickly and efficiently as possible so that you didn't miss out on precious sleep and/or the final fifteen minutes of *Prison Break*. But it didn't make your body tingle, didn't leave you with a glow that people could still pick up on a whole day later. And it certainly wasn't mind-blowing.

Still, good for Kate. It was great news, her having a boyfriend and everything.

Well, it was *kind of* great news. Sal just hoped it wouldn't change things too much. That Kate's new relationship wouldn't make her too sickeningly happy.

She sighed. Oh God, what kind of friend was she? She should be happy for Kate. And she was. Really she was. At least, she thought she was.

It was just that . . . well, it was all a bit sudden. Would this Joe character start expecting to come along to their cozy nights out at the Bush Bar and Grill? Would Kate start lecturing her on what made for great relationships, stealing Sal's only real thunder? Would the whole dynamic of their friendship change? Change meant upheaval, uncertainty, and lack of control. Change meant . . . well, *change*.

Had Ed ever told her she was special? she wondered.

Not that it mattered. Tom was right—she had a great marriage.

Although what would he know? He didn't see what her marriage was like every minute of every day. And he didn't exactly have a great relationship of his own to compare it to.

Perhaps she *had* settled. Perhaps if she'd waited, she would be going out with someone who thought she was special. Maybe if she'd waited, she wouldn't get those pangs of loneliness that resulted in those desperate moments when she let the tight control she held over her life slip and she ate copious amounts of chocolate whilst tears fell from her eyes, when she allowed herself to think all the thoughts that she suppressed the rest of the time: that she was unlovable. That Ed didn't enjoy spending time with her. That in spite of her lists and tick boxes and spreadsheets, her life was slowly but surely spiraling out of control.

Sal shook herself. Of course she wasn't a failure. She was just a happily married woman with a lovely big house.

In fact, she would prove just how happy and lovely things were. She would have a dinner party. Invite Kate and her new boyfriend. Tom, too.

Suddenly Sal got a vision of the five of them, Ed bringing up wine from the cellar as candlelight flickered on their faces and they discussed old times and teased one another. Joe would easily become a part of their group, and he would insist on buying a place in the area, and nothing would change at all, except that they would now have a more glamorous addition and might occasionally get invited to film premieres. And in no time at all, Kate and Joe's relationship would be just like hers and Ed's, and she'd laugh at herself for being so silly and paranoid and thinking that other people were so much happier than her.

Before she could have second thoughts she picked up the phone and called Kate. "Kate, it's me. I'm going to have a dinner party. For you and Joe. And Tom."

"A dinner party?"

"Yes," Sal said impatiently. "You know, fancy napkins, nice wine, genial conversation."

"That is so thoughtful! And I know Joe would love to come. He works on Tuesdays, Wednesdays, and Thursdays though. And every other Saturday."

"So things really are quite serious with him?"

"Yeah. It's great isn't it? He's . . . well, he's just lovely. And we've got this amazing connection."

Sal paused. "That's . . . fabulous. So, Friday, then?"

"Great. What time?"

"Seven thirty P.M.?"

"Done. 'Bye then." Sal put the phone down, and started to compose an e-mail to Ed. She knew he was free on Friday, but she also knew that some drinks thing was bound to crop up, because it always did. Hopefully he wouldn't see her message until late in the day when, she'd argue, it was far too late to cancel.

Penny opened Magda's door without knocking and sat down on a chair.

"You know I don't do early mornings," she said grumpily. "Mind if I have a fag?"

Magda grunted. "Yes I bloody do," she said, just as grumpily. "And for the record, I'm not wild about early mornings either, but then again, I'm not wild about viewing figures falling through the floor and the prospect of being taken off the air."

Penny's eyes widened. "They wouldn't!"

"They bloody would. We're hanging on by a thread. And if the show goes, so does the rent on your chi-chi flat, you realize?"

Penny flinched. "I *do* have other offers, you know."

"Maybe you do. But believe me, sunshine, if this show goes tits up, none of us are going to come out smelling of roses."

Penny sighed. "I'm doing what I can. It's the others you should be worrying about. We just don't have the talent on this show. Kate's color schemes are terrifying, and even Lysander's looking a bit tired these days."

"No one cares about the color schemes or fashion. We need profile," Magda said. "We need to get publicity. We get publicity, then we might just survive. Get serious publicity, and who knows, we may even move up a league or two. Attract a proper channel, like Channel Three."

"Channel Three?" Penny asked, her ears pricking up.

"It's got to be worth one last push," Magda said with a sigh. "There's already a heap of dross scheduled every night of the week. Why shouldn't our dross be amongst it?"

"I'm in *Hot Gossip* magazine every bloody week," Penny said with a sigh of her own. "I don't know what more you expect."

"I want you on the cover."

Penny raised her eyes heavenward. "Fine. I'll just call them up and ask, shall I?" she asked.

Magda frowned at her. "Look, you know how this works. Go into rehab again, shack up with some pop star, discover you've got a terminal disease. I don't give a shit. You have this job because you can generate publicity, and that's exactly what I want you to do. And if you can mention Winter Sun Holiday Breaks while you're at it, that would be lovely since they're thinking about sponsoring the show. Got it?"

Penny pursed her lips and stood up. Magda better be right about Channel 3. Otherwise she was going to seriously consider her options. She bet the car insurance gorilla didn't have to put up with this kind of shit. And she shouldn't have to, either.

"A dinner party?" Sal could practically hear Tom frowning through the phone.

"Yes, Tom. You know, food, company, wine . . ." She couldn't understand why everyone was reacting as if it was such a strange idea. People had dinner parties all the time.

She'd broached the subject with Ed, too, although she hadn't got a straight answer out of him. He'd ignored her e-mail, so she called him up. Not that she'd exactly got his undivided attention.

Sal: You know, I was thinking, we should have a dinner party.
Ed: *Grunt.*
Sal: What do you think?
Ed: I don't know. Yes, maybe. Sorry, Sal, I'm a bit busy here. Let's talk about it later.
Sal: But you're out later.
Ed: Uh huh.
Sal: And tomorrow night you're at that dinner with some clients?
Ed: Clients?
Sal: You said you had dinner. Some investment fund manager?
Ed: Oh, right. Yes. That's right. I forgot.
Sal: So what do you think?
Ed: About what?
Sal: Never mind. 'Bye, Ed.
Ed: 'Bye, hon. *Click.*

". . . just a normal dinner party," Sal finished, exasperated.

"Yes, I think I'm aware of the form," Tom said. "It's just been so long since I've been on anyone's dinner party list. Actually I'm not sure I ever have. I didn't think that we as a group really went in for the whole dinner party thing. But now that I've had time to consider the idea, it sounds great and I wouldn't miss it."

"I've invited Kate and Joe."

"Oh, marvelous. The happy couple. I can't wait."

"She sounds all chirpy," Sal said darkly. "Like she's having great sex."

Tom was silent for a moment, then he cleared his throat. "With the special man in her life?"

"She said they've got a connection."

"Ah, yes, connections. I try to avoid those, unless it concerns a train journey."

"What if she moves to LA and ends up living in some huge mansion there?"

"Sal, it's been a week. And he's a waiter, not a movie star. Are you sure everything's alright?"

"Yes, yes, of course it is," Sal said, her voice a bit calmer. "Sorry, I'm just . . . I dunno. Tired, I guess."

"Been having too much mind-blowing sex with Ed?" Tom asked mischievously.

"Chance would be a fine thing." Sal sighed. "We're married, remember."

"Ah, yes, of course."

"Presumably you're having it, though?"

Tom laughed. "What, mind-blowing sex? Right now? I'm not sure I'd be allowed to call it that if I found the time to answer the phone."

Sal sighed again. "You know what I mean. Am I the only one who has it maybe once or twice a week if I'm lucky, and usually with the light off and never anywhere other than the bedroom?"

"I think that's called being comfortable," Tom said gently.

"I guess that's one word for it. See you, then."

Tom put the phone down and frowned.

"You alright?"

He looked up to see Lucy standing in his doorway.

"Yes, yes, fine," he said. "What can I do for you?"

"I just heard you talking about mind-blowing sex," Lucy said, looking at him with a coy smile. "I wondered if it was something I could help with."

Tom startled, but Lucy just smiled, and winked.

"I'm free for a drink later, you know," she said. "If you're interested."

And with that, she smiled again, turned, and walked away, leaving Tom staring after her.

15

Sal had never noticed Jim's arms before. They looked muscular. Did he work out? she wondered.

They were sitting in her office, and she was trying to listen to what he was saying, but instead she kept drifting off, wondering about things that she never usually allowed herself to wonder about. It was far too self-indulgent. Things like what might have happened if she hadn't married Ed. Like what might have happened if she hadn't always been so determined to control everything and had instead let things just take their course. Like whether Ed was really her soul mate or whether she'd been so desperate to get married that she'd missed the man of her dreams who was now, because of her, trapped in a loveless marriage somewhere. Like whether if she'd been a bit more patient, she'd be having mind-blowing sex right now instead of wondering whether to cook chicken or fish on Friday.

"You alright, Sal?"

She blushed, realizing that Jim was looking at her oddly. She must have been gazing into thin air again. In the middle of a conversation. She was really going to have to stop doing that.

"Sorry, Jim, I was just thinking about something you said earlier," she lied. "So, anyway, you're not happy with the wording on this press release?"

Jim was the PR manager in charge of headache pills, which wasn't her area at all, but she'd acted as a go-between for him before, persuading the scientists to allow him a superlative in his press release occasionally in return for him plugging some technical data for them. Right now, she sensed that really all he wanted was to moan to someone about how difficult his job was, and she supposed she was probably more understanding—or at least appeared to be—than her opposite number in the aspirin and ibuprofen regulation team.

"If we can't say that our pain relief is faster or better, what chance do we have?" he said, shaking his head. "I mean, what the hell's the point?"

Sal looked at him sagely. The trick, she wanted to tell him, was not to worry too much about the point: You'd end up in a constant existential crisis and wind up gibbering in the corner like a halfwit. No, instead, you had to concentrate on brand values, winning concepts, and look forward to your next holiday. Or was that just her?

"We're still the best-selling brand of pain relief," she said. "Can't you focus on that?"

Jim shook his head. "I cannot get the world's health and beauty press interested in a newly packaged painkiller just because it's a best seller. I've got targets for coverage, too. I'm the one who's going to lose my bonus, not them. Their bit is easy."

Sal nodded sympathetically, although she wasn't entirely sure she'd agree that developing the world's best-selling painkiller was all that easy, and found her eyes gazing downward, back toward Jim's arms. She'd never really noticed Ed's arms. Sure, she'd seen them. There was nothing wrong with them. But she hadn't been drawn to them particularly. She couldn't even remember when she'd first seen them. Looked at them, rather. Properly, instead of just a glance that confirmed that they existed and that they weren't deformed.

Did other people marry people whose arms they barely noticed?

"Do you work out, Jim?" she asked absentmindedly. He stared at her, and she reddened again, realizing what she'd said, not to mention what she'd implied.

"I don't mean . . ." she stammered, "I mean . . . I just wondered.

You look like you do, and I've been meaning to join a gym, so I was just asking . . ."

But instead of treating her like a total freak, Jim was smiling. "I do, as it happens," he said. "Just round the corner—Holmes Place. I'll show you round if you like."

Sal nodded, not sure what to say. He'd probably leave it as an open invitation that she'd never take him up on. Within a few days they'd have forgotten all about it, she reassured herself.

"How does tonight sound? After work—say sixish?"

Jim had stood up and was looking at her, his pale blue eyes boring right into hers.

Damn, she thought. So he's not forgetting all about it, then.

"Great!" she said brightly. "Tonight would be great!"

Jim smiled again and walked out, leaving Sal shaking her head in disbelief at what she'd just done.

She rubbed her temples and tried to refocus on the product details in front of her. Jim from PR was going to show her round his gym. How had that happened? She hardly knew the guy, and hadn't been planning to join a gym, either. *I'm going to the gym with Jim.* It sounded like a children's nursery rhyme or something. Comical and silly.

But was it silly? It didn't feel particularly comical. This was the start, she realized with a jolt. The start of the decline of her marriage to Ed. She just knew it. One minute she couldn't remember what his arms looked like and the next she would be having torrid sex with Jim from PR. In the gym. He probably felt sorry for her—the sad, boring married woman from West Kensington.

Except he hadn't looked like he felt sorry for her. And what the hell else was she going to do after work—go home and wait around for Ed all night?

Anyway, it was just a gym, for God's sake. It would do her good to get some exercise. Maybe if she got herself back in shape her sex life would improve immeasurably. With Ed, that is. Not Jim. Certainly not Jim. Jim was just being friendly, and if his invitation had inadvertently turned a spotlight on the cobwebs within her marriage, that wasn't his fault. It was her fault for letting things get to this stage. And it was up to her to remedy the situation.

Quickly, as if to keep herself from changing her mind, she picked up the phone and dialed Ed's number.

"Ed Long."

"Hi, it's me. Listen, I'm going to be back later tonight because I'm joining a gym!"

"You? A gym?" Ed was laughing.

Sal frowned. "Yes, me. I'm going with a friend from work, Jim."

"Yeah, I got the bit about the gym. But what's the friend's name?"

"Ha ha," Sal said. "He's actually called Jim."

"You're going to the gym with Jim?" Ed was laughing even more now.

"Yes, I am, actually," Sal said in an irritated tone. "So I may not be back in time to cook supper."

"Marvelous. Does that mean I can order a take-away?"

Sal sighed. This was what happened when you didn't marry The One, she realized. They didn't even notice when huge cracks began to appear in the marriage.

"Yes, Ed, you can order a take-away," she said, rolling her eyes.

"Cool. Listen, got to go, got another call—probably a tip. 'Bye, honey."

And with that, Sal heard the familiar *click*. She had noticed a few months ago that she never hung up before Ed. It had struck her once when he'd hung up before their conversation had even finished because he'd got an e-mail; after that she'd realized that it happened every time. Even when she planned to end the conversation before he did, he managed to get in there first. Ed probably didn't know what an empty sound the click of someone else hanging up was, she thought despondently.

16

The hospice wasn't what Kate had expected. Somehow, the word *hospice* combined with *cancer* and *patient* had conjured up in her mind a picture of a Victorian hospital with iron grilles at the windows and a stern-looking matron in charge. Which she'd known was going to be wide off the mark, first because they weren't in the Victorian era anymore, second because they didn't have matrons these days, and third because Carole Jacobs had explicitly told her that it was more of a house than a hospital.

But it was still a shock the following morning when, having lied to Magda that she had a dentist appointment so that she could see St. Mary's Hospice for herself, she discovered that it looked like a home—not an institutional one but a real one. A place where people lived. It was a squareish building, Victorian (Kate noted that point with a certain amount of satisfaction), and very rambling for a London house. Somehow it felt as if it had been uprooted from a village somewhere and plonked down in the middle of South East London. Ivy was growing up the walls and, in some cases, through windows that had apparently been left slightly open at one point and were now permanently held that way by a green and living draft generator.

It was also a shock that Carole Jacobs seemed to think that Kate could do something with this place for next to no money. It looked as if the whole place would crumble to the ground if you took one brick out of the middle of a wall, and that was just the outside. Kate hardly dared to see the state of the interior.

"They were going to tear it down," Carole said in her cheerful way as she opened the front door and signaled for Kate to go through. "We saved it, though, and look at it now. Isn't it wonderful?"

Kate smiled cautiously. Carole Jacobs, she'd learned, was not a woman who liked to focus much on negatives. She had drive and determination, enough for a small army, and she appeared to believe that Kate could work miracles. Which was nice, really it was. But there were limits even to Kate's creativity.

Inside the hospice was even more dilapidated than the outside. Paint on the walls barely disguised large patches of damp, and wires trailed everywhere, taped to walls or floors so that they wouldn't be a hazard. The place needed to be completely rewired, Kate realized in alarm. Most of the walls should be taken back to their bare bones and replastered. And presumably it all had to be done with the patients in situ.

Still, that wasn't her problem, she told herself. It wasn't as if she was going to be involved. Advice, that's all Carole had asked for. And that's all she would be able to give, however much Carole flattered her.

Taking a deep breath, she followed Carole down a short corridor and through a door.

"And this is the dayroom," Carole said proudly. "Everyone, this is Kate. From the television. She's the one who's going to transform this place."

Kate looked at her and raised an eyebrow. "Not transform," she amended. "Advise on the transformation. Help, you know, in a *consultative* way . . ."

Her voice trailed off as she took in the sea of smiling faces in front of her. There were five men and women sitting on armchairs in front of the television, three of them wrapped in blankets. There were four more women in the corner playing a game of cards, an elderly gentleman and a boy of about seventeen hunched over a game of chess, and a girl who didn't look more than fifteen with her nose buried in a book, which she hurriedly put down when she saw Kate.

Two of the women playing cards had scarves wrapped around their heads; the other two had obviously given up trying to disguise their baldness and were proudly exhibiting soft downy hair like that found on a baby's head.

"This is Betty," Carole said, taking Kate around the room. "Betty's going back to Charing Cross for surgery in a couple of weeks, and then she'll be back here for her chemo."

Betty, a bright-looking woman in her sixties, held out her hand and smiled at Kate, her eyes twinkling. She didn't look ill. She looked like someone's mother. Maybe someone's grandmother.

"Charing Cross?" Kate asked, before she could stop herself. That was Tom's hospital.

"Yes, dear. We're just around the corner from them. And this is Margaret, who's going back home at the end of this week."

"I might not be," Margaret said quickly. "I mean, I could stay a little while. If we're going to be on television."

Kate smiled as she was introduced to them all. She talked to each of them about their stay in the hospice, about the cancers they were fighting, and about their relief to have somewhere to stay that wasn't a ward, a place that didn't remind them every minute of every day that they were very ill, that allowed them a semblance of dignity. She also found out that their favorite colors included blue, yellow, and pink, but not that nasty peachy pink color that reminded Margaret of sick. They smiled gratefully at Kate and seemed so excited about telling her small fragments of detail about themselves— about their families, their friends, the homes that they'd had to leave. Each of them had a story to tell. A story more courageous and difficult than anything she'd known in her life, and she felt at once both humbled and uplifted. She hadn't known quite what she'd expected, but the people in front of her didn't seem sick. They were fighters, locked in battle and cheerfully getting on with life in the meantime.

"So," Carole said eventually, when she'd taken Kate around the entire house, showing her the small bedrooms, the cramped staff quarters, and the dilapidated bathrooms. "I know there's a lot to do, but what do you think?"

Her eyes were shining with excitement, and Kate thought not for the first time that Carole was a dangerous woman.

She took a deep breath. "You realize it isn't just a redecoration job?" she asked. "I mean, you do realize that the wiring is shot, that there aren't enough plug sockets anywhere, that the walls are damp and the bathroom fittings need to be replaced?"

Carole's face creased into a worried frown. "Oh dear. Is it really that bad? Couldn't we just . . . brighten it up a bit?"

Kate shook her head. "It's a hazard," she said matter-of-factly. "And it's cold, too. Half the windows have got ivy growing through them."

"Fresh air is good, though, isn't it?" Carole offered.

Kate shook her head again. "Not when heating is so expensive. Look, isn't there any way of raising more money?"

Carole looked at her sadly. "The trouble is, dear, most of the people who come to us don't have much money. The ones with money have places to go. And we're such a small charity—it's really just a handful of us. We got some initial funding from Cancer Trust UK— they helped us buy the house in the first place, but the deal was that we took it from there, so to speak. We could hold a 'bring and buy' sale, but I don't think you're talking about a couple of hundred pounds, are you?"

Kate looked down at the floor. What could she do? The only sensible advice she could offer was to forget all about any ideas of redecoration until they had some serious money.

Carole studied her, then nodded. "I understand, dear. Please don't worry. It was very good of you to come and see us—I know everyone really appreciated your visit."

Kate grimaced. She didn't want to walk away. In her head she had already started doing some sketches, opening up the space, livening the place up with colors and fabrics that would make the residents feel more alive.

But it was impossible. She wouldn't even know where to start.

"If we had the money, I could do it," she said with determination, watching Carole's face light up as she spoke. "*Would* do it, I mean. But we are talking about a lot, I'm afraid. Is there no one else you could ask? No one else who'd be willing to pay . . . ?"

Carole dropped her eyes, then braced herself. "We'll just keep saving up," she said brightly. "Until we've got enough."

Kate nodded guiltily. It wasn't as if she could wave a magic wand, it wasn't as if she could just magic money out of thin air. "I'll keep in touch," she promised. "And if I think of any . . . shortcuts, I'll let you know."

Carole smiled. "Thank you, Kate. Thank you so much."

For what? Kate thought with a sigh as she said good-bye and made her way quickly back to work.

Phil walked over, his hand scratching his beard in a familiar gesture that Kate knew meant bad news. She was only an hour—maybe two hours—late, but already she'd had two text messages from Phil and a phone call from Magda, who didn't seem remotely convinced by her "I'm at the dentist" excuse.

"What is it?" Kate asked.

"You seen them ceilings in the kitchen?" he asked, his face contorting into its usual pained expression. "You can't go fixing new lights up there—the whole thing's going to come down."

Kate's shoulders dropped. She'd thought Sarah Jones's insistence on having a leather sofa was bad enough—she didn't need more problems. With a sigh, she followed Phil out from her vantage point in the hallway back toward the kitchen.

"You see where you've marked them crosses on the ceiling?" he asked.

Kate nodded. "Yes, the lights have to go there," she said firmly, "because the kitchen table's going to go right underneath. I want old-fashioned lights that come down low over the table, creating a cozy glow for family dinners when it's cold outside."

Phil looked at her. "You know that this lot'll never have family dinners, don't you?" he said, shaking his head. "They've got a sixteen-year-old son who'll be up playing computer games every night and old Mr. Jones'll probably be down the pub."

"He won't when this kitchen has become the haven he's always longed for," Kate said obstinately. "Sarah will cook delicious roasts and they'll all sit down together and talk about their day. . . ."

Phil raised an eyebrow. "I'm not being funny or anything, but from what I hear, Sarah Jones doesn't want a kitchen table with low-hanging lights. She wants a chrome and leather sofa."

"Don't you start," Kate warned, wincing as little flecks of plaster started to float down from the ceiling. "I'm just doing my job, and we've all agreed that chintz is the look we're going for here. Neither Bree Van De Kamp nor Camilla Parker Bowles would be seen dead with a leather and chrome sofa."

Phil's smile was sardonic. "Wouldn't they, now? Well, if that's what you want, we need to board up the ceiling. Nothing's going to hang from it otherwise."

"Fine," Kate said gloomily, "board the ceiling. It'll only set us back a few hours."

Phil pulled a face that suggested that 'a few hours' might be a tad optimistic, and mooched off. Kate turned to see Gareth walking into the room. Or, rather, flouncing in.

"She hates it all!" he said desperately. "Kate, she just looked at it and shook her head. Didn't even say anything. I'd done a whole drawing of her with darker hair with some beautiful subtle highlights and she winced. Winced! Oh, God, it's a disaster!"

"You just explain it's so she looks good sitting underneath the low kitchen light," Phil said, pausing at the door, the corners of his mouth creeping upward. "I'm sure she'll love it then."

"Ignore him," Kate ordered. "He's on his way to do some work, *aren't you Phil*?"

Phil grinned and departed. "And don't worry," Kate said, turning to Gareth. "She was the same with me. It was as if she hadn't agreed to the concept or something. Ah, Magda!"

Magda had just appeared, her forehead creased into lines. "What?" she asked.

"Mrs. Jones seems to be having some second thoughts about the concept," Kate said. "I wonder if you could maybe have a quick word with her—remind her what it was she agreed to. Otherwise this week is going to be seriously difficult."

"The concept. Yes," Magda mused. The week before filming, paperwork was always biked to the next week's victim, outlining the concept and budget and other details of the show. Until they had signed the papers, including a whole load of legal jargon that basically said they couldn't blame the show for anything that went wrong whatsoever, work didn't start. They usually left the courier there waiting, just to further encourage the victim(s) to sign it and quickly.

"The thing is," Magda said, looking nowhere in particular, "last Friday I got a bit sidetracked."

Kate frowned. "But they got the paperwork. Right?"

Magda bit her lip.

"Magda!" Kate shrieked. "If she hasn't signed the paperwork we're in serious trouble."

"Look, I'm on it," Magda growled. "I do have other things on my mind, you know. Like whether we're going to have a show to worry about in a few weeks."

"Are things really that bad?" Kate asked. "I mean, could they really pull it?"

Magda sighed. "No one ever bloody cries on this show. We need life stories that blow people away, drama that has people sitting on the edge of their seats, and instead we get overweight housewives who can't be arsed turning their lives around. I sometimes think we don't deserve to stay on air."

Kate looked at her hesitantly. Drama and life stories? That's what she wanted?

"Have you ever thought about us taking on something . . . bigger?" Kate asked tentatively. "Like, say, a hospice, or something?"

Magda shrugged. "That's where people go to die, isn't it? I can't really see that working. We want *life* stories, not death ones, Kate. Anyway, look, I better get on. Don't worry about the paperwork. You just concentrate on getting that ceiling filmable, yeah?"

She hurried off, and Kate's brow furrowed in thought. Magda was wrong. The hospice would make great television, and that way she'd get the funding for the transformation. She just had to think of a way to persuade her.

"Okay, so Joe, you sit right there. You're going to be fed cream cheese on a cracker, and I want you to lick your lips afterward. But make sure there's no cream cheese on your tongue when you do it." The director pointed to a leather chair and Joe obediently sat down.

"And then I say my line?" Joe asked.

"No. We're going to film it before and edit it in. Can't risk you having a mouth full of cream cheese."

"And when do you think my costar might get here?" Joe asked with a loud sigh. "What's keeping her, anyway?"

The director frowned. "Where's Penny?" he demanded. "What's holding her up?"

"Makeup," someone shouted. "They're having problems achieving the dewy skin you wanted."

"Well, tell them to get a move on," the director shouted back.

"So, Joe, why don't you practice your line? Remember, you need to look right into the camera."

Joe cleared his throat. "Mmmm, creamy," he said.

"Yeah, that's great. But maybe with a bit more sex appeal? We want housewives to get excited by this, okay?"

Joe nodded and tried again. "Mmm. Creamy," he said lasciviously.

"Hmm. Sexy, but not porn film. We want that All-American Boy feel, you know? Flirtatious but not threatening. You know what I mean?"

"Sure," Joe said. "All-American. Gotcha."

He opened his mouth to say the line again, but before he could, a scrawny-looking woman with peroxided hair arrived on the set.

"These fucking makeup people are a joke," she seethed. "I could do a better job than them. And where's the director? I want to talk about my lines."

The director walked over and smiled. "Hi Penny, I'm Andrew. And don't worry about lines—yours is a visual role."

"That's the problem," the woman said angrily. "Either you give me a line, or I'm out of here."

"You want a line?" the director asked.

The woman smiled. "There, that wasn't so hard. Now, who's this?" She was looking at Joe and he flinched.

"Joe Rogers," he said. "I'm Joe Rogers, ma'am."

She appraised him. "Well, yes, I think you'll do."

"*You* think I'll do?" he asked. "Andrew, what the hell is this?"

Andrew gave a patient smile. "Penny, Joe is a successful actor, so we're very lucky to have him here. Joe, Penny Pennington is a bit of a British institution. I'm sure you'll get along famously."

Joe frowned. "Penny Pennington from *Future: Perfect*? You had a hit single way back when?"

Penny's eyes narrowed. "Well, you do know your stuff. And it wasn't that way back, if you don't mind." She moved closer to Joe and sat down on the arm of his chair. "So you're a successful actor, are you? Why have I never seen you in anything?"

"I've been working in the States until recently." Joe smiled thinly. "I've worked on some big shows over there."

Penny met his eyes and licked her lips. "And now you're over here. Looking for fame and glory?"

"Looking for interesting work."

"Like cream cheese advertisements?" Penny asked silkily.

Joe's eyes narrowed.

"So tell me, Joe," Penny continued. "Have you got yourself a girl-friend over here in England?"

Joe nodded.

"Shame," Penny said. "Because I think we'd make rather a photo-genic couple, don't you? I can see a double page spread in *OK!* mag-azine coming out rather well."

Joe's eyes widened slightly. A double page spread? "Right. Well, I'm taken, so I guess that won't be happening." He allowed a little un-certainty into his voice.

"I guess it won't," Penny agreed with a pout. Then she smiled again. "So who is this girlfriend? She must be quite something."

"I think you know her, actually," Joe said, shrugging. "Kate Heth-erington. From your show."

Penny's eyes widened. "Kate?"

Joe nodded, and Penny laughed. "God, and there I was thinking your girlfriend would be competition. Now I'm just questioning your judgment." She looked at him meaningfully, then turned to An-drew.

"So, Andrew, about my lines. I was thinking that as I feed Joe here the cream cheese, I could say 'So, honey, how do you like this?' "

She smiled, winningly, and Andrew, defeated, turned to his assis-tant. "We're going to need more coffee." He exhaled deeply. "I think this is going to be a long day."

17

Keeping Romance Alive

Starting a romance is easy. You may not think so, but believe me, people start romances all the time. It's keeping romances going that's the difficult bit—keeping the interest going, keeping the romance alive. So what can the hopeless romantic do to make sure her dreams don't just come true but stay true, day after day, week after week?

The answer is simple: You must look after yourself, and you must look after the man in your life.

Looking after yourself is covered in the next chapter, where we'll look at the preparation required to look naturally, effortlessly beautiful. Looking after the man in your life is just as important. A man who feels that he is the center of your world, who knows that he will always have your full attention, and who can rely on you to put him first and address his needs before your own, will be a man who loves you, honors you, and stays true to you. . . .

Joe was exhausted. Eight hours he'd been filming for an advert that was going to last less than two minutes. And they said they might need him back tomorrow, too. With that woman. God, Penny Pennington drove him crazy. All she talked about was herself, her line, her shot.

He hated big-headed women. They were such a pain in the ass to be around. So much better to hang out with women who were interested in him, who wanted to make *him* happy. Like Kate. She always seemed to want to listen to what he had to say. Which was exactly as it should be, Joe thought.

Just wait till he told her he'd been working with Penny, he thought with a smile. Of all the people. She wouldn't believe it.

Still, it was money. And it would be profile. His agent had promised great things from this. Just yesterday he'd auditioned for a crime show, and he had a good feeling about it. Frowning, he dug out his phone. Might as well check in. Might as well see how things were.

"Bob!" he said, when his line connected. "It's me. Just finished filming. Thought I'd see how my audition went yesterday, what else is in the cards, that kind of thing."

"Joe! Great to hear from you. So filming went well, did it? How did you get on with your leading lady?"

"Nightmare," Joe said. "So, about my auditions?"

Bob drew in his breath. "Joe, I'm not going to lie to you, you didn't get the part. But I don't want you to get downhearted. Something good will come your way, I know it."

"Right," Joe said uncertainly. "They give you any feedback?"

"They loved you," Bob enthused. "Really loved you. But it's that profile thing, Joe. It's a problem for us. People like a recognizable face."

"Recognizable. Right."

"The advert will help. Only it's not due to air for another three months . . ."

"Three months? What the hell am I going to do for three months? Man, this is a joke."

"I know, I know. Joe, I'm on your side. But it's competitive out there. If you're not a celebrity already, it's hard to get people's attention. I'm working on it, though. When the ad comes out, we'll see if we can't get you a little snippet in *Hot Gossip* magazine. Get people talking about you."

"*Hot Gossip* magazine."

"Sure. Or maybe not *Hot Gossip*, but certainly one of the listings magazines. I'm sure we could get you an inch or so in one of them. With a photo."

"And that's how you get acting work around here? You get your face in magazines?"

"Bear with me, Joe. I know it's tough." Bob encouraged him. "But you can do it. I know you can."

"Sure," Joe said morosely. "Whatever."

The doorbell went, and Kate put her book down and got up to open it. "Hi!" she said, leaning up to put her arms around Joe's neck. "How was the filming?"

"Yeah, it was okay," Joe said. "You'll never guess who my costar was."

Kate frowned. "Who?"

"One Penny Pennington."

"No! Oh, God, you poor thing. Was she horrible?"

"Worse than horrible. You have my full sympathy for working with that woman." He made his way to the kitchen and sat down with a sigh. "You ever been in *Hot Gossip* magazine?" he asked.

Kate looked at him strangely. "Me? No. Why?"

"You're on television, right? I mean, you're like a mini-celebrity. You could get yourself in there, couldn't you?"

Kate laughed outright. "Joe, I am not even a Z-list celebrity. I'm on a crappy show on cable that no one watches and I can guarantee that *Hot Gossip* magazine would never be interested in me in a million years."

"Shame," Joe said. "So you don't think they'd be interested in our relationship? You know, television star and LA actor?"

"Like Teri Hatcher and George Clooney, you mean?" Kate giggled. "Yeah, I'm sure they'd be all over it."

Joe smiled wryly. "Hey, it was just a thought. So what have you got cooking there? Something good? I'm starving."

"How does lasagna followed by chocolate pudding sound?" she asked. "All cooked by hand, from scratch."

"You know, I think I'm in love with you," Joe said, his eyes shining as he looked at Kate.

She gulped. "In . . . in love?"

"Sure. What, you're not in love with me?"

Kate looked at Joe hesitantly, then broke into a broad, happy smile. Maybe Americans fell in love quickly, she found herself thinking. Maybe the problem with English men was that they took too long to make their minds up. "Of course I am," she said, reaching her arms around his neck and resting her head gratefully on his shoulder. She'd found love, she realized. Found true love. And it had all been so easy.

"Well, that's good," Joe said easily. "So, this food, is it ready? I'm famished."

"Just another ten minutes," Kate said, pulling herself away and walking to the oven. "Now, tell me about your day. I want to hear everything."

Sal thought she might be about to throw up. She felt wretched, and she'd only been on the bloody machine for about ten minutes. She used to be able to run the 1500 meters with no sweat, and now she had been decimated by a pathetic jog.

She stepped off the machine slowly and luckily had the forethought to hold on to its side; as her feet touched the ground, her legs almost buckled beneath her. Crumpling to the floor was hardly a good look on her first visit to the gym. With Jim.

He'd been really sweet, signing her in and showing her around, all smiles and flirty little comments like "Oh, I'm sure you'll find it a breeze." She wasn't used to people saying nice things. It wasn't that

Ed wasn't *nice*—of course he was. But he was Ed. Very early on in their relationship they'd been relaxed enough in each other's company to forgo all the niceties like saying "you look good today," instead choosing to bestow affectionate insults. Neither of them was a terribly romantic person; they weren't the sort to send red roses or call the other the love of their life. So rather than call Sal "gorgeous" or "darling," Ed called her "midget" because she was only 5′4″ to his 6′1″; instead of calling him "my love" or "my destiny," she called him "chunky hunk" because of his expanding girth. They regularly referred to themselves and each other as "dull middle-aged bores" in a self-deprecating-but-actually-quite-smug way. After all, she'd always thought that they were dull because they were happy. Married. Settled.

But now it didn't seem quite so a warm. Last night, when Ed had looked all grumpy at the idea of spending two weeks on holiday with her, she'd started to think that maybe things were even more serious than she'd feared. Two weeks with his wife was too much for Ed to contemplate.

The truth was that now the word *settled* had a very different ring to it. *Dull* seemed to be a description of her marriage. And real middle age was only just around the corner.

"You alright?" Sal looked up to see Jim grinning at her with a concerned look. "Yes. Oh, yes, I'm fine. Just . . . well, haven't been to the gym for a while," she lied, forcing a smile onto her face and hoping that the nausea would go away.

"Well, I'm going to be done quite soon—maybe we could have a juice? They've got a nice café downstairs."

"Great!" Sal could see spots before her eyes and needed desperately to shove her head between her legs, but until Jim walked away, she knew she would stay upright, grinning inanely at him.

Thankfully he turned round and made his way to the free weights section, leaving Sal to run to a mat and flop down, pretending to stretch her hamstrings. A juice. That would be nice. And there was no reason to feel even a smidgeon of guilt. It was a juice, not a drink!

Well, okay, it was a *drink*, but not an alcoholic one. Not one that had any suggestion of anything other than rehydration to it.

So why was she feeling a tremor of fear, anticipation, and excitement? Why had she packed some eyeliner and foundation in her gym bag so that she could make herself presentable after her shower? Why had she blushed—only figuratively, since her face had been so red already from exertion that it just wasn't possible to flush any further—when Jim had brushed his arm against hers just now?

She knew why. Of course she knew. She'd already committed the crime, that's why. Just one little word. Not even a whole word. And by saying it, she might as well have taken off her wedding ring, put on a low-cut top, and gone to some cheap bar an hour before closing time. Even now, she wasn't sure why or how she'd said it. How she could be so brutal, so cruel, so . . . honest.

On the way to the gym, Jim had said, "You're married aren't you?"

She'd replied, "Yes, that's right."

Then he'd asked, "Happily?"

And she had said . . .

Sal cringed and felt the guilt flare up inside her like a fire in a paper factory.

She had said *ish*.

18

"What time is Ed going to be back?"

"God knows," Sal said, rolling her eyes as she peeled vegetables at her large double sink whilst Kate chopped. Kate couldn't help noticing that all the surfaces gleamed. Only Sal could cook a three-course meal and still have a kitchen that looked as if it should be photographed for a catalog.

"You know what he's like," Sal continued. "I mean, he said he'd be here by eight p.m., but only if nothing crops up at work. Frankly, your guess is as good as mine."

Kate grinned. Ed's timekeeping was legendary—he'd even been late for his own stag do because there had been a deal going through and he hadn't been able to get away from work. She noticed that Sal was frowning, deep lines embedded on her forehead that Kate had never noticed before. "Everything alright?" she offered, cursing as she nearly sliced off one of her fingers for the fifth time.

"Me? God, fine. No, I'm just wondering why I had to marry a financier, that's all."

"Being a financier was on your list, remember?" Kate said with a smile. "You wanted someone who could cover a mortgage and school fees on his salary. Which basically means a financier or a pop star, and you also wanted someone dependable, which kind of ruled out Robbie Williams. . . ."

"I suppose," Sal conceded. "So come on, tell me about Joe. Where is he, by the way?"

"I sent him to buy wine," Kate said lightly, then turned to face Sal. "It's amazing, actually. I mean, I don't want to jinx it or anything, but I actually think he could be the one."

"The one? Seriously?"

Kate smiled. "Maybe. We just get on so well. The sex is amazing. And we've got loads in common, too. Like, guess who he did an advert with this week? Who, incidentally, he hates now as much as I do."

"Um, I dunno, that girl off *Big Brother*?"

Kate rolled her eyes. "Penny Pennington, of course."

"Really? Oh God. Poor him."

"I know. Apparently it was awful. But the point is, we're in similar worlds, you know?"

"So he's got some work, too. That's good," Sal said.

Kate shrugged. "Only an advert, but his agent is really excited about the interest in him. He's just being really choosy, you know. To make sure he gets the right thing."

"That's great," Sal said sincerely. "Really great."

Kate gave a deep, happy sigh. "It is, isn't it. It's like we were meant to find each other, you know? I mean, I know Tom always takes the piss because he thinks I'm a hopeless romantic, but maybe that's not such a bad thing. Maybe all my waiting has paid off."

Sal raised her eyebrows. "God, you are serious."

"Maybe I am." Kate grinned. "Tell me . . . when you met Ed, what was it like? I mean, how did you know he was the one?"

Sal frowned. "He had a lovely face," she said. "I remember looking at his face and thinking it was so open, so honest. And then we had a lovely evening—we were having dinner at a new restaurant. And we had lots to talk about, I remember that. We barely ate any of our food because we had so much to say. . . ."

"Yes, yes, I know that," Kate said impatiently. "But how did you know? You know, deep down? How did you know that he was the person you wanted to marry?"

Sal reddened a little and moved over toward the cooker. "I just did, I suppose," she said, biting her lip. "I mean, he was a nice guy. Look, I know you believe in thunderbolts and stuff, but sometimes things just make sense. At the time, I mean."

Kate looked at her curiously. But before she could probe any more, the doorbell rang.

"Can you answer that?" Sal asked. "I need to keep an eye on the veg."

Kate nodded and nipped down the corridor. She swung open the front door to find Tom standing there, clutching a bottle of wine.

"Well, if it isn't our romantic heroine," he said, smiling darkly.

Kate returned his smile with the sweetest in her arsenal. "And the great cynic himself. We were just talking about you, actually."

Tom raised an eyebrow and followed Kate into the kitchen. "That's bad news," he said. "People never say nice things about me.

"Ah, Sal. Smells divine, whatever it is," he added, planting a kiss on her cheek, which was hot from standing by the stove.

"Tom," Kate said as he turned to kiss her, "remind me later that I need to ask you about a hospice. St. Mary's Hospice. It's near your hospital, I think."

"St. Mary's? I know it well. Several of my patients have either been there or are going there. Why do you know about it?"

Kate shrugged. "They might want me to do a refurb, that's all."

"Really? Kate, that's amazing. What a great thing to do."

Kate's smile was embarrassed. "I'm not actually doing anything. Yet, I mean. There's no funding, to start with, and it's a huge job. But I was thinking about maybe getting Magda to look at it. You know, as a television thing."

Tom frowned. "Right. I see. Well, yeah, you know, whatever you need to know . . ." He rummaged around for a corkscrew and opened his bottle of wine. "So, Joe not coming?" he asked with a little smile. "Have you decided that his hair's the wrong color, or that you don't like his accent after all?"

Kate rolled her eyes. "No, actually. He's buying wine."

Tom handed her a glass. "How very good of him," he said.

"Kate thinks she's in love," Sal said suddenly. "She thinks Joe might be the one."

Tom frowned. "Don't talk rubbish." He looked searchingly at Kate. "You can't possibly know something like that after a week."

"Nearly *two* weeks," Kate said. "And Sal, I told you that in confidence."

"Tom is in confidence," Sal said. "I just thought he should know so that he makes sure he's polite to him."

"I'm always polite," Tom said, gulping his wine and pouring himself another. "But Kate, come on. You're not serious, are you?"

Kate raised her eyebrows. "Thirsty, are you?" she asked, then sighed. "I don't know. I think so. It's different with Joe. I'm different. I listen more, and I actually like looking after him."

Tom, who had started on his second glass of wine, nearly spat it out with laughter. "You like looking after him? You know, that's worrying on so many levels. For one, is he a man or a child? And for another, Kate, you can barely look after yourself!"

Kate narrowed her eyes at him. "Look, I like him. Okay? And after years of telling me I'm a perfectionist or a hopeless romantic or that I should just stop complaining and find myself a husband, I think the two of you should be a bit more supportive."

"Sorry, Kate," Sal said with a sigh. "You're right. He sounds lovely. I'm sure he is lovely."

Kate turned expectantly to Tom, who sniffed. "I still think you're being very premature," he said, becoming very interested in Sal's notice board. "He could be a serial killer, for all you know."

As he spoke, there was the sound of keys in the door, and Ed came rushing through. "Sorry, sorry, got caught up. Hello, darling. Kate, Tom, good to see you as always. I found this chap loitering outside, too. Seems to think he's invited."

He turned and grinned at Joe, who was standing behind him, and moved aside to let him in. Joe, who looked a little nonplussed, smiled.

"Joe!" Kate said, rushing over to give him a kiss. "This is Sal, and this is Tom. And this is Joe!"

"Lovely to meet you, Joe," Sal said quickly, wiping her hands on her apron so she could shake his. "We've heard so much about you."

Joe smiled easily. "And you," he said. "And thanks for having me over here. Much appreciated."

"Oh, it's nothing," Sal said, turning back to the stove. "Ed, can you get some more wine? And lay the table? Right, everyone, food will be ready soon, so why don't you go and sit down in the dining room so I can get on with serving?"

Everyone made their way to the dining room, Tom carrying his wine bottle with him and pouring himself a refill as soon as he had sat down. Kate shot him a look, but he didn't appear to notice.

"Right, well, here we are," Sal said emerging from the kitchen a few minutes later when everyone was sitting around her formally laid dining table. "I thought I'd dispense with starters because we're having sticky toffee pudding after this and it's quite rich."

She placed a large fish pie on the table, along with a medley of vegetables, and sat down, looking with irritation at Ed, who was staring at his BlackBerry.

"Not at the table, please," she hissed, and he rolled his eyes before putting it back in his pocket.

"This is wonderful," Tom said, as soon as he'd taken a mouthful.

Kate nodded in agreement. "Completely delicious. Really amazing." She turned to Ed. "So, Ed, how are things? How's work?"

Ed sighed. "Oh, you know. Market's up so things are busy, but it's getting more competitive. Investment houses setting up their own analysis divisions doesn't help."

She nodded seriously. "Right." Kate never knew how to talk to Ed. She'd never managed to find a subject on which they both had something to say.

"And you're an actor?" Sal said, turning to Joe, who grinned.

"Guilty as charged," he said, his eyes twinkling.

"That must be so interesting," Sal continued. "So exciting. Have you worked with anyone famous?"

Joe nodded. "You heard of Cindy Taylor? Or Brad Anderson?"

Sal shook her head, looking regretful. "No, sorry, I don't have much time to watch television, I'm afraid. I've heard of Cindy Crawford and Brad Pitt, though," she added helpfully.

Joe frowned. "How about Randy Beat and Stu Edwards? I worked with them on a show before I got the part on *Everything I Do*."

Sal flushed. "I might have heard those names. . . . I mean, I'm sure I'd recognize them. If I saw them."

"Joe's huge in LA," Kate said. "But he wanted to come to London because there's more interesting work. It's really easy to get type-cast in LA, isn't it, Joe?"

Joe nodded seriously.

"And have you found any yet? Interesting work, I mean?" Tom asked. He was looking intently at Joe, Kate noticed, but his focus seemed to be a little off. She noticed that his wine glass was empty again, and felt herself frowning.

"Hey, it hasn't been long." Joe grinned, though it seemed a little forced. "I've had some offers, but nothing that's really grabbed me, you know?"

Tom nodded thoughtfully. "Is it theater work you're after?" he asked.

"Stage?" Joe looked at him, incredulous. "God, no. I'm a television actor, really."

Tom's eyes widened in surprise and he shot a little smile at Kate, who glared at him.

"Tom doesn't watch television either," she said, rolling her eyes. "You can imagine how excited he and Sal were when I got the job on *Future: Perfect*. I made them watch it once, and I think that's still the only episode they've ever seen."

Sal frowned. "That's not true. I saw the one where someone

threw paint at Penny, too. Anyway, the only reason we never watch it is because you made us swear we wouldn't."

"Television is vacuous," Tom said loudly. "Television is responsible for society's ills. Isn't that true, Joe?"

Joe looked at him as if he was speaking a foreign language. "You're joking, right?" he said, his voice faltering. "Television is, like, bigger than film these days. And it's not just shows and stuff. There are documentaries, too. . . ."

"Of course he's joking. Aren't you, Tom," Kate said, shooting him a meaningful look. She smiled at Joe. "I think acting on television is just wonderful. And I'm sure Tom does, too."

Tom grinned and poured himself another glass of wine, taking a large gulp as soon as the glass was full. "Very well, I'm joking. Although I thought there were fewer opportunities for actors nowadays. Isn't it all reality shows and hidden cameras? Like your show, Kate?"

Kate put her knife and fork down noisily. "Which you obviously consider vacuous, too. Thanks, Tom. You really are a ray of sunshine this evening."

Ed picked up the bottle of wine next to Tom, realized it was empty, and reached for another. "I think television is a wonderful invention," he said. "And I'm sure being an actor beats working in the City."

"Yes," Sal said tightly. "At least Joe seems to be around in the evening on occasion."

Ed looked at her strangely, and poured her some wine. "You must have some good stories, though, Joe," he continued. "Haven't you?"

Kate gave him a grateful smile. "Joe, why don't you tell everyone about that advert you did with Penny. It was such a great story."

Joe grinned and held out his glass to Ed for a refill. "Sure. No problem."

An hour later, Kate excused herself to go to the loo. She had to admit, she'd been to better dinner parties. Sal kept glaring at Ed when he tapped surreptitiously on the keypad of his BlackBerry. Tom, she suspected, was very drunk—either that or in a very belligerent mood. Whichever it was, he was being incredibly patronizing and wasn't laughing at any of Joe's stories. And Joe seemed bored, which was hardly surprising, since no one apart from her appeared to be listening to a thing he said. For her part, she had laughed noisily and heavily every time Joe had even attempted a joke, and every time the conversation switched to her, she had done her best to throw it back to Joe. But whatever he said seemed to result in either incredulous looks or stilted pauses, which she then found herself either filling with more "interesting" facts about Joe or asking him yet more questions about himself, which just seemed to rile Tom further.

Making her way back, she ducked into the kitchen to get herself a glass of water. As she turned on the tap, she felt someone come up behind her.

"You cannot tell me that he is The One," she heard a voice say right behind her, and she turned round irritably to see Tom shaking his head at her. "There's nothing to him," he continued. "He's as vacuous as the television shows he works on."

"He is not!" Kate shot back. "He's lovely, and interesting, and if you weren't so bloody pompous about television, you'd think so, too. You've never even seen him act. He's great."

Tom raised his eyebrows. "I doubt that very much. Look, he's good-looking—even I can see that. But that's all he's got to offer."

"How dare you!" Kate exploded. "How dare you be so arrogant? Just because he isn't a doctor doesn't mean he hasn't got a lot to offer. And at least he doesn't go round pronouncing things that he's never even seen as *vacuous*. What, is it your word for the day or something? Are you moving on to words beginning with w tomorrow?"

Tom shook his head and staggered slightly as he lost his balance. "Fine. Don't listen to me. You certainly seem to enjoy listening to him. You're different around him, you know. Worse different, in case you're wondering. Hanging on his every word, asking him questions all the time like he can't talk for himself. It's like he's turned you into a Stepford wife, or something."

"You're drunk," Kate said. "And I'm not a Stepford wife. Being thoughtful and attentive are considered good qualities, you know."

"By whom?" Tom asked, incredulous. "I prefer the Kate who talks over other people's conversations and tells us all where to go. Like now, in fact. This is the most animated I've seen you all evening."

"What are you two doing in here?" Sal said, appearing in the doorway. "I was wondering what you'd got up to."

Kate walked toward her, folding her arms as she did so. "Tom was just telling me that he doesn't like Joe," she said hotly. "In that supportive manner he has."

Sal frowned. "Come on, you two, make friends," she urged them. "Kate, I think Joe's lovely. And Tom does, too. He's just being a grumpy bastard as always. Aren't you, Tom?"

Tom looked at her sternly. "I just don't think he's good enough, that's all," he said, swaying a little.

"God, you're pissed," Sal said, rolling her eyes. "Right, drink some water."

"Ed doesn't like him either," Tom said, as Sal found a glass and filled it with water. "He'd rather send e-mails than listen to *his* stories."

Sal gave the glass to Tom. "Ed is being unforgivably rude, and I will be telling him so later," she said in a low voice. "But right now, we are all going to go back to the dining room and have a nice time. Okay?"

"I'm just being honest, that's all," Tom said, putting the glass down on the side. "Kate's nearly thirty, so she's trying to convince herself that this American chap is right for her, when it's obvious that he isn't."

"And what the hell would you know?" Kate asked in a furious undertone. "You wouldn't know a mature relationship if it bit you on the ass. And Joe *is* right for me. Unlike you, he doesn't look down on what I do. Unlike you, he isn't mean about people behind their backs. And unlike you, he isn't twisted and bitter and convinced that there's no such thing as a happy ending."

Tom shook his head. "On the contrary, I think there can be happy endings. Look at Sal here. She's got her happy ending. But she didn't have some half-baked idea about The One; she was sensible, knew what she was looking for, and found Ed."

Sal stared at Tom. "You think I settled, don't you?" she burst out accusingly. "You think that my marriage is just a practical arrangement to pay the mortgage."

Tom frowned. "I didn't say that."

"But you were thinking it. You both think it. I can see it in your eyes."

"No!" Kate said.

"*Yes*," Sal said. "Well, fine, you're right. There was no thunderbolt. It didn't occur to me to wonder whether Ed was The One or not; he was there. And I wanted to get married. . . ." Her voice cracked.

"Sal, don't be stupid," Tom said, grimacing. "We were talking about Kate, not you. You got married because you wanted to, and we're very happy for you. And you know we love Ed."

"But do I? Do I love him?" Sal asked desperately. "That's what I don't know."

Kate swallowed as she looked over to the door and saw Ed and Joe standing there with startled expressions on their faces.

"We . . . we wondered where you'd all got to," Ed said. "Didn't realize it had turned into a kitchen party."

Sal stared at him for a second or two, then appeared to pull herself together. "God. Sorry. Yes. I was just getting dessert."

Ed nodded awkwardly. "I'll just . . . I'll be . . ." He turned back vaguely toward the dining room.

"Actually, we should get going," Kate said. "I mean, it's getting late."

Sal nodded. "Yes. Yes, I suppose it is."

In the charged silence, Kate grabbed her coat and she and Joe said their good-byes. She barely dared meet Ed's eyes, gave Tom a cursory wave, and embraced Sal in a huge hug.

Tom picked up the glass next to him on the counter, poured the water out, and filled it with wine, as Sal saw Kate and Joe to the door.

"Well," she said, kissing Kate on the cheek, "at least now I know why I don't throw dinner parties very often."

19

Tom woke up feeling like death. His head pounded, his mouth felt like the Gobi desert, and he had a nagging feeling that he'd done something he'd regret when he remembered it.

Then he sighed. Of course. Sal's bloody dinner party. He'd known it was a bad idea.

Then again, going to the pub beforehand for a swift one and ending up having rather more than that probably hadn't been the best idea, either. The trouble was knowing when to stop. One drink eased the guilt of having lost a patient that afternoon, managed to dilute the blackness that filled his head at the realization that he wasn't good enough or early enough or lucky enough to save her. A second drink made the world seem almost acceptable again as a place to live, made him feel that things weren't entirely and utterly pointless after all. A third, and he began to feel able to socialize, to speak without barking, to listen without wanting to scream that everyone was so bloody preoccupied with such stupid mundane things that they didn't notice what a fucked-up world they were living in where people died senselessly all the bloody time, and there was nothing anyone could do about it.

A fourth drink—a double—made the dinner party seem quite inviting.

He opened his eyes briefly and winced as daylight brought memories of the night before. Laying into that guy Joe for no real reason except that Tom couldn't believe that after all the hype, all the talk about him being The One, this was the best Kate could come up with. Half the guys she'd turned down because their noses were too long or they didn't like Billie Holiday were better than him—brighter, funnier, more engaging. All Joe seemed to do was look at himself in the mirror, smile, and talk about himself. And the way Kate was fawning over him, listening to him like he was some bloody guru or something . . .

God, his head hurt.

Still, maybe that was what Kate wanted. And if it was, good luck to her.

"You alright? You didn't half toss and turn last night."

Tom jumped. He opened his eyes again, shielding them with his hand, and saw Lucy grinning at him. He frowned. He could vaguely remember calling her as he stumbled out of Sal's house after sharing another bottle of wine with Ed, telling her to come over. But he'd never thought she would. Had they . . . ? He had no idea.

"You don't mind if I have a fag, do you?" she asked conversationally, sitting up so that her breasts appeared from under the duvet and rested on it gently. "I know I shouldn't, but sometimes you've just got to live a little, haven't you?"

"It was awful," Kate said, sitting back on her chair and looking at Gareth morosely. "Everyone was arguing and Tom was being a complete arse, and by the end I just couldn't get out of there fast enough. Joe didn't say anything, but I know what he was thinking—are these really her best friends? The ones she kept going on about how nice they all were?"

Gareth nodded. "They're all just jealous," he said. "Joe's better-looking than any of them, and it's making them paranoid."

"You think?" Kate frowned.

The two of them were reviewing footage from the Moreley shoot in the small, dark editing suite. Gareth nodded again. "That's the thing with people you think are friends," he said matter-of-factly. "They like it when you're down, can't take it when things start going well."

Kate looked at Gareth, uncertain.

"Happened to me," he explained with a shrug. "Got myself a gorgeous—and I mean *gorgeous*—man a couple of years ago and suddenly my friends were bitching and freezing me out. Went on for a whole month. Soon as he dumped me, they wanted to hear all about it."

"Hmmm," Kate said. "You could be right. It didn't help that Tom was drunk and Sal was pissed off with Ed for something or other."

Gareth patted her shoulder. "So, come on," he said, "let's hear what Penny's come up with to say about the Moreleys."

He pressed "play," and the credits were soon replaced with the image of Penny outside the Moreleys' house, a pained expression on her face.

"The couple who live in the house behind me, Marcia and Derek Moreley, have found themselves in a rut," she said, as if it was the worst thing she'd ever heard. "Having succumbed to middle age, they're now hurtling fast toward old age with drab looks, a drab house, and nothing to look forward to. They called us because the two of them want to get some magic back in their lives, but they're not sure how. But they needn't worry, because the *Future: Perfect* team is here to help. In the next hour stay with us, and you'll be able to see for yourself their transformation from frumpy to fabulous!"

At this point, Penny smiled flatly into the camera, a facial expression that Kate knew she tried to avoid as far as possible because of the pressure it put on her beyond-Botox crow's feet. Then the screen was filled with the image of Marcia and Derek, sitting on their sofa and explaining why they were on the show. Kate giggled as she remembered how many takes the researchers had been forced to do because Marcia couldn't seem to understand that they were being filmed and that she couldn't interrupt the interview to ask questions. She also hadn't really appreciated that "because we both have big noses and can't afford a nose job" wasn't an appropriate answer to the question of why they'd contacted *Future: Perfect*. "Maybe you want to revive the passion you felt all those years ago?" the researcher would ask, only for Marcia to shake her head. "No," she'd say, "I just want a nose job. . . ." Somehow someone had managed to coerce her, however, and now she sat on screen talking about personal growth and reviving their youthful enthusiasm as if she'd been born to be on daytime television.

"And now, let's meet the *Future: Perfect* team," Penny was saying, and suddenly Kate was on screen, sitting next to Lysander.

"Kate Hetherington is our interiors specialist. So, Kate, tell us what we're going to be doing to brighten up Marcia and Derek's home!"

"We need to bring some more light into this house," Kate heard herself say, and she made a face at Gareth. "Why didn't you tell me my hair was sticking up at the back like that?" she squeaked. "Oh, God, I look dreadful."

"Shhh," Gareth hushed her. "I want to listen."

"And now Lysander Timlington, our fashion guru. Tell us, Lysander, what look are you going to be going for?"

Kate frowned. Penny never referred to her as an interiors guru. Why was she just called a specialist?

"I want to get some more structure in their wardrobe," Lysander said smoothly. "This season it's all about volume, but we need to tread carefully so that the volume is all in the right places!" He winked as he said that, and Kate rolled her eyes.

"Thanks, Lysander. And what about hair and makeup? Let's ask our *Future: Perfect* specialist, Gareth Mason."

Hah, Kate thought. Gareth's only a specialist, too.

"Marcia has been ignoring her skin care for far too long," Gareth-on-the-screen said soberly. "I want to update her makeup, and perhaps introduce Derek to some of the male skin-care products currently on the market to revive his complexion. Then we need to update Marcia's hair, losing her old perm and creating a bit more bounce, and, as I say, updating Derek's look with a shorter but less stern coiffure."

The Gareth next to Kate gasped at the screen. "Update! Update! I said it about five times. Why didn't someone tell me? Oh, it's just too horrible."

Kate put her arm around his shoulders in a show of solidarity. Repeating the same word a few times was nothing—she'd once said the word *absolutely* ten times in one sentence onscreen. Magda would never let them retake unless someone had obviously screwed up, like Marcia, or had said something libelous. "It's good enough," she would say, clapping her hands, and moving on, oblivious to—or willing to ignore—the faces being pulled behind her.

They continued to watch as Dr. Proudfoot, the show's silky-voiced plastic surgeon, told Penny in sympathetic tones that for those people sadly afflicted with facial features that didn't allow them to reach their full potential, surgery was really a godsend.

"Is that the new term for big noses?" Kate asked Gareth. "Features that don't allow you to reach your full potential?"

Gareth didn't answer and Kate pouted. He pretended to agree with her when she bitched about Dr. Proudfoot and his needles, but she knew full well that Gareth had asked about the price of Botox, and he'd admitted once that if he ever got fat he'd get liposuction right away.

The camera panned around the "before" shots—the house, dismally lit and looking even worse than it actually did before Kate got to work; Derek and Marcia's drab outfits; and finally, their faces (with a nice profile shot of their noses), made significantly worse by the pained expressions they had been asked to assume.

"Well, now that we know what we're working with," Penny's voice could be heard saying, "it's time to get to work!" She put on a hard hat and picked up a hammer and Kate rolled her eyes.

"Like she knows what work is," she said. "I can't believe she actually gets paid all that money to just talk crap and act like a prima donna."

"Talking of work, what happened to that woman who was stalking you?"

Kate frowned. "Stalking me?"

"Carole whatsherface. The one who was going to sue you. I thought you were going to call her."

Kate grinned. "Ah. Carole. Yes, well, turns out she isn't suing me after all. She loved the makeover."

Gareth looked at her curiously. "She loved it?"

Kate nodded. "Apart from the lipstick you put on her, but she's agreed not to call in her lawyers." She giggled. "No, she wants my help refurbishing a hospice."

"A hospice?" Gareth's face was still indignant from the lipstick comment.

"Yup. A hospice. Only she doesn't have any money. I thought Magda might be interested but she wasn't, so . . ."

"You think it would make good television?" Gareth asked with interest.

"Definitely. I mean, it's heartwarming, isn't it? And it's such a good cause. The people there are amazing, and it's all run by this small charity, and—"

"So take it to another production company," Gareth interrupted her.

Kate looked at him dubiously.

"Seriously," he said. "Someone's bound to buy the idea. Bringing hope to ill people. It's bloody perfect."

"Maybe you're right." Kate mulled over the idea. "Do you know any other production companies?"

Gareth shook his head. "But you could try the Yellow Pages."

Kate heard something that sounded like a dry laugh, and spun round. "Is there someone there?" she asked nervously. "Gareth, turn on the lights."

"No need," she heard Penny say. "I've got what I was looking for. And I'm leaving now."

Kate sat open-mouthed as the door of the editing suite opened, and Penny's outline could be seen leaving.

"How long was she here?" she gasped, looking at Gareth, who had gone white.

"It's alright," he said, as if trying to persuade himself. "We didn't say anything bad. At least, I didn't. You said she was talentless and lazy, but she can't blame me for that."

"Thanks, Gareth," Kate said, sighing. "So basically, Tom and Sal get antsy and argumentative as soon as things start going well for me, and you scarper as soon as things go wrong?"

Gareth managed a weak smile. "No one's perfect," he said. "Not even me."

20

Sal tapped her fingers against her desk and looked around furtively, trying to work out if anyone had noticed that she was a bit flushed. Relieved to discover that no one was in the least bit interested in her or the state of her body's thermostat, she turned back to her computer.

> Following last week's detox in the gym, fancy retoxing? Having a shitty day and wouldn't mind a drink after work if you're free? J

The e-mail had arrived twenty minutes ago, and Sal had been rooted to her chair ever since, reading and rereading it until she felt she could have written a five-thousand-word essay on its possible interpretations.

It was just a friendly drink with a colleague.

Or it was the beginning of the end of her marriage.

Or anything in between.

She never thought she'd find herself in this position. For one thing, she wasn't the sort—Sal had never been a flirt and had never considered herself particularly attractive to the majority of men. She was sensible, down-to-earth. The guys she went out with always told her how refreshing it was to have met someone who wasn't up and down all the time, who didn't cry at nothing, shout at everything, and insist on being taken out to ridiculously expensive restaurants or bought luxurious gifts.

And it was true: Sal rarely got hysterical, didn't argue unless there was a very good reason, and preferred money to be spent on sensible things like mortgages and pensions rather than squandered on frivolous things like meals out and jewelry.

But that wasn't to say that every so often, she hoped against hope that maybe Ed would buy her something that came in a small box and was an indulgent surprise instead of something practical that she needed and wanted. That maybe Ed would one day come home and whisk her away somewhere, ignoring her protests that there was no need and that she hadn't taken his suits to the dry cleaner yet.

She knew, though, that he wouldn't, because that wasn't who she was. She was practical. Pragmatic. Organized.

Boring.

But now . . . now she didn't feel boring. Boring, pragmatic people didn't get e-mails from people like Jim suggesting a drink after work. Dull, settled people didn't get a flutter of excitement every time he walked near her office and turned to flash a little secret smile at her—smiles that she had ignored at first, assuming they were aimed at someone else, and that now she waited for, on tenterhooks, every time she saw him stand up.

Now she felt a bit like Cinderella must have on her way to the ball. As if she was someone else completely—someone who flirted with colleagues, who went for illicit drinks, who was fun and decadent and . . .

Except she wasn't, was she? And unlike Cinderella, she'd already married her prince.

Sighing, Sal closed the e-mail and picked up the phone.

Penny smiled to herself and held her phone close to her ear.

"Joe?" she purred. "It's Penny here. Penny Pennington. Remember me?"

"Penny?" He sounded surprised.

"I hope you don't mind me calling you like this. Your agent kindly passed me your number."

"Sure. I guess," Joe said, still sounding a bit nonplussed. "Is it about the ad? Do we need to reshoot?"

"The advert?" Penny laughed. "No, Joe. No, it's not about that."

"Okay," Joe said uncertainly. "Then . . ."

"Joe," Penny said, her voice low, "I know that you're going out with Kate. And it's sweet. I'm sure you make a lovely couple. But I thought you should know that she isn't going to have her job here for much longer. It's a long, boring story, but the management here have just had enough of her—her lack of professionalism. I thought you should know, because I'm sure you'll want to support her, to step up and help her out—financially, emotionally. . . . I imagine she's going to go through a bit of a hard time, Joe."

There was silence on the other end of the phone, and Penny smiled to herself.

"Or," she said softly, "you may want to reconsider my offer. You may want to get out whilst you can, before you're dragged down by Kate. You and I, Joe, we could create a bit of a storm. So think about it, okay? You have my number, and I'm free tonight."

She hung up and marched straight into Magda's office.

Kate looked around Sarah Jones's kitchen–cum–sitting room proudly and grinned at Phil.

"Looks alright, this room, doesn't it?" he said from his vantage point on a ladder, methodically painting the cornice above Kate's head. "You've really brightened the place up, you know."

Kate shook her head. "You mean you have," she corrected him. "You're amazing. And in only a week."

"I knocked the wall down," Phil agreed. "But it was your idea to do it. I hope she likes it. Mrs. Jones, that is."

"Well, she cried, so Magda's happy. I couldn't tell if they were happy tears or devastated ones, to be honest."

"So where's she now, then?"

"Don't tell Gareth," Kate said with a wicked grin, "but she's gone to the hairdresser. Wasn't wild on his interpretation of Bree Van De Kamp meets Camilla Parker Bowles. I think he took it a bit literally and gave her Camilla's hair in bright carrot orange."

Phil smirked. "Leather sofa looks alright, too."

Kate rolled her eyes. The sofa had been Magda's concession in order to get Sarah Jones to sign the release and waiver forms. Kate had shoved it up at the top of the room, behind where the camera crew were positioned, and covered it with cushions. But in the event, she'd ended up doing a piece to camera on it. Bizarrely, in spite of it being completely wrong in the room, being—in Kate's view, at least—the totally wrong piece of furniture and actually kind of ugly if she was completely honest, it had somehow worked.

"I suppose it's not too hideous," she relented. "Right—shall we get on with the final coat of paint?"

She looked up at Phil, and he motioned to something behind her. She turned to see Magda standing in the doorway with her arms crossed.

"Got a moment, Kate?" she asked, her voice tight and strained.

Kate nodded. "Of course. We're just finishing the painting. Do you want to see the—"

"Now," Magda said. "In the front room."

Frowning, Kate followed her out and down the corridor. It was only when they were in the front room with the door closed that Magda opened her mouth to speak.

"Kate," she said, pacing up and down and failing to meet Kate's eye. "Enjoy working on *Future: Perfect* do you?"

"Of course," she said with a wary nod.

"We don't have big budgets," Magda continued. "Don't have fancy offices or big parties. But you know what we've got?"

Kate looked at her blankly.

"Loyalty," Magda said. "Loyalty and teamwork. That's how we get a show on air every week. That's how we make ends meet and keep ourselves going. Right?"

"Right," said Kate, confused. "We're a great team. Is there something wrong, Magda?"

Magda looked at her for a second, then away again.

"That's what I asked myself," she said sadly, "when I heard that you were approaching other production companies with programming ideas. Why, I asked myself, wouldn't Kate come to me? Why didn't she feel any loyalty?"

Kate stared at Magda incredulously. "But I haven't!" she exclaimed. "I haven't spoken to anyone. I don't have programming ideas, anyway. I have a project that I'm involved in, and I ran it past you and you said no. That's it."

"Ran what idea past me?" Magda asked. "I haven't seen any proposals. I haven't had a thing from you."

Kate stopped herself just before she rolled her eyes. "I told you there was a hospice that needed a refurb and you said it wasn't good television material," she said.

"I said no such thing." Magda's eyes narrowed. "A hospice? Ill people? Crying relatives? It's bloody brilliant television."

"But you did," Kate cried. "It was last week."

Magda frowned. "You expect me to believe that?" she said. "So you're involved with this hospice, are you?"

Kate felt herself getting hot.

"Even though you know that your contract specifically prohibits you from taking on additional work without getting approval from your manager? AKA me."

"When I say involved, all I mean is that I've been approached," Kate said quickly. "I haven't done anything yet. It was Carole Jacobs. You know the woman who was trying to get hold of me? She's one of the trustees and wanted me to help do it up a bit. . . ."

She looked at Magda hopefully, but Magda's frown was now furrowing into her brow. "You contacted a former victim? When I specifically told you not to? This just gets better and better, Kate. And here I was thinking that Penny must have got the wrong end of the stick."

Kate stared at her. "Penny?" Suddenly this was making a bit more sense.

Magda sighed. "You know Penny wants you out, don't you? Thinks she can do the interiors herself. Probably looking to launch her own furniture line or something."

"Magda, you can't," Kate said indignantly, wide-eyed. "I've been on this show since day one. I'm here every day, every week. . . ."

Magda looked at her. "What choice do I have?" she asked. "You break your contract. You approach other companies. And Penny, who is this show's only bloody selling point, is demanding that I fire you. Can you see any alternative option?"

"But I didn't approach anyone!"

"Penny heard you discussing it. Whether or not you've actually made the phone call is neither here nor there."

Kate swallowed. She suddenly felt very hot and very uncomfortable. "But . . . but what will I do?" she asked.

"That," Magda said, "isn't really my business anymore, is it? That's a question you should have thought about before. You'll be paid up till the end of the month, Kate, but I'm afraid we won't be needing you on set. You understand, don't you?"

"I . . ." Kate started to say, but left it hanging. Her legs were trembling and she felt as if the room was closing in on her. She was being fired. She'd never been fired. It didn't feel real.

Magda pursed her lips. "Right, then," she said. "I'll tell Penny."

She walked past Kate and opened the door. Then she turned around.

"So which company did you approach?" she asked. "You may as well tell me now—I'll find out soon enough anyway."

"I didn't," Kate said pleadingly. "I haven't approached anyone."

Magda shook her head. "Have it your way, then." She left, closing the door behind her.

Kate made her way to Mr. Jones's large armchair and sat down, leaning over and cradling her head in her hands. She sat there for a few minutes, maybe longer—she wasn't sure. Then the door opened.

"You alright?" Phil ventured, coming over and hovering a few inches away. "I thought you might want a cup of tea."

He pressed a mug of hot, milky tea into her hands, and she took it gratefully. "I've been fired," she whispered, hardly daring to say it because it might make her situation more real.

"Fired?" Phil asked. "What do you mean, fired?"

"I mean, Magda's sacked me. For breaking my contract. Penny told her I'd been approaching the competition with ideas."

"And have you?"

"No," Kate said miserably. "Gareth told me to—there's this hospice that I was hoping to refurbish. Thought it might make good telly. And Penny overheard and used it to make Magda fire me. Apparently she wants to do interiors now."

Phil laughed, then stopped short when he saw that Kate couldn't even manage a smile. "So what are we going to do, then?" he asked.

Kate looked at him curiously. "We?"

"I'm not hanging around here and working for Penny," he said matter-of-factly.

"But you haven't been fired," Kate said. "Don't leave on my account."

Phil rolled his eyes. "I'm not. I'm leaving on my account. If that woman thinks she's going to be able to boss me around, she's got another thing coming. Anyway, I'll be getting my pension through in another six months. It's you I'm worried about."

Kate smiled at him. "Thanks, Phil. But, look, I'll be fine. I just need to think, you know, about what to do next."

"Sounds like you want to make over this hospice," Phil said. "So contact those companies you're meant to have contacted already."

Kate sighed. "Yeah," she said. "Maybe."

"Or," Phil said, more gently, "you could go home, forget all about it, have a nice bath and get that boyfriend of yours round to cheer you up."

Kate grinned. "Now *that* sounds like a plan. Thanks, Phil."

"No problem. I've just got one question," Phil said.

"What?"

"You're fired, right? And I don't have a contract, so I'm free to walk away whenever I want?"

Kate shrugged. "I guess so."

"So there's not much point me leaving my ladders and the paint that I was going to finish off tomorrow, is there?"

"I . . . guess not."

"And if I just get word out, you know, casually, in the pub, that this isn't a job any builder in London would want to take, there wouldn't be any harm in that, would there?"

Kate's eyes widened.

"And," Phil continued, his face lit with mischief, "it won't take Penny *that* long to work out which color paint she needs to finish the wall off, will it? Seeing as how there's about a thousand different colors to choose from? I'm sure she'll be able to work it out in time for filming tomorrow afternoon. . . ."

Kate found a little smile inching its way onto her face.

"You really think she'll manage?" she asked innocently.

"She's an interiors guru," Phil said, deadpan. "I'm sure it won't take her any time at all."

21

Joe frowned; things were not going according to plan. Not that he'd exactly had a plan, but his LA agent had assured him that coming to London would be great for his career. Said it was either London or Tokyo—Tokyo would mean money, London would mean credibility. What he couldn't do was hang around in LA for much longer because it was getting hard for his agent to convince producers that Joe was in demand when they could see him waiting tables or hanging out, restless, in the various bars along Sunset Boulevard.

And now he was still waiting tables, only the rent was more expensive, the tips were smaller, and the weather sucked. Kate might be cute, but she'd proved to be useless in terms of hooking him up with important television executives, which was what he'd hoped for when he'd first asked her out, and that awful cream cheese ad, his only professional job in the two months he'd been in London, hadn't even aired. For some reason they kept delaying the launch of the campaign, which meant that, apart from a slightly healthier bank balance, he had nothing to show for it.

Frankly, it sucked. It sucked big time.

He looked around the cramped studio apartment that was his current home, and sighed. Then he dug out his phone and pressed redial.

"Bob?"

"Ah, Joe. How're things?"

"You know how things are. I was hoping you might have some news. Some work. Something."

Bob sighed. "Joe, we're working on it. Just give it a bit more time, okay? There's an audition coming up next week that I'm hoping to get you into. A comedy. I'll call you as soon as I know anything."

"I just feel like *I'm* always calling *you*, you know?"

There was a pause that suggested Bob agreed with this sentiment and wasn't exactly wild about it.

"Joe, we're working really hard for you here. I give you my word."

Joe nodded silently.

"Okay, then," Bob said, sounding relieved. "I'll talk to you soon."

"Wait," Joe said. "Listen, Bob, if I . . . hooked up with someone famous, would that . . . would it make a difference?"

"Someone famous?"

"Sort of famous. If I was in celebrity magazines, I mean. That kind of thing."

"That could definitely help," Bob said, sounding much more interested. "You mean a model or an actress?"

Joe bit his lip. "Does the name Penny Pennington mean anything to you?"

"Penny Pennington?" Bob seemed surprised. "I thought you said you hated her."

"Bob, this is my career we're talking about. I do what I have to do. You gotta have focus, you know?"

"Right, of course," Bob said. "Well, she certainly knows the publicity game."

"Yeah." Joe frowned. "That's what I figured."

"Joe, it's definitely worth a shot, if you're up for it. I mean, all publicity is good publicity. You know that, right? People recognize you, it's easier to get you parts. Simple as that."

Joe nodded. "Okay, thanks, Bob."

"You'll keep me posted?"

"Sure."

No sooner had he hung up on Bob than his phone rang again. He frowned and picked up.

"Joe?"

"Kate. How's my favorite girl?" he asked, smiling easily and immediately putting all thoughts of Penny out of his mind. After all, he hadn't made any decisions. No reason to rock the boat. She was a sweet girl, and she hung on his every word, which was quite nice, if sometimes a little annoying. There was no need to burn any bridges until he absolutely had to.

"Awful. Well, pretty rubbish. Are you free tonight? I was hoping you might be able to come over."

Joe frowned. "Tonight?" He paused, about to make an excuse, then smiled. Now was not the time to say he was tied up. "Sure I am. What's up?"

Kate sighed. "What isn't up? I lost my job today. I'm still in slight shock, actually."

Joe's eyes widened. So Penny had been right. Well, that made his decision a little bit easier. "You . . . you lost your job?" he asked, trying to sound sympathetic, but already planning his escape route. "Why? How?"

"Don't ask," Kate said, her voice tense. "I'll give you the full story later. So, you realize you're going to have to get an Oscar-winning part now so you can support me, don't you?"

Her voice suggested she was joking, but it didn't stop little beads of sweat from appearing on Joe's forehead. "You'll walk right into another job," he said. "No problem."

"Maybe." Kate sighed. "Or maybe I'll take a bit of a break. You know that hospice I told you about?"

"Hospice?" Joe was distracted, his mind racing. She wanted to take a break? Why?

"Yeah, the one I went to a week ago? I'm still thinking about trying to help them, I just don't know how."

"Great," Joe said unenthusiastically. "So there you go, then. Listen, honey, I gotta go—got a call coming through. Could be work."

"Okay. But I'll see you later? Sevenish?"

"Sure. I mean, hopefully."

"Hopefully?"

"I've got some loose ends to tie up, that's all. Yeah, I'll see you later."

"Thanks, Joe."

Joe hung up and took a deep breath. She sounded dreadful. Like she really needed a shoulder to cry on. Poor Kate.

And yet, was it really a good idea to get involved? He'd start by comforting her, and the next thing he'd be supporting her, just like Penny said. Right now, he needed to be focused. In control. A free agent, whose number one priority was his career.

He reached hesitantly into his pocket and pulled out the pink card Penny had given him. Maybe just one drink. He could always see Kate later. It was really no big deal.

Slowly, he picked up his phone again and dialed Penny's number.

Beauty Care

The hopeless romantic knows that beauty is only skin deep and that true love is based on so much more than the clearness of our skin or the shape of our calves. Nevertheless, she also knows that in looking after herself, she is showing that she holds herself in high esteem and wishes to please the man she loves. And every woman feels better when her nails are manicured, her hair coiffed, and her figure trim.

The hopeless romantic also knows that whilst following fashion is easy, being constantly, casually, and naturally chic is so much more attractive and so much more difficult. Simple, unfussy hair that looks natural and is soft to the touch will appeal to a man far more than hair that is set and rigid.

Skin that is fresh-looking and blemish-free is so much prettier than skin that is caked in powder.

And so, the hopeless romantic knows that investment is everything. The hopeless romantic eats well—eggs, fish, and wheat germ for shiny hair and clear skin—and takes the stairs to maintain firm legs. She avoids shabby heels by using hand cream on them daily, and keeps her legs eggshell-smooth with a razor or wax treatment. The hopeless romantic never knows when she may be swept off her feet, so dressing beautifully only for important occasions is simply not an option; she must be radiant at all times.

This applies just as much when we are down at heel or sad. For, although it is tempting to match our mood with drab, dull colors and little or no makeup, this will never do. How will our broken hearts be mended if we wear our sadness on our sleeves? How will we find sunshine if we are dressed for rain?

Indeed, focusing on one's beauty when one is feeling lonely or saddened by something can truly lift the spirits. A splash of perfume, a hint of lipstick, and a little smudge of gray pencil along the upper eyelid can transform not only your look, but your entire mood, and the moods of those around you, including your beau or prospective beau! Cheer yourself up and fix a smile upon your face; say to the world that you expect great things from it, and you will soon not remember why on earth you were feeling so blue in the first place.

Kate blinked onto the mascara wand and stared at her reflection in the bathroom mirror. There was no getting away from it—Elizabeth Stallwood knew what she was talking about. An hour ago, she'd felt dreadful. Sick to the stomach with anxiety, mad as hell with Penny, and utterly bereft.

Now she felt like none of it really mattered. Not for the time being, anyway. Her face was made up, her hair freshly washed and blow-dried, and her nails sported a lovely pale pink varnish that she'd bought months ago and never got round to wearing because her nails always got trashed on set. Now she didn't have to worry about that. Good-bye career, hello grooming.

Kate took a look at her watch: seven thirty P.M. Any minute now, Joe would arrive and would sweep her up in his strong arms. And then maybe they'd talk, or maybe they'd make passionate love, or maybe he'd insist on taking her out somewhere to take her mind off things. She didn't mind which; she was just grateful she had him. It wasn't as if she had much else at the moment, after all—her friends seemed intent on shouting at each other and trading insults, and her job . . . well, the less said about that, the better.

Satisfying herself that her eyelashes were clump-free, Kate wandered into the kitchen to wait for her beau.

"This is a funny sort of local," Lucy said, grinning. "What is it, a West London thing? You can't just go to the pub like the rest of us?"

Tom reddened slightly. "You can eat here, too," he pointed out.

"Yeah, if you've got ten pounds to spend on a plate of chips. Look, thanks for this. I really appreciate it. And for letting me stay with you. You know, I think this might be the start of something special. If my plan works, that is!"

Tom shook his head. "It's no problem. And this way I'm not drinking alone, so you're helping us both out."

"I suppose," Lucy said, her eyes twinkling. "And, after all, you never did buy me dinner. That's the least a girl expects these days. I suppose someone's got to spend that doctor's salary of yours, haven't they?"

"So, enjoying your fish?" Tom asked.

Lucy nodded. "It's lovely. And the wine, too. Quite a treat."

Tom smiled, but then his eyes caught sight of something and his brow furrowed.

It couldn't be. It looked like it, but he must have got it wrong.

"What is it?" Lucy demanded, swiveling round on her chair.

Then she turned back again, her eyes dancing in delight. "It's that woman, isn't it? Penny something. Bloody hell, so you get celebrities down your local. I'm pressed, Dr. Whitson."

She swiveled round again. "Ooh, and look at her date—he's nice and all, isn't he? I wouldn't mind a bit of him. . . ." She swung her head round and winked at Tom. "Not that you're not lovely, but jeez Louise. Must be at least ten years younger than her, too. Lucky cow. D'you think she's rich? Tom? Dr. Whitson? Are you okay?"

Tom stared over at the other table, feeling more and more agitated. It was him. It was Joe. And he looked very cozy with that woman whom Kate hated. Horrible-looking specimen.

Still, there would be an explanation. Of course there would.

Tom swallowed, forcing back the urge to walk over and punch Joe. He didn't even know why he wanted to punch him. "Lucy, I'm just going to make a quick call, if that's okay. Do you mind?"

Lucy shook her head. "'Course not."

Tom nodded and wandered over to the bar. Then he maneuvered himself so that he was near Joe and Penny's table.

"Now, I spoke to my agent," he heard her say in a harsh, nasal voice. "If you were better known, we'd want to deny our involvement for a few weeks, to get everyone's attention. But since you're not . . ." Penny raised her eyebrow at Joe. ". . . we need to go for maximum impact instead. I've tipped off a couple of photographers so they'll snap us leaving in a couple of hours. And then I'll start doing interviews about my newfound love."

"*We'll* start doing interviews, you mean."

Penny smiled. "Of course. Silly me."

Tom blanched and made his way outside.

Once on the pavement, he took out his phone and dialed Kate's number.

"Joe?" she said immediately on picking up. "Is that you?"

She sounded so hopeful. So excited. Tom bit his lip. "No, Kate, it's me."

"Oh. Tom. Hi. What's up?"

"Expecting Joe to call, were you?"

Kate laughed self-deprecatingly. "Sorry, that was a bit sad, wasn't it? No, he's coming over, actually. He was meant to be here a while ago, so I thought it would be him."

Tom looked up at the sky.

"Tom? Are you still there?"

He sniffed. "Look, um, Kate, do Penny and Joe know each other?"

There was a pause. "They did an advert together. Joe told you about it at Sal's dinner, if you remember? Or were you too drunk?"

With a flash, Tom remembered, and immediately he felt like a fool. It was work. Nothing more. "Well, that explains that, then," he said. "I couldn't work out why they'd be having dinner together, that's all. But if it's work. . . ."

"Having dinner together?" Kate asked, surprised. "When?"

"Well . . . now," Tom said. "They're at the Bush Bar and Grill."

"Now?" Kate's voice grew strained. "Tom, is this some kind of joke? Some crude attempt to rile me? Because if it is, it isn't bloody well funny."

Tom swallowed. "No joke, Kate. I promise."

"Well, I'm sure there's a perfectly good explanation," Kate said quickly. "Anyway, he hates her guts so if he is there, it'll be under duress. You're there now, I take it?"

"Yup."

"Well, maybe I'll just call him," Kate said, sounding distracted. "Find out why . . . um, so look, thanks Tom."

"No problem. I'll be here for a while. In case you . . ."

"Great! Okay, then, 'bye!"

Tom frowned and made his way back to his table. "Have you finished?" he asked Lucy, watching Penny and Joe like a hawk. "Only I've rather lost my appetite."

Kate smiled at her reflection in her hallway mirror as brightly as she could, but the smile didn't get past her lips. She'd called Joe. Asked him in a sweet, relaxed way if he was on his way. And he'd told her that he was "in the middle of something." That he might not make it round tonight after all. Just like that.

The thing was, though, she told herself firmly, he still could have been telling the truth. He and Penny had worked together—there was no reason why they might not be discussing some future project. The fact was, he hated the woman, so there was no reason to feel remotely worried. Okay, so Penny was the biggest bitch in the world and had pushed Kate out of a job, but Joe didn't know that. Maybe the advert had been really well received and they were going to do a follow-up.

Kate smiled again, and this time she managed to bring a little sparkle to her eyes. She would just wander down to the Bush Bar and Grill, she decided. She wasn't meant to know Joe was there, so he couldn't accuse her of checking up on him. And when Joe saw her, no doubt he'd be relieved to be able to get away from Penny. Kate would think of some cutting comment to direct at her archnemesis, and then she and Joe would leave. And hopefully Tom would still be there to witness it, too. After the other evening Tom was the last person she wanted feeling sorry for her.

Pulling on a coat, and turning her mind to a biting insult that would cut Penny to the quick, Kate grabbed her keys and made her way outside.

It was a warmish, drizzly evening—not wet enough for an umbrella, but wet enough to sabotage any attempts at non-frizzy hair. So much for her coiffure, she thought grumpily. Elizabeth Stallwood would no doubt have her wear a headscarf, but you had to draw the line somewhere.

She got to the Bush Bar and Grill in less than five minutes and stood in the entrance for at least another five, trying to calm her heart, which was racing with adrenaline. It was just Penny and Joe, she kept telling herself. Her boyfriend and a washed-up has-been who was probably desperately trying to seduce Joe, whilst he was no doubt laughing at her. The two of them would giggle about it later, and she would wonder what on earth she'd got so worried about.

Not that she was worried. She wasn't worried at all.

Tossing her hair back, she fixed a smile back on her face and walked along the little alley that separated the Bush Bar and Grill from Goldhawk Road, then stepped inside.

It was warm and smoky, and she took off her coat, then made her way to the bar. The trick was to look casual, she told herself, turning round surreptitiously to survey the room. There was no sign of Tom anywhere, she noticed. And no sign of Joe and Penny . . .

Then she frowned. There they were. Sitting at a small table to the left.

Quickly, she turned round again, her heart thudding. Then she ordered a drink, picked it up, and, taking a deep breath, made her way over.

"Darling!" she said, a few feet from the table. Neither Joe nor Penny noticed her, and she cleared her throat. "Joe!" she said as she arrived at the table and saw with some consternation his shocked face. "What a surprise!"

Then she looked at Penny. "Penny. How *sweet* of you to look after Joe for me." She smiled confidently and waited for Joe to spring into action. To get her a chair, to tell her that he and Penny were just finishing their work discussion, to stand up and kiss her and make it completely clear to Penny and anyone else that he and she were crazy about each other.

But instead, he just looked at her awkwardly and said in a strangled voice, "I thought you were at home."

Kate swallowed. "I was," she said, as brightly as she could manage in the circumstances, "but I decided to come out for a drink."

"On your own?" Penny asked. "How sad."

Kate narrowed her eyes at her. "Not on my own, actually. With a friend. So, Joe, are you going to be long? Talking work with Penny,

I mean?" She smiled at Penny. "I mean, I can't imagine that you two would have anything else to talk about."

"Actually, we've got rather a lot to discuss," Penny said silkily. "And Kate, by the way, I was so sad to hear that you lost your job today. Such a shame."

Kate put her hand on the table. Her legs were beginning to feel rather weak.

"Well, at least I won't have to work with you anymore!" she said with a bright smile. "Every cloud certainly has its silver lining!"

Penny's eyes hardened. "Joe," she said smoothly, "maybe it's time you told Kate about us."

Joe shifted uncomfortably in his chair.

"Joe?" Kate asked, frowning. "What's Penny talking about? Are you doing another job together or something?"

Penny laughed. "A job? Oh, dear me, you really are naïve, aren't you?"

Kate looked at Joe and swallowed. "Joe?" she asked pleadingly.

He sighed. "Jeez, Kate. I'm sorry. I just . . ." He looked at Penny, then stood up to face Kate. "We . . . I mean, Penny and I . . . we . . . ."

"We're together," Penny said, cold as ice. "Joe and I have fallen in love. The poor boy's been too terrified to tell you. So it's probably best if you run along now."

Kate felt like her legs might buckle beneath her.

"But you hate her," she said, her voice almost a whisper. "You said she was arrogant and selfish and self-absorbed. . . ."

Joe shrugged helplessly. "I guess I was wrong," he said, looking at the floor.

"Kate, love, have some dignity, why don't you?" Penny said with a sigh. "You've lost your job and lost your man—maybe you need to start asking yourself a few questions about yourself, huh?"

Kate stared at Penny. "You total bitch," she said, very low. "You are an evil, horrible woman."

Penny smiled brightly. "Who has a job and a very good-looking boyfriend, wouldn't you say? Now, Joe, I think it's time to go. Don't you?" She stood up and clicked her fingers at Joe, who reluctantly handed her her coat.

"I'm real sorry," he said to Kate. "I was going to call you. Tell you some other way."

Kate said nothing. She simply watched as Penny slipped her arm through Joe's and started to walk toward the entrance.

It wasn't until they were nearly there that she ran after them.

"But you can't . . ." she yelped as she reached the door and saw Penny and Joe walking along the alley toward the street. "Joe, we've got a connection. You said I was special. . . ."

As she spoke, she was blinded by flashing lights, and she stumbled, falling back against the wall. Confused, she watched as Joe wrapped his arms around Penny and they both smiled beatifically for the cameras, as if they were on a red carpet somewhere, not coming out of a bar in Shepherd's Bush.

She allowed herself to sink down to the ground.

But before she could, someone appeared at her side.

"Quick, let's get out of here," a familiar voice said. "Take my hand. And repeat after me: Men are pigs. The whole bloody lot of them."

22

"You may as well say it," Kate said unhappily.

"Say what?"

They were sitting on her sofa, Kate holding a cushion defensively to her stomach, her legs curled underneath her, and Tom beside her, his legs stretched out onto the coffee table.

"That you were right. That I'm an idiot and a hopeless romantic and that you knew it was all going to end in tears."

"You're not an idiot. Joe's an idiot."

Kate nodded. "Penny," she said in a wondering tone. "I mean, of all the people. Why Penny?"

"It was probably voodoo," Tom said. "I can't think of another reason why anyone would contemplate sleeping with her."

"You think he's slept with her?" Kate asked, clasping her hand to her mouth. "Oh, God. Oh, how horrible."

"No, no," Tom said, appalled. "I didn't mean that. . . ."

"But he's going to, isn't he. He's going to go to bed with her and he's going to kiss her and . . ."

Tears started to prick at Kate's eyes and she vigorously wiped them away. "He was my perfect man," she whispered. "It was all going so well."

"Your perfect man is one who doesn't even have the courtesy to dump you before running off with Penny Pennington?"

Kate shrugged. "She'll have made him do it. The point is, I was promised love, and along came Joe, and now he's out with that . . . that bitch."

Tom raised his eyebrows. "You were promised love?" he asked. "Look, we all think we've been promised all sorts of things, but there are no guarantees in this life—"

"No, but there are!" Kate said indignantly. "Find love or your money back. And now I probably won't even qualify, because I *did* find love."

"You got a money-back guarantee?" Tom asked, taken aback.

Kate blanched slightly but admitted, "It's a book I got. *The Hopeless Romantic's Handbook.* It said on eBay that I was guaranteed to find love."

Tom's eyes widened. "You're reading a book called *The Hopeless Romantic's Handbook*? You don't think you're hopeless enough without getting advice on the subject? And don't believe everything you read on eBay, either. Poor little Kate. It's no wonder you get so upset about things."

"I don't get upset about things; I get upset about manipulative cows like Penny," Kate said fiercely. "God, I hate that woman. I hate her so much."

"No point," Tom said. "You hate her and she won't even know. And it'll eat you up and make you angry and you'll blame her even more, but there'll be no point because she barely knows you exist."

Kate frowned. "Are we still talking about Penny here? Because I guarantee she knows I exist."

Tom smiled. "Sorry. You're right, she does." He sighed. "I've just learned over the years that letting anger go is the best thing you can do."

Kate nodded, remembering the hurt in Tom's voice the first time he told her that his mother had left. He'd said it so casually, on the way home from school one day; just dropped it into conversation as if it was normal, as if, if he didn't attach any significance to it, it wouldn't *be* significant. But could you really let go of anger over that kind of betrayal? she wondered. She didn't think she could.

Kate studied him silently. "Is that why you don't believe in happy endings?" she asked, her voice small.

Tom frowned. "I believe," he said pointedly, "that this subject is now closed. I also believe in the healing powers of Billie Holiday, whiskey, and dancing. What do you say?"

Kate couldn't help but grin. "You actually expect me to dance with you? I've lost my boyfriend and my job and been totally screwed over by a bitch with straw-colored hair and you expect me to dance?"

"I'm a doctor," Tom said. "People always do what I tell them to do. So come on, stand up." He grabbed her hand, tossed the cushion away, and dragged her to a standing position. Then he put a CD in Kate's stereo, took her hands again and, as the music played, he started to sing. Badly.

"Stormy weather," he crooned.

"'Cause my man and me ain't together," Kate joined in.

"Keeps raining all the time . . ."

Tom grinned and pulled her closer. "See, not so bad now, is it?" he asked. "Billie feels your pain, and spits it out. She's a miracle worker, really."

As they started to spin around her sitting room, Kate smiled nervously. She had danced with Tom plenty of times before—even sung Billie Holiday songs with him—but something felt different this time. Their bodies were pressed so close together that she could smell the skin of his neck, feel his heart beating in his chest. She had an almost overwhelming urge to pull him even closer, to kiss him, to . . .

"Didn't you promise me whiskey?" she asked quickly, pulling a bit away.

"So I did." Tom met her eyes and for a second Kate was terrified that he could see what she'd been thinking, but then he grinned and made his way to the kitchen. "Do you still keep your alcohol in the same cupboard as the ketchup?"

Kate took a deep breath. This was very silly. It was just Tom. And any strange feelings were just due to her hurt over Joe, nothing more.

But when Tom reappeared at the door carrying whiskey and two glasses, and when she met his eyes for a second time and this time couldn't tear hers away, she wasn't so sure anymore. Suddenly Tom didn't seem like Tom anymore. He looked like an incredibly attractive man who had saved her from the stone floor outside the Bush Bar and Grill.

Still smiling nervously, she finally pulled her eyes away and went to sit back down on the sofa. Tom poured her a glass and passed it to her before sitting down. The sofa was old and sagging in the middle and as soon as he sat, they found their legs touching. Tom pulled his away self-consciously and shifted to a different position, but it was no use—however he sat, his legs ended up almost on top of Kate's. Neither of them had said a word since he'd gone to get the whiskey, and the air felt tense and heavy.

"Shall we . . . put the television on?" Kate suggested.

"Ah, the television," Tom said with a little smile. "The panacea to modern life."

"Fine, no TV," she said quietly. She took a sip of the whiskey and coughed when it burnt her throat.

"That's my girl," Tom said. "By the time you've finished that glass you won't remember who Joe or Penny are, let alone why you're upset with them."

Kate smiled weakly and took another sip, then another, and another, until the glass was empty.

"Joe who?" she said.

"There you go," Tom said, grinning. "And now, madam, it's late. Time for you to go to bed."

The word *bed* seemed to hang in the air for a few seconds, and Tom stood up, Kate following him.

"Stay a bit longer?" Kate said before she could stop herself.

"You . . . you want me to stay?"

Kate nodded. And as she lifted her head, she saw Tom looking at her with an unreadable expression. She held his gaze, challenging him, and they stood for what felt like hours, staring into each other's eyes, each daring the other to look away.

And then she suddenly felt Tom's lips on hers. Tender at first, then urgent, his arms around her tightly. Her hands reached around his back, up to his neck. It felt exciting, thrilling, but safe, too. Like she was coming home. Like she'd finally found her place.

And then he pulled away.

"I'd better go." His voice was hoarse. "Now is not the time."

Kate nodded mutely, knowing he was right, but not wanting to see him leave.

He looked at her for a moment, then kissed her forehead. "Sleep well," he said. "I'll call you tomorrow."

"Tom?" Kate said, as he headed for the door.

"What?"

"You were wrong," she said, a little smile on her lips. "Men aren't all pigs."

"Right," Tom said uncertainly, then grinned. "Right."

23

Sal picked up the phone as soon as it started ringing. It was a reflex—anything that happened before ten A.M. at the weekend was dealt with by her, as quietly as possible. Ed survived on six hours of sleep a night Monday to Friday, and without a lie-in at the weekend he simply couldn't function. And last night he hadn't got back until late. Very late. Sal knew the exact time, because she had only got in twenty minutes before. It had been the first time she'd been thankful that Ed's work kept him out with clients into the small hours.

And, in many ways, it was Ed's fault that she'd been so late back. If she thought about it enough, she could even persuade herself it was entirely his fault. But she knew it wasn't.

The truth of the matter was that she hadn't wanted to go for a drink with Jim. Or at least, she'd rather hoped that something would stop her. She'd called Ed at work and asked if he fancied getting a take-away that evening, but he'd apologized profusely, said he thought he'd told her that he had a thing that night, and could they do it on Saturday instead? She'd even asked if he wanted her to accompany him on his soulless client entertainment evening, something she had never ever done since a disastrous occasion two years before when Ed's boss had stared at her cleavage all night and tried to grope her ass as he helped her on with her coat at the end of the evening. But Ed had said no—said it would be bad enough for him, but that there was no reason she should endure it, too. He even said that she should go for a drink with her friends. That she didn't seem to have been out much lately. When she'd said pointedly that she hadn't been out with *him* much lately, he'd told her to get off his case: He was busy and the last thing he needed was her nagging him.

So she'd said yes to Jim's invitation. Telling herself that he was just one of her friends. That there was nothing remotely untoward about going for a drink with a single man after work, not mentioning it to anyone else, and not going to a bar anywhere near work lest someone they knew should see them. Now, with hindsight, it seemed utterly brazen.

Sluttish, even. She might as well have had a placard on her forehead saying UNHAPPILY MARRIED AND TOTALLY AVAILABLE.

That's probably how Jim saw her.

But was she? Was she really unhappily married?

She just didn't know anymore. What constituted a happy marriage anyway? She was fairly sure that she and Ed did care about each other. That they still enjoyed each other's company. But was that enough? Ed never looked into her eyes and told her she was special. Half the time he barely seemed to notice she was there. He came home, buried himself in paperwork, snapped at her, and spent hours furtively tapping e-mails into his BlackBerry as if whoever was at the other end was far more important and interesting than her. Maybe they were. Maybe the person at the other end was special.

So she'd gone out with Jim. And worn her sparkly top—the second outing for it, the first being that disastrous dinner party when she'd worn it and no one had even noticed it or commented on it at all, especially not Ed.

Jim had noticed it right away. He'd told her how nice it was, how it was so nice to see her out of work clothes. Or gym clothes. He smiled when he said that, almost suggestively, but Sal wasn't sure and so she just moved the conversation on with a smile. She'd been so on edge to start with—simply being in the bar seemed to her to be the logical precursor to a horrible, painful divorce and an admission of failure where her marriage was concerned. But after a couple of vodka tonics, she started to relax a bit, and after a while longer, she began to enjoy herself. Jim was an interesting guy—he used to be a journalist, covering big stories about the side effects of drugs that had been covered up or the damaging impact of the high cost of drugs around the world. Now, he told her sheepishly, he'd jumped to the other side because the money and security were so much better, but he might go back to writing one day. She told him about her doctorate and how she enjoyed regulation because she could understand the scientists, being one of them, but also enjoyed the business and marketing side of things. He said she was the best person by far on the regulation team, that everyone thought so. And she basked in the praise, her whole face lighting up at the thought that people actually rated her.

They'd talked nonstop, actually, with no awkward pauses or hesitations. Until the end of the evening, that is. And then suddenly things got very awkward. Sal said she was going to get a cab. Jim offered to share it with her. There ensued a long discussion about whether or not it was worth sharing a cab when she lived in West Kensington and he lived in Clapham, and eventually he grinned and put her in a cab and said there was another one right behind, even though Sal could see that there wasn't and that he was just being nice because she was obviously uncomfortable with the idea of sharing a cab, let alone more. And then, just before he closed her cab door, he leant over and kissed her. On the lips.

Until then, Sal had been able to kid herself that this was just a friendly evening. That Jim was a work colleague—hell, they'd been talking about work most of the evening.

That kiss changed everything. On the way home, Sal replayed it a thousand times—sometimes she imagined pulling away in horror and telling Jim that he'd got the wrong idea, that she was married and not interested in anything more than friendship. But a couple of times, she imagined pulling him into the cab, imagined his lips on hers, on her neck, him holding her in his arms with an urgency she hadn't experienced in years and whispering that he couldn't believe how lucky he was to have met her, that she was the only thing he could think about, every minute of every day.

"Hello?" she whispered into the telephone receiver, suddenly terrified that it would be Jim, in spite of the fact that she hadn't ever given him her landline number. She looked over at Ed and saw to her relief that he was snoring gently.

"Sal? Gareth here. Kate's friend from work. We need to get over to her place."

"What? Why?" Relief was flooding through her. She was safe. It wasn't Jim.

"Do you want the long version or the short version?"

Sal looked at Ed, who might wake up any minute. "The short one."

"She's lost her job and Joe's left her for Penny Pennington."

"You're joking!"

"Nope. I heard it from Will, a runner on the show, and he heard it from Adam the cameraman, and he heard it from Penny herself. Apparently she's shouting it from the rooftops. So look, I've got chocolate," Gareth continued. "But we'll need more than that."

Sal's mind was racing. Joe and Penny? Was everyone having affairs now, even the ones who professed to being in love?

"I've got HobNobs," she said eventually. "And ice cream."

"Might be a bit early for ice cream."

"You're right. Okay, HobNobs and maybe a bottle of something. Where are you now?"

"Outside your house."

Sal jumped up and looked through her bedroom curtains to see Gareth standing in the middle of the street, his dyed blond hair glowing in the sun. She waved at him, suddenly relieved to have an excuse to get out of the house before Ed woke up. "Give me five minutes."

◆ ◆ ◆

"You really needn't have come," Kate said, grinning as her kitchen counter filled with biscuits, chocolate, milk, bread, and more biscuits.

"Don't be silly," Gareth said. "You're what's known as a friend in need. Although . . ." He looked at her closely. ". . . you don't seem all that upset. Are you in denial? Have you buried the trauma deep within yourself?"

Kate shook her head. "I'm fine. Really."

"I still don't understand," Sal said, bemused. "Joe and Penny? Of all the people. He was bitching about her at dinner just last week."

"Love and hate," Gareth said knowledgeably, turning on the kettle. "They're very close, you know. And probably he was protesting too much, you know, to disguise his real feelings."

Sal frowned at him. "Maybe it was a mistake," she suggested. "I mean, maybe he just got carried away in the moment. It happens, doesn't it? It doesn't have to mean anything. . . ."

Kate shook her head. "I don't understand it either," she said with a sigh, "but it wasn't a mistake. Me and Joe . . . well, it's over."

"Gareth's right," Sal said. "You're in denial or something. You don't even seem that upset. Just the other day you were talking about marrying this guy."

"I know." Kate smiled slightly. "But, you know, I got it wrong. He wasn't the guy for me. You have to move on, don't you?"

Sal's eyes narrowed. "Not this quickly. You move on after spending a weekend listening to Bette Midler and eating ice cream. You don't just get up and say, Oh well, not to worry. It's not normal. What aren't you telling us?"

Kate turned pink. "Nothing!" she said defensively. "There's nothing I'm not telling you. I'm just . . . well, I'm just okay." She took a mug of steaming tea from Gareth and sat down at the kitchen table, trying to focus her mind. She was upset by Joe and Penny. Of course she was. But that all seemed a long time ago now. That was before Tom kissed her.

And now she had no idea what she thought about anything.

"She's gone mad," Gareth announced. "Complete basket case."

"I think you might be right," Sal said, not at all certain. "So, Kate, have you thought any more about your job situation? What you might do?"

Kate frowned. "I dunno. I'll think of something."

"I've got the numbers of some producers," Gareth said, digging a piece of paper out from his back pocket. "D'you want me to call them for you? I could be your people. You need to have people to be taken seriously."

Kate raised an eyebrow. "You think if I had people they'd be like you?" she asked, smiling.

Gareth shrugged. "Suit yourself."

The phone rang and they all stared at one another.

"What if it's Joe?" Gareth asked excitedly.

Kate frowned again. What if it was Tom?

"I'll get it," Sal said, picking up the receiver. "Hello? Kate Hetherington's apartment." She passed the phone to Kate. "It's someone called Heather."

Kate frowned. "I don't know a Heather." She sighed and took the receiver. "Kate speaking," she said. "How can I help you?"

"Kate! Hi! It's Heather here. Heather from *Hot Gossip* magazine. I just wanted to say all this stuff with Penny and Joe must be really hard. How are you feeling today?"

Kate stared at the phone. "Sorry, do I know you?" she asked, slightly taken aback.

"I heard about last night. Our photographer got a photo of you, all slumped up on the ground. Just awful, and I felt so sorry for you, I just wanted to get your thoughts, really. You know, toward Joe, toward Penny. How long had you two been together? Have you ever gone to LA? I mean, did you think you were going to move to LA with him? Has he shattered your dreams?"

"I . . . I . . . I have to go now," Kate said, quickly putting the receiver down.

Sal raised her eyebrows and Gareth looked at her expectantly.

"Sales call?" Sal asked sympathetically. "I get those all the time. If it isn't double glazing, it's credit cards or accident insurance. I mean, does anyone actually buy that stuff over the phone?"

"It was *Hot Gossip* magazine," Kate said, still reeling. "They wanted to know if Joe had shattered my dreams of moving to LA."

"*Hot Gossip?*" Sal repeated in disbelief, her eyes wide. "Why? I mean, really?"

"Yes, really," Kate said. "She . . . she said they've got a photograph of me on the ground outside the Bush Bar and Grill."

"You were on the ground? Oh my God. How dramatic! Did Penny push you? Have you got any bruises?"

Kate looked at Gareth sternly. "I was just pissed off. No one pushed anyone. But I didn't think they'd photograph *me*."

"Why were they photographing anyone?" Sal asked, confused.

Gareth rolled his eyes at her. "Publicity. Come on, Sal, keep up. Penny would get the paparazzi to photograph her getting out of the bath if she thought they'd be interested." Then he grinned. "Give them an interview," he said, his eyes glinting. "Make like Princess Di on *Panorama* and tell the world what a bitch Penny Pennington is."

Kate shook her head. "No way. There is no way I'm doing an interview. I can't think of anything worse than being in one of those magazines."

Gareth bit his lip. "So you're not keen on being in the papers, either?"

"Of course not." Kate frowned. "Why?"

"Yeah, the thing is, I wasn't going to show you this until, you know, I was sure you were feeling strong enough. . . ." Gareth said awkwardly.

He slowly pulled out a copy of the *News of the World*.

"I saw it when I was buying the chocolate," he explained. Opening it up at page sixty-three, he winced as he turned it round to show Kate and Sal.

There, on a columnist's gossip page, was a slightly out-of-focus photograph of Penny and Joe with a small but clear image of Kate in the background, sitting outside the Bush Bar and Grill with her head in her hands. The caption read, "Daytime dramas: *Future: Perfect* star Penny Pennington has her mitts on a new man, actor Joe Rogers. But our spies tell us that all isn't happy on the *Future: Perfect* set, particularly for Kate Hetherington, interiors stylist, who until recently was Joe's girlfriend. More like *Future: Imperfect* for Kate, it seems. But the new couple are Perfectly happy with that!"

Kate stared at the photo and grabbed the paper away from Gareth.

"Oh my God!"

"I know!" Gareth said. "They don't know you've been fired yet. Journalists are so clueless these days . . ."

Penny triumphantly held up the newspaper to show Joe, then picked up the phone.

"Magda? It's me. Seen the *News of the World*? . . . I know! . . . Couldn't be better if we tried. Look, got to go, just wanted to make sure you'd seen it. . . . Oh, and I hope you don't mind but I'm not going to be in on Monday. . . . No, important publicity stuff . . . Yes, yes, I will, don't worry. Byeee."

She made a kissy face at Joe and dialed another number.

"Me. What've we got? Uh huh. Yup. Okay. No, I don't want to do it here—you'll have to find me another flat. Something interior designed. Yeah. Oh, really? Oh, I think so. . . ." She turned to Joe. "You ski?"

He frowned and shook his head.

"Yup," Penny said, "skiing's not a problem. Great! Alright, well, keep me posted." She put down the phone and turned to Joe, elated.

"*OK!* is going to do an interview with us in our lovely new home," she said, licking her lips. "So we need to find a hotel suite that looks suitably glamorous. And *Tittle Tattle* is going to take us to Verbier for their celebrity holiday pullout special. *Hot Gossip* magazine is going to run the pics from last night and the story. You and I, Mr. Rogers, we're hot property!"

Joe looked at her in disbelief. This woman was incredible. In less than twenty-four hours he'd gone from being a no one to half of a celebrity couple. His agent had already been on the phone congratulating him, telling him that he'd have some more auditions lined up for next week. And all he'd had to do was kiss Penny in front of some cameras and tell a couple of journalists that he was in love. Oh, and then, when they'd got home, he'd had to . . . Actually, he didn't really want to think about what he'd done back at Penny's flat. He only had to do it until he'd got some recognition, anyway. Then he'd never have to see Penny's scrawny body again.

And in the meantime, Penny said he could stay here. In her Chelsea apartment. Man, he'd landed on his feet this time. He was going places. He was going to *be* someone.

"Okay, just one question," he said firmly.

Penny smiled. "What?"

"Where's Verbier?"

24

On Monday morning, Kate woke up at seven thirty with an odd feeling in her stomach. She had no job to go to. No one was expecting her anywhere. And Tom still hadn't called.

She'd reluctantly gone to bed at midnight the night before, convinced that no sooner would her head hit the pillow than the phone would start to ring and he'd be apologizing for being so busy, wondering if he could come over. . . .

And while she waited, she'd tried to imagine life with Tom as her boyfriend, tried to imagine walking arm in arm with him, having picnics on hot sunny afternoons, going to Paris by Eurostar, floating around Venice on gondolas. It was impossible. She could conjure the pictures with the Tom from the other night, alright; the Tom she'd kissed, the Tom who sent little shivers down her spine every time she thought about him. But as soon as those pictures were safely in her mind, the Tom she knew far better—the cynical, sarcastic, best friend Tom—appeared in her head and sabotaged the pictures, making stupid remarks and taking the piss out of her little fantasies. Cynical Tom wouldn't be able to keep a straight face floating around Venice on a gondola, she thought. Sarcastic Tom didn't even believe in love.

Eventually she'd fallen asleep rather like a cat with one ear cocked, waiting to spring into action should the phone ring or the doorbell go. She'd even dreamt that he turned up in the middle of the night. She went to open the front door and found him standing there, wearing a hat pulled down over his face, like Alec's in *Brief Encounter*. It was pouring with rain, and he pulled her to him, kissing her firmly on the mouth, and little droplets of rain from his hat cascaded down onto her skin, and the next thing she knew they were in a car driving off to the country without a care in the world.

And then she woke up, and he wasn't there, and there weren't any messages on her answer machine. Which was . . . disappointing. But there would be a good reason for it, she was sure. Anyway, she was fine. It was just a kiss, after all. And it was just Tom.

At seven forty Gareth called to find out if there were any messages she wanted him to relay to Magda and Penny or any stories about fabulous new jobs she wanted him to make up, but, to his evident disappointment, she declined his kind offer.

"You're sure?" he asked. "I mean, you don't want Penny thinking she's won, do you? I could just say you're on holiday in the Seychelles or something?"

Kate smiled but stayed firm. "Don't say anything," she ordered.

"I can't believe you're not coming in," Gareth wailed. "I'm going to have no one to play with anymore. No one to bitch with or anything."

"I know. I'm a bit sad, too," Kate said. "But then again, I think in many ways, it might be a good thing. You know, a catalyst."

"Right," Gareth said. "Um . . . catalyst. That's something to do with cars, isn't it?"

Kate grinned. "Not exactly. I think maybe it was time I left *Future: Perfect*, you know? I mean, there are other production companies, right?"

"'Course there are. I'm going to miss you, though. And as for that Penny . . . I'm just going to blank her, I've decided. Show her she can't go pushing people around without consequences."

Kate smiled. "Penny's got filming today, hasn't she?" she asked mischievously. "At Sarah Jones's house? I think she'll have enough on her plate finishing the painting and decorating without worrying about what I'm up to."

Gareth considered. "But Phil'll be doing that, won't he?"

"Phil works for me, so he won't be in today." Kate smiled to herself. "But I'm sure Penny will be fine. I mean, she's always saying how much she knows about interior design."

"You're a clever little minx, I'll give you that," Gareth said, giggling. "Maybe today isn't going to be a total washout, after all."

By eight fifteen Kate had eaten her breakfast, had two cups of tea, read all the junk mail she'd received that morning—along with a few leaflets on double glazing that had appeared over the weekend—and loaded the dishwasher. She'd also checked in with Phil, who was fitting a kitchen for his sister-in-law which she'd been asking him to do for several months now; knowing that the nagging was going to stop, he told Kate, made his life suddenly seem a million times better.

By eight forty-five, she had called her landline from her mobile, and her mobile from her landline to check both were working.

At nine sharp, having dialed Tom's number five times and each time forced herself to hang up before it started ringing, she went online instead and found the numbers of five production companies to approach.

And by nine thirty she discovered that Footprint wasn't the only production company to hold a Monday meeting which tied up all their executives for at least two hours.

Still, she told herself, she had all day. There was no rush.

She had all the time in the world.

In an office on the other side of London, Sal sat staring at her computer screen.

She'd barely slept the night before. How were you meant to sleep when you realized that your husband was lying to you? That your marriage was in its final stages?

It had been such a small thing that betrayed him. The oldest mistake in the book. Ed had been playing golf with clients, as he often did at the weekend. Unavoidable, he always told her—if he didn't play, he wouldn't get nominated by them in the quarterly analyst voting rounds, and that would mean no bonus, which would mean no money to throw at the mortgage. He was doing it for their future, he told her over and over again until she believed him, until she accepted it as fact.

And then Sal had decided to clean her car. She had no idea why—perhaps it was her subconscious pushing her, or perhaps it was just the early spring sun that made her want to make everything feel clean and new again. So she'd driven it round to the carwash, and they'd asked if she wanted the inside done, too, and she'd thought about it briefly and then said yes, why not. And they'd asked if there was anything in the boot, and she'd frowned and said she didn't think so, and she'd opened it to check, and there were the golf clubs. Ed's only set. The set they'd moved into her car months before when they needed to fill Ed's car with Christmas presents on the way to his family's for the holidays.

All this time, he'd been disappearing at weekends to play golf with no golf clubs.

She hadn't said anything. Hadn't dared to. Sunday night at eleven P.M. was not, in her book, the time for confrontations. And anyway, she needed to think. Needed time to absorb the horrible truth. Needed to pull herself together so that she could challenge him without bursting into tears, without falling to the floor and weeping because her life was over.

"Ed is my husband."

She said the words aloud as if to remind herself or to check if the statement still rung true, still carried the reassurance and excitement with it.

She still remembered the first time she had said the words *my husband.* It was in the car on the way home from their wedding, and they were stopping briefly at their flat to get changed and pick up their bags before hurtling off to the airport. She'd said, "My husband will get the bags." There had been no need to say it; the driver hadn't asked her about the bags and nor did he appear to be interested in them, but she'd said it anyway because she wanted to feel the shape of the words in her mouth, wanted to see how they sounded in her voice.

My husband.

My husband, Ed.

Have you met my husband?

Oh, I was just telling my husband the other day . . .

For at least a year she'd managed to steer every conversation back to her husband. For slightly longer, she'd had her nails manicured every week because she wanted to draw attention to her hands, to her left hand, to her wedding ring. It symbolized something so fundamental: She was married, she was no longer searching, she was safe and sound.

Funny, she thought as she looked at her ring now, that she'd seen it almost as a shield when it was first placed on her finger. As if the ring would protect her like something out of a sci-fi movie; no one could touch her so long as she wore it.

In the event, it hadn't turned out to be a particularly strong protective shield. In the event, it turned out that marriage didn't protect you at all. It just diverted you for a while. Gave you the illusion of safety so that you didn't notice the dissatisfaction creeping up behind you and gaining ground slowly but surely until it was walking at your side and it was too late to disentangle yourself from it.

Until your husband was lying to you and you were receiving inappropriate text messages from male colleagues.

Free tmrw fr drnk? x

She turned and reviewed the message again. Jim had inadvertently stumbled upon the key question, she realized. Was she free?

She hadn't thought so. But now she wasn't so sure. Perhaps Ed would be relieved if he found out that she'd kissed Jim. Perhaps he would see it as letting him off the hook. Ed would recommend a clean break. Luckily they didn't have children to worry about. They could sell the house, split the proceeds. . . .

Sal went white at the thought. She'd heard people talking about divorce, of course, but it had never been something that would happen to her. She and Ed . . . they loved each other. They did. They were good together. . . .

Sal swallowed fiercely, closing her eyes and forcing the tears pricking behind her eyes to go back to where they came from. How dare Ed put her in this position? How dare life conspire to render her helpless and out of control? It wasn't fair. It wasn't right.

The truth was that she had no one, and she hadn't even noticed it happening.

Sal found herself smiling sadly. She had planned her life meticulously so that she would never find herself in this predicament. Had been so careful to manage her relationships, friendships, house, and job into neat, ordered compartments to make absolutely sure that she had no areas of weakness, no breaches where the floodwaters of despair could find their way in. She'd seen what happened when you left things to chance—when you found yourself pregnant and alone and unable to cope. Her mother hadn't been able to come to grips with the life she'd made for herself, failing to turn up on time to collect Sal from parties because she got waylaid or distracted, because the pills she took to keep herself on an even keel sometimes made her forgetful or sleepy or both. Sal's mother had descended gradually into an all-consuming depression that made her so selfish and self-absorbed that sometimes she seemed not to remember who Sal was. She hadn't turned up to Sal's graduation from Oxford. Had asked her once how her degree was going when she was a year into her doctorate. And had killed herself two days before Sal's twenty-fifth birthday. She hadn't even left a note.

Sal missed her mother. Missed the mother she remembered from the old days, the mother who used to plait her hair when she was five and sing her songs and read her stories about dragons and princesses. Missed the mother who always wanted to hear about her day, who would put everything to one side so that she could focus entirely on Sal, her eyes lighting up as Sal told her about her lessons, her adventures, her friends, and her mortal enemies.

And now she missed Ed. Missed him so much she ached inside. Missed him like Adam and Eve must have missed paradise, because, she realized now, that's what it had been like, being the center of Ed's world, having him smile at her and tease her and desire her and make her feel that she was human again rather than the machine that everyone else thought she was. He was the only one who'd seen her armor for what it was, who'd got inside and loved what he found so that she felt happier than she ever imagined possible.

Heavily, Sal reached for a tissue and took a deep breath. She would get over this, she told herself. She would figure out a way to get things back to normal. She would pull her socks up and paint a smile on her face, and she and Ed would work through their difficulties together. Sal did not do despair or depression. *Would* not do them.

This present mood was probably hormonal anyway, she told herself. In a couple of days' time she'd get her period and then she'd feel much more able to cope. She'd no doubt wonder why she had allowed herself to be seduced into self-pity by a collection of hormones that she really ought to be able to control by now.

Bringing up her e-mail inbox, she clicked calendar. Last month her period came an hour before that awful presentation, which would make her next one due . . .

She frowned. That couldn't be right.

Quickly she recounted the days. Forty-two. That was impossible. No one had a forty-two day cycle. Not unless . . .

Wide-eyed, she stared at her stomach. It was impossible. Had to be wrong. She couldn't be pregnant now—not by mistake, not when her husband was having an affair and she was on the brink of her own. It simply couldn't be true.

And then it dawned on her. She had spent her entire life micromanaging everything to avoid ending up like her mother, pregnant and alone, only for history to repeat itself anyway. Her worst nightmare had been organized so carefully out of the realms of possibility that she hadn't noticed it slip in and bite her on the arse.

Tom looked worriedly at Mrs. Sandler. She was still losing weight. If she couldn't keep her food down, they were going to have to stick her on a drip again.

"You realize, Mrs. Sandler," he said, "that if you don't eat, you'll be here longer? I mean, I know the food here is a disaster, but the more you can eat, the sooner you'll be able to eat food that doesn't make you want to puke. A kind of virtuous circle, if you will. . . ."

"Call me Rose, please, doctor. I do try, you know," Mrs. Sandler said with a weak smile. "I just can't seem to keep it down."

Tom grimaced. "I can't see why," he said, shaking his head. "You should be able to tolerate food by now."

Rose smiled sheepishly. "It's my nerves, Doctor," she said. "Can't ever seem to eat when I'm stressed. My Pat's always on at me to eat more. He's on the chubby side, see. Can't see how I'd let myself get this thin."

"And he's got a good point," Tom said. "So come on, what shall we do? How about I go and buy some nice fresh soup from the supermarket across the road? And some fresh bread. We'll hide it from the nurses, ignore every health and safety regulation in the book, and have a gastronomic feast. What do you say?"

"You're very kind, Doctor. But the hospital food's fine. Really it is. My son's coming in today. I'm sure I'll feel better when I've seen him."

Tom looked at her for a few seconds. "Well, good. That's good."

"He's ever such a good boy, Doctor. Says he wants to be a doctor himself when he grows up. He was saying to me just the other day that he's been really studying his science—"

"Which is great news," Tom interrupted. He didn't want to know about her son. Personal information led to personal involvement. "But about your eating, Rose . . . shall we try and focus on that?"

"It's his school concert this week. Keeps asking me if I'm going to be there," Rose continued sadly. "Told him I would be, but it's looking less likely, isn't it, Doctor?"

Tom sighed. Why did everyone always want to involve him in their lives? Why did they think that school plays and sons who wanted to be doctors had anything to do with him?

"If you don't eat, Rose, how can you get better?" he asked pointedly.

"My boy's only seven, that's the thing, Doctor. Seven's very young to lose a mother, isn't it?"

Tom stared at her and found his throat tightening. "Rose, no one is losing anyone," he said. "You are going to eat, then you are going to have another operation in a couple of days, and then you will get better. I've spoken to your consultant, and we're just waiting for you to get your strength up before we schedule you in."

Rose nodded. "But you couldn't get it all last time, could you, Doctor?"

Tom shook his head. "We usually leave the traces to chemo," he said. "It's horrible, I know, but less invasive. But now we're going back in. We'll get it all out, Rose. We will."

"I know you'll do your best, Doctor," Rose said with a small smile. "But this is cancer, not a splinter. I know what my chances are. And Liam, my son, well, he's so young, and I've been in and out of hospital, losing my hair, throwing up. . . . I'm worried that the only memories he's going to have of me are those. Being ill. Illness is so terribly selfish, Doctor, that's the problem. It takes you away from the people you love. And I'd like him to have a happier memory. You know, maybe if I could go to his school concert tomorrow. See him play the violin. He's been practicing so hard, you see. . . ."

Tom sighed. "It's out of the question. You're in no fit state to leave the hospital," he said sternly.

She bit her lip. "You see, it's not guaranteed, is it? The surgery, I mean. It might not work."

"Nothing is ever guaranteed in this world," Tom said quietly. "Except . . ."

"Yes, Doctor?"

Tom reddened slightly. "Nothing. Sorry. Just this book a . . . a friend of mine bought. Promised love or her money back. Stupid thing. Forget I mentioned it."

"Lucky her!" Rose said with another little smile. "Has it worked?"

Tom looked uncomfortable. "No. Well, no, no, it hasn't."

"Shame," Rose said. "Yes, that is a shame. It's all anyone really wants isn't it? Love, I mean. That's what I'm most scared of. That if I die, Pat and Liam will forget how much I love them. Loved them."

Tears started to cascade down her face and Tom swallowed hard. It would be foolhardy to let her go to that stupid school concert. Against every policy.

"When's the concert?" he found himself saying.

Rose's eyes lit up. "Five o'clock, tomorrow afternoon, Doctor. It only lasts for an hour and a half."

"You'll go straight there and straight back. No detours. No popping in to see a neighbor. You go, you see your son, and you come back."

"Yes, Doctor," Rose said, her eyes shining.

Tom nodded curtly and started to walk away. Then he stopped and turned back. "Nothing's going to happen, Rose," he promised. "You're going to be fine. The surgery will be successful. And your son—Liam, is it?"

Rose nodded.

"He's very lucky to have a mum like you," Tom said. "He's very lucky indeed."

As he walked out of the ward, he passed Lucy. "Lucy, Mrs. Sandler needs to go to a school concert tomorrow," he said, his voice businesslike.

"A school concert?"

"That's right. It's at five P.M., and she'll be gone for a couple of hours, no more. I want you to make sure she's got steroids with her and that she eats a proper meal before she goes."

"You're letting her go to the school concert?"

Tom raised his eyebrows. "That's right, Lucy."

Lucy smiled mischievously. "This is the same Mrs. Sandler whose personal problems you're not interested in?"

Tom narrowed his eyes. "You'll make the arrangements, Lucy?"

"Yes, Doctor," Lucy said, grinning. "By the way, how come you didn't come back the other night? I thought you just popped out for some milk."

Tom startled a bit. "Work," he said at once. "I . . . I realized I'd forgotten some paperwork. Needed to be in by eight A.M. for a patient's insurance . . ."

"Whatever." Lucy looked unconvinced, but shrugged. "So, doing anything tonight? Got more paperwork, have you? Because I noticed we're both off from four this afternoon. And there's a certain someone I want to bump into, arm in arm with you, if that's alright."

Tom hesitated for just a moment, then shook his head. "Your ex-boyfriend, I assume?" he asked. "Well, okay then. I'm not doing anything else. In fact, I'm all yours."

25

"Could you try looking a bit more romantic, Joe? If you could gaze at Penny adoringly, that would be just great. . . . Yeah, that's better. Okay, now, Penny, you look toward me. . . . Try to make your eyes a bit softer, love. There we are, that's what we're looking for. . . ."

The photographer started clicking and Joe wondered if anyone ever got frostbite doing this. They were in Verbier. On the top of a mountain. In the freezing cold. And there was one other thing playing on his mind, too: At some point he was going to have to get down, and the only way people seemed to be doing that was on skis. Bearing in mind that they were on what was referred to as a red run, which Joe discovered meant "difficult," and bearing in mind that he had never so much as stepped foot in a pair of skis before, he wasn't entirely looking forward to it. Actually, he was terrified. And they wanted him to look romantic?

Eventually, the photographer from *Tittle Tattle* stopped and the journalist lady, Miranda Ridgeway, joined them instead.

"So," she said brightly. "Your first skiing trip. Are you both outdoorsy people?"

"Not really," Penny said, annoyed. "I thought you were going to ask about my career? Channel Three is interested in *Future: Perfect*, you know. It's about to really hit the big time."

Miranda smiled, slightly less brightly. "Absolutely," she said. "But

I'm sure our readers would like to know a bit about you as a couple. So, Joe, when did you first realize that Penny was the one for you? When did you—dare I say it?—fall in love?"

Joe stared at her. Oh, man, did he really have to answer that?

The truth was that Penny was a total nightmare. She bitched from the minute she woke up until the minute she went to sleep. She looked like death without her makeup—he'd stumbled on her in the bathroom by mistake and, boy, he wouldn't be doing that again in a hurry—and she didn't seem to even notice other people, let alone acknowledge them. The way she acted, you'd think she was the hottest property in LA, up for a million Oscars, rather than presenting some daytime drivel on British television. If his British agent, Bob, hadn't been so excited by the idea of a spread in *Tittle Tattle*, Joe would have bailed out by now. This was the hardest work he'd ever done. And he kept having to kiss her for the cameras. Off the cameras, too.

"Well," he began with a gulp, "I guess I knew when I first saw her."

"He saw me on the show," Penny put in immediately, "and fell in love with me. Thought I lit up the screen and showed such empathy with the people on the show. He's from LA, so he can really recognize talent."

Miranda frowned and made some notes in her notebook. "And when you met Penny," she continued. "What did you think then?"

Joe thought hard. Jesus, it was freezing up here. He couldn't feel his feet anymore.

"I guess, well, you know, I just thought 'wow'," he said, wracking his brain. "I mean, she's hot, right? And funny, and intelligent . . ."

Good thing I'm such a great actor, he thought as he spoke. If a casting director could just see me now . . .

"That's great, Joe, thank you," Miranda said enthusiastically. "And you're an actor, aren't you?"

"That's right, ma'am. I was in the well-known American show *Everything I Do*. And now, I'm keen to build my career in London, you see. Keen to take advantage of the opportunities on offer . . ."

Miranda nodded. "Well, great. Okay, so Penny, did you see Joe on *Everywhere I Go*? Did Joe light up the screen, too?"

"*Everything I Do*," Joe said quickly. "It's *Everything I Do*."

"Of course, sorry," Miranda said. "So, Penny?"

"I don't have time to watch television," Penny said with a loud sigh. "I'm too busy being on it."

Miranda looked slightly taken aback. "Right. Um, okay. So tell me about the first time you saw Joe. Was it love at first sight?"

Penny looked at Joe lasciviously. "Lust you mean?" she said, smiling, then obviously thought better of it. "I was deeply attracted to Joe," she said, suddenly soulful. "And I could see that he wasn't happy with his girlfriend. That she was holding him back. And when our eyes met, well . . ."

Joe looked at her in shock as she dabbed at her eyes with a handkerchief that had appeared out of nowhere. Were those real tears?

"I suppose, I just suddenly felt that life made sense after all. That I'd met my soul mate."

Miranda sniffed. "That's lovely," she said, shaking her head. "Right, well, perhaps we could reconvene at the hotel—I'd love to hear a bit more about how you met, and about your plans for the future, Penny. And about the show in the U.S., Joe. *Everywhere I Go*. Was it a travel program?"

Joe smiled thinly. "*Everything I Do*," he said, through gritted teeth. "It's *Everything I Do*."

"Great!" Miranda said. "So, I'll leave you two to ski down the slopes—hopefully get some great action shots for the spread—and I'll see you later for a bit of après-ski!"

She left, and the photographer reappeared. "Okay, so you just ski as normal down the slopes, yeah? My assistant, Jon, is going to ski after you with a camera and get some shots. Okay?"

Joe looked at Penny, waiting for her to explain that Joe couldn't ski, that he had absolutely no idea how to get down what looked like a vertical slope without breaking his neck. But she just smiled. "Last one down has to buy the drinks!" She grinned, putting her boots into her skis and throwing her head back in laughter when she saw Jon begin to click.

Joe walked awkwardly toward her. He couldn't believe how uncomfortable these boots were. Now not only could he not ski, he could barely walk.

"I can't ski," he hissed when he was close enough for Penny to hear him without having to alert anyone else.

"You'll be fine!" she said, rolling her eyes. "Honestly, it's not that hard, Joe. Look, there are children doing it. Don't be such a wimp."

Joe swallowed. "I'm guessing those children have had maybe a lesson or two," he said, trying to remain calm, and talking with a smiling face just in case Jon decided to snap a picture or two.

Penny sighed. "Okay, look. Legs together, you go fast. Snowplow like this and you'll slow down. Go side to side so you don't build up too much speed. See? Easy. Look, watch me."

And to his dismay, Penny turned and immediately whizzed across the ski slopes as if she'd been doing it all her life. Jon frowned and quickly followed her, whooshing elegantly on the snow.

Actually, it looked kind of fun.

Concentrating, Joe put his boots into his skis like Penny had, wondering vaguely why they didn't seem to match, and made his way to the top of the slope. It seemed like a big drop. And he couldn't figure out how you'd stop once you got started. But hey, if Penny and Jon could do it, if children could do it, then Joe Rogers would find it a piece of cake.

Holding his breath, he forced himself off the top of the mountain and felt the incredible exhilaration of speed as he found himself skiing hell for leather right down the middle of the slope.

Magda stared at the rolls and rolls of bright pink velvet that had been ordered at Penny's instructions and were now cluttering up the home of Maggie and Charles Kitchin. Several times already, one or other of them had looked at them, smiled a bit anxiously, and asked what they were going to become. Each time Magda had smiled weakly and said that Penny had some exciting plans that she herself couldn't possibly reveal.

Because she didn't have the slightest clue.

Which meant that Magda had a big problem. Following Penny's publicity stunt, she'd managed to get a meeting with two executives from Channel 3 to talk about commissioning the show for a major evening slot. She'd promised them that *Future: Perfect* was developing into a different kind of show, one that would appeal to a mass audience, that would get high ratings. And instead, she didn't have a show at all. Filming still hadn't been completed at the Joneses' because the bloody walls weren't painted and no one could find a painter or decorator who was available for love or money—Magda had even called round a few herself and had been told blankly that no one was available, at all, period—and the Kitchins were meant to be signing off the concept for their makeover and the bloody concept didn't even exist yet. She was going to look a bloody fool. Those Channel 3 people were going to laugh her out of the meeting.

And Penny, in spite of all her promises, was still not here.

Magda took a deep breath and tried to calm herself. It was only Tuesday. Lysander had kept the Kitchins busy shopping for clothes that flattered the older person whilst giving them a youthful air, a job Magda could tell he hated by the way he kept grinding his teeth and staring into the middle distance. Penny could film her pieces to camera tomorrow, and she'd be able to do something with this place by the end of the week, Magda was sure of it. No walls were coming down, after all. Nothing major had to be done.

As for the Joneses, Magda would think of something. No problem was insurmountable. She'd paint the place herself if need be.

No, everything would be fine. Penny knew what she was doing. And she'd certainly pulled it out of the bag this time. If Magda had doubted her for a moment, she wouldn't again. Interviews, photographs—Magda's phone hadn't stopped ringing. Holiday Choice had signed up as sponsors for an entire year, and the chief exec himself had been down to see her. He'd never done that before.

Of course, he'd wanted to see Penny, but Magda had managed to divert him. Penny had an appointment with *Tittle Tattle* magazine, she'd said, watching his eyes light up greedily. She hadn't mentioned that the appointment was in flipping Switzerland.

The important thing, though, was to focus on the big picture. This week's show would sort itself out; what mattered was how Magda played this positive turn of events. Now was the time to get out there, to start talking to other production companies.

No, no it wasn't. They had to come to her. If she started calling people up it would be too transparent and she'd lose any bargaining power. Better to stay put and wait for viewing figures to go through the roof, then sit back and let the phone start to ring.

This week *Future: Perfect*; next week, *Panorama*. And failing that, *Extreme Makeover*, where they at least had proper budgets and company cars.

"Would you like some hot chocolate? Maybe something stronger? Maybe some food?" Sarah Ridgeway was looking at Joe with a concerned look on her face.

He shook his head.

"You came down very quickly," she said cheerfully. "Shame about that tumble at the end. I think you're very brave going skiing in the first place. I mean, it's alright for people like Jon and Penny who've been skiing all their lives, but I don't suppose there's much snow in LA, is there?"

Joe turned to Penny. "You've skied all your life?" he asked, his voice strained.

Penny frowned. "'Course I have. I grew up in bloody Switzerland, didn't I? I was skiing before I could walk. Why?"

"No reason." He took a deep breath. "Hey, would you excuse me? I need to make a phone call."

He stood up stiffly, every bone and muscle in his body crying out in pain. Even his neck muscles were in agony from having been tensed in utter terror as he hurtled down the slope. But nothing in his body had been dented as deeply as his pride. How was he to know that there was a right way and a wrong way to put on skis? He'd thought that maybe his skis weren't a matching pair when one appeared to be shorter at the front than the other, but it turned out that he had one of them on back to front. Which helped somewhat when he ended up traveling backward down the bottom portion of that horrible mountain. It helped less when Penny didn't stop laughing about it after she and Jon discovered him in a crumpled heap at the bottom. She told everyone, too. It was her latest funny little anecdote.

God, he was beginning to hate that woman.

Slowly, he eased his way to a nearby table and managed to sit down, pulling out his mobile. The minute he was back in the UK, he was going to knock this whole farcical relationship on the head. He just wanted to make sure that he'd gotten enough publicity mileage out of it.

"Bob," he said, "it's me. Joe."

"Joe! Great to hear from you! How's the skiing?"

Joe chose not to answer that question. "Do I have some auditions? I don't know how long I can keep this thing going with Penny. So, I was wondering, maybe we could break up and I could get some publicity out of that?"

Bob whistled. "Joe, right now you're really flying on Penny's coattails. I'm not sure you breaking up with her is such a good idea, you know? If we could get you on *Celebrity Sing a Song for Sixpence*, or next year's *Celebrity Big Brother*, then you'd have your own profile, but for the time being, I think this thing is really working for you. . . ."

"Next *year*? I cannot do this for a year!"

"I'm sure it won't be that long. We're making some calls, and when you get back I just know we're going to have some exciting things lined up for you. Okay?"

"Fine. See ya." Disgruntled, Joe put his phone in his pocket and sighed, looking over at Penny and the *Tittle Tattle* crew.

Then he stood up, cringing at the pain, and walked back to his interview.

At five P.M., Tim from NorthWest Productions finally took Kate's call.

"Hi!" she said brightly. "I'm Kate Hetherington. Formerly the interiors stylist on *Future: Perfect*, a makeover show you may know about on—"

"I know who you are," Tim cut in. "You're the one who was in the papers. Penny Pennington nicked your boyfriend, right?"

Kate blanched. "I wouldn't say *nicked*, exactly," she said. "I mean, I wasn't really that into him anyway."

"Right. So my assistant tells me you have an idea you want to pitch?"

"Yes," Kate said. "A makeover project with a difference. It's a hospice, you see. A hospice for cancer patients and it's run as a charity, and the place really needs to be brightened up. . . ."

"A hospice."

"Yes, with these great patients, so some really good life stories there . . ."

"Any celebrity interest?"

Kate frowned. "Celebrity interest?"

"We could get a bunch of them," he said with growing excitement. "Each one could design a room and it could be a competition. The patients could vote. Viewers could vote. Maybe they could get voted out, one each week?"

Kate cleared her throat. "Yeah, I was actually thinking not so much of celebrities and more of getting builders in, you know. More of a warmhearted program than a celeb one, if you know what I mean?"

"You, Penny, and that bloke. If all three of you were on it, that would be great," Tim continued obliviously. "Could you stage an argument? Fall out over something?"

"There's this patient. Betty, her name is," Kate tried. "I think she'd be great on television. She's bright, and funny, and brave, and—"

"Kate, I love the idea. Get me a proposal. Suggest some celebrities, and we'll brainstorm here, too. Penny and whatshisname are definites. We'll need a few more, though. Maybe it could all be warring couples. Or new couples. Peter and Jordan, maybe. Yeah, this is great. Thanks for thinking of us. So, shall we say you'll have something with us by the end of today?"

Kate frowned, unsure that they had been having the same conversation. Then she shrugged. "Sure," she said. "That sounds great."

Jane from Panther Productions was less enthusiastic. "Yeah, I think hospitals have been done," she said. "Thanks, though, and if you have any other ideas . . ."

"Not a hospital," Kate said. "A hospice. It's like a house where patients go after treatment and they're looked after there and—"

"Yeah, I think it's the whole medical genre that's been a bit overdone," Jane said in a South London drawl. "Sport's big right now. Since we've got the Olympics everyone's going crazy for it. Got any ideas around sport, have you?"

Kate bit her lip. "No," she said, "no sport. Just the hospice, I'm afraid."

"Shame," Jane said with a sigh. "Well, let me know if you come up with anything, yeah?"

"Sure," Kate promised. "You'll be the first to know."

Despondently, she put the phone down. Out of the five producers she'd contacted, Tim seemed the only one who was even remotely interested, and his version of the idea bore absolutely no resemblance to hers. She'd rather spend a year renovating the hospice her-self than involve Penny and Joe in the project.

And Tom still hadn't called.

Was he angry with her about something? Should she have called him, maybe? No, he said he'd call her. The cardinal rule was that you couldn't call someone when they said they'd call you. Even if that person was Tom. Even if until that kiss, calling Tom had been the most natural thing in the world to do.

Maybe she should just call him and tell him the whole thing had been a bad idea, she thought. That would clear the air. Get things back to normal.

But had it been a bad idea? Or had it been an incredibly good one?

Maybe she should call him and see what he thought. Maybe he was waiting by the phone right now, hoping that she'd call him up. . . .

Her hand reached tentatively toward the phone, but she stopped herself. She'd buy some food instead, she decided. She'd buy some food for supper, cook it, eat it, and then if Tom still hadn't called by, say, ten P.M., she'd call him.

She grabbed her bag and keys and headed out of the flat.

A brisk walk later, Kate opened the door to the supermarket and made her way to the fresh foods counter. She'd decided to buy a freshly made pizza, which she would eat in front of the television be-fore having a long, hot bath. That way, if Tom did call, she wouldn't have been waiting by the phone. That way, she was less likely to give in and call him instead.

She stared at the board above the counter, trying to decide which toppings to go for and drawing a blank because her mind was too tired to concentrate.

Then she frowned. In the mirror beneath the toppings board, she thought she could see a familiar face. Turning round, she smiled, wondering why she suddenly felt so awkward.

"Tom!" she said. "You're here!"

Tom stared at her for a second, then grinned broadly. "Kate," he said, rushing over and giving her a hug. "So sorry I haven't been able to call. So, how are things?"

"They're good. Really good," Kate said quickly. "I was just buying pizza. Are you hungry?"

Tom gave her an unreadable look. "Actually," he said, "I'm, uh, going back to the hospital in a bit. Just came out to grab some things, you know."

"Oh." Kate nodded uncertainly. "And later?"

Tom shrugged. "Kate, I just don't know, I'm afraid. This patient . . ." His eyes moved away from hers shiftily, and she got a sudden pain in her stomach, as if she'd been punched. She knew that look—had seen it on other people, had no doubt had it on her face a few times over the years. She'd just never expected to see it on Tom's face.

"Right," she said. "Of course. Well, you know, I'll see you when I see you, I suppose."

"You're okay, though?" Tom asked hopefully. "I mean, things are okay?"

Kate forced herself to smile. She might have mistaken the look. Tom was a doctor, after all. Of course he was busy. "They're fine, Tom. Really. Don't worry about it."

Tom ducked his head.

"Ooh. You buying pizza, Tom? Do they do pepperoni?"

Kate frowned and stared at the strange girl who had just appeared beside him.

"I'm sorry?" she asked, her voice rather more cutting than she intended.

The girl looked at her in surprise. "Do I know you?" she asked, then turned to Tom. "Make sure you get pepperoni," she said, and pinched his bum. "I feel like a bit of meat tonight!"

Tom looked at her, then at Kate, and gulped. "Kate. This is . . . Lucy."

"Lucy," Kate said levelly.

"Hi!" the girl said, holding out her hand, then gasped. "Hey, you're that girl from the newspaper, aren't you? Oh, shame, wasn't it? Oh, poor you."

Kate suddenly felt sick to her stomach. She attempted a smile.

"Lucy's a nurse at the hospital," Tom said.

"That's right," Lucy said brightly. "I was just looking for some wine. Can't have pizza without wine, can you?"

Kate shook her head, numb. "No. I don't suppose you can. Well, Tom, I'm glad to hear that you'll be fed. Can't have you working all those hours and not having time to eat, can we?"

"It's . . . it's not what you think," Tom said, looking at Kate intently. "It's not . . ."

"I don't think anything, Tom," Kate said lightly. "I never have."

She turned a brilliant smile on Lucy. "Enjoy your pizza," she said, then turned and hurried out of the shop. Suddenly the thought of pizza made her want to gag. Actually, the thought of eating anything made her want to throw up.

She walked along the street and turned in to her own, walking briskly back toward her flat. But with each step that she took, the brittle smile on her face eroded a little. And by the time she opened her front door, it was all she could do to get inside before her tears began to flow. Their kiss hadn't meant anything. Tom had a girlfriend with large breasts and curly blond hair. No doubt tomorrow he'd have a different one.

And she couldn't bear it. Couldn't bear the idea of him being with anyone else but her. Which was ridiculous. This was Tom, after all. Tom, one of her oldest friends. They'd only kissed once, and it was really no big deal.

Except it was a big deal, Kate realized now. Everything about that night had been a big deal. Just not to him.

Suddenly, Kate knew why she'd been feeling so unsettled by the kiss, had got over Joe's betrayal so quickly. She was in love with Tom. And yet she hated him, too. Because he'd let her fall for him when he wasn't interested. Because she realized that she needed him, and he didn't need anyone; he considered love a weakness. As for the kiss, he'd probably done it just to stop her crying. It wouldn't have meant anything to him. She shuddered at how close she'd come to calling him, to asking how he felt about the whole thing. *Silly Kate and her romantic fantasies*, he'd have thought. *When will she grow up and accept reality?*

Well, now she would accept reality. Now she would forget her romantic fantasies and her dreams of a happy ending. Slowly, she walked into the kitchen and picked up *The Hopeless Romantic's Handbook*, which was sitting on the table.

"It's all your fault," she muttered. "Making out that everything's fine. But you're wrong. Things aren't fine. There is no Prince Charming. There is no beau with a jaunty hat and pleasing manner who's going to make everything okay." She looked at the book for a moment or two, flicking through and seeing chapters she hadn't yet read: "Spreading Romance—and Making the World a Better Place" and "Following Your Dreams."

Then she marched to her front door, opened it, and threw the book into the trash bin.

"You've ruined my life," she said bitterly. "Tom was right—there *is* no such thing as a happy ending."

And with that, she ran to the bathroom to throw up.

26

Magda frowned and banged the telephone receiver down. This was just too much. This was not acceptable. Not in the least.

It was Wednesday now. Wednesday afternoon and Penny still hadn't shown her face on the set of *Future: Perfect*. She hadn't even called to give Magda an update or to apologize. And when Magda called her for the umpteenth time this week, some assistant or other had answered the phone and said apologetically that Penny wasn't available right now.

Wasn't available? Did she know who was paying Penny's wages?

"'Scuse me, Magda, sorry to trouble you, but we've just had the builders you booked for the Joneses on the phone. Their job's over-running so they won't be able to get there till next week now."

Magda stared at the researcher in front of her. It was almost as if the entire building community in London was conniving to make things difficult for her. She'd had enough problems tracking down one firm who would take the job, and now even they were letting her down.

"Next week? But we need them now. We need that place finished *now*."

The researcher shrugged. "That's builders for you," he said, grinning, then wiped the smile from his face when he saw that Magda was in no mood for humor. "I'll, uh, try to find someone else, shall

I?" he suggested. Magda nodded curtly, waited until he'd disappeared, and then let her head drop onto the top of her desk.

Everything was a mess. The Kitchins' house was a tip, the pink velvet was unused, and without a presenter they had no links filmed, no introductory sequence, nothing—and now the Jones house was going to be useless, too.

Bloody Penny Pennington. Magda had trusted her when she said, "Leave the interiors to me." Trusted her when she said the skiing trip would be a day, or a day and a half tops. Trusted her to come back to work and sort this mess out before it cost Magda her job for gross mismanagement.

And now she had an e-mail from someone at NorthWest Productions asking her to give them a reference for Kate, and saying how excited they were to work with her. Frowning, she picked up the phone and dialed a number.

"Hello?"

"Kate. It's Magda."

There was silence at the other end.

"I was just wondering how you were getting on. I see you've been in touch with NorthWest. Nice little company. No money, of course, but I suppose you knew that. . . ."

Kate cleared her throat. "Magda, what do you want?"

Magda frowned. Kate sounded different. Impatient. Miserable. Maybe the girl would have a career in television after all.

"Okay," Magda said. "Cards on the table. I was maybe a bit hasty, with that firing business. Wondered if you'd be interested in coming back."

"Come back?" Kate snorted. "You're joking. Absolutely no way."

Magda took a deep breath. "Just a few days, Kate. I'll pay you double. We just need you to finish off the Joneses' house for us. And the Kitchins', too. Do that, and then we can talk about the future. Pay rises, that sort of thing."

"Finish off the Kitchins' house? What have you done so far?"

Magda sighed. "Okay, to *do* the Kitchins' house. Please, Kate?"

There was a pause. A pause had to mean she was thinking about it. That was good.

"I'm sorry, Magda. But it's a matter of loyalty, you know? I'm just not sure I can work with you anymore."

Magda scowled. Bloody girl was getting too clever for her own good. "The people at NorthWest Productions are cowboys. You know that, don't you?"

"Thanks, Magda. If I decide I want career advice from you I'll ask, okay?"

Magda raised her eyebrows. Was this really the same Kate? "Okay," she said briskly. "Bottom line is that maybe I was a bit hasty. Maybe our little chat was an overreaction."

"Maybe you're sorry?"

"Don't push your luck. So, look, talk me through this hospice idea."

"You want to know about the hospice now?"

Magda gripped the telephone receiver. "Yes, Kate, I want to know about the bloody hospice."

Kate sighed. "Fine. Basically, it's a hospice affiliated to the Charing Cross Hospital cancer unit. People go there when they've had surgery but are still doing chemo—like a halfway house. It's in really bad repair, so the plan is to do the whole place up."

"Cancer," Magda said, picking up a pen on autopilot and scribbling notes. "And there are patients with interesting life stories?"

"Of course there are. One or two in particular whose stories the show could follow from surgery through recovery."

Magda thought for a moment. This was the sort of thing Channel 3 would love.

"Look," she said. "We might be interested. I've got a meeting with Channel Three later today, and it just might appeal. They're lobbying for a share of the BBC license fee and they're looking for programs with a social conscience."

"Channel Three?" Kate asked, her deadpan tone suddenly forgotten.

Magda smiled with satisfaction. Now she had Kate's attention.

"That's right," Magda said matter-of-factly. "So what do you say?"

There was another pause. "I say that if you can get me some details, some assurances, and some indication of budgets, I might consider it," Kate said. "Until then, I suggest you contact Penny and hope that she can bring her interiors flair to the Kitchins' house. Because I'm afraid that I'm rather busy."

Kate hung up, and Magda shook her head, smiling. She was actually beginning to like that girl.

"And if it goes ahead, we'll be on television?" Betty asked.

Kate nodded. She'd gone down to the hospice as soon as she'd hung up the phone with Magda to make sure everyone was comfortable with the idea and to start putting together her proposal. She'd been planning to come down again before she started contacting production companies, but it wasn't until she chucked that book away—that stupid, hopeless book for hopeless cases—that she'd finally realized that sometimes you had to take the bull by the horns.

"But only if," she warned. "It might not come off. Television people can be very . . ." She searched for the right word. "Flaky," she said eventually.

She looked around the dark dayroom. Paint was peeling, and miscellaneous pipes crawled up the walls, disappearing into the ceiling, with no indication as to what they were for or where they led. The radiators on each side of the room clanked ominously, and she could smell dry rot. Television people might be flaky, but they were also the best hope the residents had for transforming this place. It might also be the best hope Kate had for staying sane. By hook or by crook, she was going to see this hospice transformed into the home-from-home that the residents deserved. And in doing it, she wasn't going to take any prisoners. No one was ever going to take her for a fool again.

Betty nodded. "But there'll be cameras here? We'll be asked to answer questions?"

Kate nodded again. "Which is why you've got to be completely okay with it. It's a big commitment, and the cameras can be quite intrusive. . . ."

"Like *Big Brother*," Margaret said knowledgeably.

"Will they have cameras behind the mirrors? Even when we're in the bathroom?" Betty asked, worried.

Kate grinned. "No, Betty. Just the ones you can see. And they'll only be here sometimes."

Carole smiled. "So what do you say? Are we in favor?"

Betty nodded vigorously. "Of course we're in favor," she said. "So long as I don't have to go on television without my makeup. And I don't want that Trinny and Susannah manhandling me, either."

Kate kept a straight face. "Okay, I'll make sure they're barred. In fact, none of the crew from 'What Not to Wear' will be allowed anywhere near us. Anything else?"

Edward, a middle-aged gentleman who spent most of his time playing chess against a machine, put his hand up.

"Yes, Ed?" Carole asked.

"When will it be on television?" he asked, his voice wheezy.

Carole looked at Kate, who frowned in thought. "It's hard to say," she said. "Probably three to four months after filming is finished. So if we started next month and the whole thing took four months, then we'd be looking at maybe December, or early next year."

Ed nodded seriously. "Have to make sure I'm still around then," he said, returning to his chess.

Carole grimaced. "Of course you'll be here, Ed. Don't be silly. Now, does anyone else have any questions? Any concerns they'd like to raise?"

The residents of St. Mary's Hospice looked at one another and shook their heads.

"Then I'd like to thank Kate for taking the time to come down here again," Carole said with a smile. "And to wish her luck in her negotiations with those flaky television people."

Magda called first thing the next morning.

"Hello?"

"Kate, it's me, Magda."

"Magda!" Kate did her best to sound surprised and casual. "How are things?"

"Things?" Magda asked. "Screw things. I had my meeting with the Channel Three executives, and they're interested."

Kate said nothing.

"I said, they're interested. They think it's got legs."

"Right," Kate said, playing it cool. "Well, I suppose you'll want to know my conditions?"

"Your conditions?"

"Absolutely," Kate said. "Do you have a pen and paper handy?"

"Of course," Magda said tightly.

"Okay, then. First, this is not a weeklong shoot. We're talking several weeks minimum, probably three months. We can't cut corners and I want staple guns to be banned. Second, no one is to refer to any of the residents as a victim. Cameras must not be intrusive, and I don't want anyone trying to make the residents cry at any point. Third, the residents will need separate accommodation whilst the electrical and piping work is done. And fourth, I want commitment in writing to stumping up the cash for the work. We're talking about a renovations budget alone of two hundred thousand pounds."

She waited for Magda to tell her where to go, or to shout at her for being so demanding. But to her surprise, she did neither. "Labor or supplies?" Magda asked instead.

"Sorry?" Kate said blankly.

"The two hundred k. Is it for labor or supplies?"

"Um, about half and half."

"Supplies we'll get through sponsorship. Labor we can probably get for nothing, too, if we credit the builders."

"You won't get Phil for free. And he's going to manage it."

"Fine, so we'll pay Phil." Magda reviewed the notes she'd just taken. "So that's it?" she said dubiously after a pause. "We'll treat the residents with respect. And we'll use discreet cameras. We can be nice. Do we have a deal?"

Kate hesitated but pressed on. "Not yet. I want no Penny. I don't want her anywhere near the program. I won't let her exploit these people for publicity. She can't even do a voice-over once it's finished."

"Fine," Magda said. "Now, here are *my* conditions. You get me a proposal in twenty-four hours with background on the hospice, outline of the major players and their televisual appeal, timelines, budgets—just give me your time and Phil's time, I can do the rest—and a couple of paragraphs selling the concept. I will talk to people here and get the wheels in motion. Deal?"

"Deal," Kate said, slightly taken aback.

"And you finish the Joneses' and the Kitchins' houses. After that it's anyone's guess whether we'll stay on the air, but all I know is that I've got fifty meters of pink velvet and much as I'd love to stick them up Penny's arse, she's nowhere to be found so you're going to have to do something with them instead. Okay?"

"Okay."

"Good. Then I'll see you tomorrow."

Kate put the phone down numbly and dialed Phil's number.

"Magda's okayed the hospice idea," she said. "With a budget of two hundred thousand. And Channel Three wants it."

"Channel Three," Phil said, as if it was the most normal thing in the world. "So, quite a few people watching, then."

"She wants us to finish the Kitchins' house," Kate continued. "And the Joneses'."

"Well, should be alright," Phil said lightly. "I've finished at my sister-in-law's anyway. The woman could give Penny Pennington a run for her money on the annoying stakes 'n' all."

"Channel Three!" Kate whispered.

"Two hundred k," Phil said, and whistled. "So that's quite good news, then."

"Quite good," Kate agreed. "So I'll see you tomorrow?"

Tom took a detour into work. A detour that took him past Kate's flat. Just to check that she was okay. He wasn't going to go in or anything.

He walked up to her door and stood against it for a few seconds. Kate's flat. Kate's flat where he'd been a thousand times, more even, talking until the early hours, passing out on her sofa, eating home-made casseroles whilst the rain beat down outside. It was like his home away from home, a place of sanctuary.

At least it had been.

Now it was a place of danger. A place where he'd been unable to control himself, unable to keep his rigid armor on. Jesus, he'd nearly told her how he felt about her, nearly prostrated himself before her and embarrassed her beyond belief with his protestations of love.

She might not think so, but in the circumstances, failing to call her back a couple of times was letting her off easy. Right now, she was pissed off, but she'd thank him later. At least she would if she ever discovered why he did it, which she wouldn't because he would never tell her. She'd meet some other big-jawed superstar and be married with children in a jiffy. And he'd be able to put this excruciating memory behind him and pretend to live a perfectly normal life again. He was pretty good at it, really. Been doing it long enough.

The trick was never to let on. And that didn't just apply to the big stuff; it applied to the small stuff, too. Tom knew that if you made an emotional connection with someone, however small, you were done for. They'd chip, chip, chip away at you until you were a defenseless, needy wreck. And then they'd leave you. Leave you to cope, alone, with no one to confide in anymore and no understanding of how to deal with the big bad world.

On which note, Tom thought, it was time to get back to the hospital.

He paused for a moment, then frowned as his eyes caught sight of something in Kate's bin. *Hopeless Romantic* something.

He reached over and dug it out of the trash, then gulped. *The Hopeless Romantic's Handbook*. The book that Kate was talking about. The one that had promised her love. Guaranteed it, even.

And now she'd chucked it in the bin.

Tom's heart started to race in his chest as he fought the temptation to push the door down, put the book back on her shelf, track Kate down, and tell her that he loved her, hopelessly, madly, completely, even if she was a hopeless romantic.

But that would be stupid. It would go wrong. Tom had had his heart broken once and he wouldn't risk it happening again.

He looked at the book again and felt his heart thud painfully. It was okay for him to avoid emotional entanglements, to maintain a dispassionate approach to relationships and life. But not for Kate. Had he done this to her? Had she chucked it out because of him?

Uncomfortably, Tom dusted the book down and put it in his pocket. Hopeless romantics like Kate were dangerous creatures, irresponsible and naïve and stupidly optimistic. But without them, he feared that the world would only ever be the depressing gray battleground that he saw every single day.

27

Everyday Romance

For many, romance is a very specific thing, concerned with love between a man and a woman, the giving of flowers and the excitement of a dinner engagement.

But romance need not be so limited. Romance might be the call of a morning bird or a jaunt down the river with friends. Romance might be the smile of a loved one or a shared experience.

To bring true romance into our lives, we must do our best to experience romance every day. Once we are used to romance being all around us, we will be more open and prepared for more serious romantic entanglements.

And so, Reader, do something romantic today! Call in on a friend, grant a request you might usually turn down. Remind your parents of your deep affection for them. Put on a bright scarf. Cheer up a glum companion with funny tales. Fill your home with colorful flowers. And buy yourself some rose-tinted spectacles, for when we see the world in a pinky hue, it is always so much more pleasing. . . .

Tom raised his eyebrows and wondered if this book was for real or some kind of piss-take. Was this seriously the reading matter that Kate chose?

Make the world pink or pale blue. Brilliant. This woman had more insight than Einstein.

He shook his head and smiled ruefully. No wonder Kate was such a hopeless case. Sweet, silly Kate. Maybe he'd take the book into the hospital. Try telling his patients that all they needed to do was to choose to see the world in a pinky hue and everything would be alright again.

People could be so foolish. So . . . emotional. Rose Sandler, for instance. She'd left a couple of hours ago to go to her son's concert, all made-up and dressed as if she was going to the opera. Her husband had brought in several outfits for her to try on; Tom had been forced to turn a blind eye to the fact that Lucy had spent over an hour doing her makeup, and all to sit in a hall and listen to her son play the violin. He probably wouldn't even notice she was there.

The fact of the matter was that the world was an arbitrary place. An unfair place. Catch cancer early and you could rip it out, kill the bastard with chemo. And when people got the all-clear, it was like the ending of a million great books tied up together—tears, joy, relief, wonderment, and a sudden feeling that it was all worth it. That good could conquer evil, that happiness was more than an advertising slogan. Seeing people hold each other, the look in their eyes as they realized that they weren't going to lose their husband/wife/child/parent after all, was . . . well, it felt good. But it never lasted. Because five minutes later there was some less lucky bastard to give bad news to. Some other husband/wife/child/parent to destroy with the news that it was too late, that the surgery hadn't worked, that the hospital had done all it could, but . . .

He hated that word. *But.* You could be saying the nicest things and as soon as you uttered the word *but*, everyone knew it was game over. "I love you, but . . ." "The surgery was successful, but . . ." "I don't want to leave you, but . . ."

But rendered everything else a lie. Why not just say "I don't love you"? "The surgery was a hopeless cause because whilst we removed the tumor, the cancer is now out of control." "I want to leave you because someone else is offering me a better life and I'm not sure I ever wanted you anyway, and please don't bother trying to get in touch because I'm going to have better children with my new husband. . . ."

Tom's beeper went and he dug it out. Mrs. Sandler, he read, curiosity piqued. Maybe she was back and regretting her excursion. Well, it would serve her right, and he'd tell her so very sternly.

Putting his beeper back in his pocket, Tom closed *The Hopeless Romantic's Handbook* and left his office.

Lucy was waiting for him in the ward when he got there.

"Tom . . . Doctor. She's . . ." She bit her lip and put her hand on his arm. "She said she wanted to see you and I thought you'd probably . . . well . . ."

Tom looked at her. "What?"

"Tom . . ." Wide-eyed, Lucy returned his gaze. ". . . she had a seizure."

Tom shook her off. "A seizure? Where is she?" He raced to her bedside. "Rose, what happened?"

Rose smiled weakly. "It was beautiful," she whispered. "I was in the front row, you know, and he played so well. And . . ." She took a breath, with difficulty.

"He knows that I love him," she said, a few moments later. "Thank you, Doctor. I really can't thank you enough."

"You shouldn't have gone," Tom said. "Look at you. It was too much stress. I shouldn't have allowed it. . . ."

Rose shook her head very gently, wincing at the pain. "I needed to go," she said quietly. "I needed to have a moment, a memory for Liam that didn't involve a hospital bed."

Tom stared at her, furious. "Stop talking about memories, Rose. You are getting better. You will *be* better. As soon as you're strong enough I'll operate, and we'll get the rest of the tumor. . . ."

Lucy appeared at his side and squeezed his hand, and Tom silently studied the machines around Rose, willing their readings to be different, begging them to tell a different story. "You just need to eat," he whispered hoarsely. "Need to get your energy up."

Lucy pressed his arm, and ushered him a few feet away. "Tom, the doctors found out this afternoon that she's got a liver infection. On top of the tumor."

"And you still let her leave the hospital?"

He walked back over to Rose and took her hand. "I'm so sorry," he said. He could feel tears appearing at the corners of his eyes, tears that hadn't been allowed to fall for more than twenty years.

"Don't be sorry," Rose said, smiling serenely. "I saw today how my boys—Liam and Pat, I mean—how they've got so close. Him and his father never used to have much to say to each other, but now . . . well, they're wonderful together. The thing is, Doctor, I know they're going to be alright now. I'm not worried anymore."

"But what about you?" Tom said tightly. "You can't just . . ."

Rose put a finger to her lips. "They'll be here soon. Liam and Pat. I'm going to have my boys next to me. You can't ask for more than that, can you, to die surrounded with the people you love. Who love you."

Tom swallowed, doing his best to ignore the large lump in his throat.

"And I wanted to thank you," Rose continued. "You're a good man, Doctor. A very good man."

Tom shook his head as Rose's husband and son appeared at the door of the ward, their faces worried and pale.

Rose saw them and smiled. "Good-bye, Doctor," she said. "You take care of yourself, now."

"Good-bye, Rose," Tom managed. He held her eyes briefly, then turned and walked out of the ward, nodding a greeting to Mr. Sandler as they passed each other, but failing to look him in the eye. He didn't dare to.

28

Kate decided to walk home from the hospice. For the past few days, she'd been there constantly, and when she wasn't there, she was on the phone, dealing with suppliers, organizing timetables, and making demands. Everything felt surreal, as if she'd got in a lift to go up a floor and instead it had taken off like the Great Glass Elevator, and now she was in a place that seemed vaguely familiar but that differed from her own world in very significant ways. Channel 3 had jumped on the commission. Magda was treating her like someone important. Suppliers were bending over backward to give her everything she needed for free. She had a team of researchers working just for her. She was thrilled and excited about her work for the first time in absolutely ages. And each day that went by made the pain of Tom not calling lessen just a little bit, made the world a little bit more bearable.

As she walked, she found herself outside Charing Cross Hospital, and she glanced up at the large gray building, wondering if Tom was inside. He was probably studying someone's charts, she thought. Or maybe he was talking to a patient. Doing some paperwork.

Not knowing quite why, she found herself walking through the doors and into the reception area. She hadn't been here for years—Tom had studied to be a doctor here, and she remembered coming here with Sal for a party at the end of Tom's first year. There had been a disco, and at some point in the evening they'd played lots of fifties tunes and Tom had flung her around the dance floor until she'd been sure she was going to be sick. And then the three of them had played lift-jumping with the lifts-with-no-doors-that-keep-moving-constantly-that-probably-had-a-very-important-medical-use but which they had huge amounts of fun with, leaping in and out with gay abandon until an angry woman told them to leave. That had been a different time. A time when all that mattered was the here and now, and how much fun could be had.

But in recent years there had never really been a reason to come to the hospital. It was strange that this place, such a huge part of Tom's life, should be so unfamiliar to her.

A bit like Tom himself.

She stared at the hospital map and idly wondered where Tom would be. The cancer unit was on the fourth floor. Would Tom be there? Or did he have an office somewhere? She frowned—on television, doctors were always racing down corridors holding calibrators in their hands. Or was that just *ER*?

Not that it mattered.

She turned to leave.

"Can I help you?" A woman in blue was smiling at her expectantly.

Kate smiled brightly. "Um, no, thank you." Then she frowned. She did need help. She had a television show to organize; in the beginning she had assumed she'd just talk to Tom about getting permission to film, but that seemed less and less likely.

"Actually, I'm doing a television show, with Channel Three," she said. "Renovating a hospice around the corner for cancer patients who've had surgery here. I was just having a look around. Do you know who I'd need to talk to about getting permission to film here?"

"You'll need to talk to the press office," the woman said. "Have you made an appointment?"

Kate shook her head.

"Maybe you'd like to call them and arrange one," the woman suggested.

Kate nodded quickly. "Yes, of course."

She headed out of the hospital. It had been a mistake coming in. She was still hoping that somehow things with Tom would work out. That he'd realize he was in love with her. And it wasn't going to happen.

As she reached the doors, her phone buzzed furiously, and she dug it out.

"Hello?"

"Hi, Kate! Heather from *Hot Gossip* here. Listen, I was just wondering if you felt you wanted to talk yet. I mean, you know, if there's anything you'd like to say. . . ."

Kate sighed. "No, Heather," she said firmly. "I have nothing to say to the readers of *Hot Gossip* magazine. Nothing at all."

Then an idea hit her.

"Wait," she said. "I might. Would you be interested in a project I've got on the go? Renovating a hospice for cancer patients?"

"Charity?" Heather said cautiously. "Possibly, I mean . . ."

"Television," Kate said. "It's going to be a television show."

"And you'll give us your side of the Penny and Joe story?"

Kate sighed. "There's nothing really to tell. . . ." she began.

"Only, I'm not sure some charity thing is going to be enough," Heather said.

"Fine," Kate said reluctantly. After all, she told herself, two could play at the publicity game. If Penny and Joe were going to use her to get themselves in the papers, then she was going to use them right back to promote the hospice. "You'll get my side of the story."

"Fabulous!" Heather said. "I mean, that's great. Shall we arrange a time and place now?"

"Sure," Kate said, "why not."

Ed seemed worried when he came in that evening, the result, Sal recognized, of her phone call that afternoon insisting that he be home by seven and telling him that she urgently needed to talk to him. She was sitting, waiting for him, at the breakfast bar in the kitchen, her hands on top of her knees where she could regularly wipe the sweat off them.

He looked at her curiously, then poured himself a glass of wine. He offered one to Sal, who declined.

"So," he said with a sigh. "What's this emergency summit all about, then?"

Sal looked down at the ground, then back up at Ed. "Do you know where your golf clubs are?" she asked.

Ed frowned. "My golf clubs? You get me home early to talk about my golf clubs?"

"Answer the question, Ed," Sal said levelly.

"In my car," Ed said. "Next question?"

"In your car," Sal said. "Well, that would make sense, since you took your car to golf last weekend. And the weekend before that."

"Is there a point to this?" Ed asked, tensing.

Sal stared at him. "I was just curious, you see," she said, her voice quiet. "Because I thought they were in your car, too. And then I got my car cleaned. And I found them in my boot. Where we put them at Christmas."

The color drained from Ed's face.

"And I just wondered how you'd been managing to play golf without them," Sal continued, looking Ed right in the eye.

"I . . . I borrowed clubs," he said weakly. "I need some new ones anyway, so I was trying out some different . . ." He trailed off, and closed his eyes briefly. "Fuck, Sal," he said with a sigh. "I'm sorry. I'm really sorry. . . ."

"Who is she?" Sal spat. "Who is the woman that you've been leaving me for every weekend? Who knackers you out so you barely have the energy to touch me anymore. Or is that just lack of desire? Do I not do it for you anymore?"

Ed's face crumpled. "You think I'm having an affair?"

"What am I meant to think?" Sal cried. "You tell me, Ed. What am I meant to make of our marriage? I never see you, and when I do you snap at me. You say you're playing golf, but you leave your clubs behind. . . ."

She shook her head. "I'll leave, Ed. I will. And you're not the only one with opportunities to play around. But unlike you, I know the meaning of restraint. Unlike you, I value our marriage. I was kissed, Ed. Kissed. And it ate me up so that I couldn't bear to even look at myself in the mirror anymore. But now, now I wonder what I was so worried about."

As she spoke, she found tears forming at her eyes and she blinked them back furiously.

Ed looked stricken. "You . . . you kissed someone?"

Sal shrugged, tears now falling freely. "He kissed me. I didn't kiss him back. And now I'm going to be a single mother and I don't know what to do, Ed. I don't know what to do."

"A mother? What?" Ed asked.

"I'm pregnant, Ed."

"You're pregnant? You kissed this guy and now you're pregnant?"

Sal gave him a withering look through bleary, tear-filled eyes. "I think the actual order of events was that you and I actually found the time to have sex about seven or eight weeks ago and now I'm pregnant. I'm not sure the kiss really featured, actually."

"You're having a baby? We're having a baby?" Ed looked dumbstruck.

"Yes, you idiot. And you don't have to be involved if you don't want to. I mean, I'll need some money, but I don't want you staying with me just because I'm pregnant. I've got my pride, you know. . . ."

"Oh my God." Ed stood up. "Oh my good God." He wrapped his arms tightly around Sal. "My darling girl. We're having a baby. We're having a frigging baby. God, I can't believe it. That's the most wonderful thing I think I've ever heard."

"But . . ." Sal said in confusion. "What about the affair? What about the state of our marriage?"

Ed swung her stool round and stared at her. Then he sighed. "Sal, you have to believe me when I tell you that since I met you, I have not looked at another woman. Apart from Helena Christensen, but that was in a magazine, which doesn't count."

Sal looked at him indignantly. "The golf clubs, Ed. What exactly have you been doing every weekend for the past four months?"

Ed sat down and took her hands in his. Then he looked down at the floor.

"What, Ed?" Sal whispered. "What is it?"

He swallowed with difficulty and took a slug of wine. Then he looked Sal right in the eye. "Sal, I'm being investigated. By the Financial Services Authority."

"What? What do you mean?"

Ed sighed. "I mean that for the past five months, the FSA has been listening to every single phone call I've made, going through every e-mail I've sent, and talking to every single one of my investment clients. They think I was involved in some inside dealing."

"And were you?" Sal asked, shocked.

"Of course not," Ed said wearily. "But if they think I was, I lose my license. I'll never work in the City again. We'll lose the house. We'll lose everything."

"And why do they suspect you?"

Ed shook his head. "It doesn't matter."

Sal frowned. "Of course it does. Tell me."

Ed blinked. "Several of my clients bought shares in your company, a day before it announced that the trial for the new nicotine patches had been a success. They put two and two together and . . ."

"They think I passed you confidential information?" Sal gasped.

"They think you may have inadvertently told me. That's not the crime. The crime is acting on it."

"But I wasn't even involved in that trial. I had no idea. . . ."

Ed shrugged. "They don't know that."

"So I'll tell them. Ed, I couldn't have known anything about that trial. I don't get passed records until the product packaging is being developed. Why didn't you get them to talk to me?"

Ed couldn't meet her eyes. "I didn't want you to be involved. I wanted to protect you. That's why they're going through all my records."

Sal took a deep breath. "Why didn't you tell me?" she asked in a small voice. "Why didn't you tell me this at the beginning?"

Ed bit his lip. "I was afraid you might lose your job, too. Afraid you might be angry. And then, when they didn't clear me right off, I couldn't tell you. I . . . I was afraid of losing you, Sal, and I thought that if I could just deal with it, it would go away."

"Losing me?" Sal asked incredulously. "But I love you."

"You love me because of who I am, Sal," Ed said with a sigh. "I'm successful, I got you the house you always wanted, the stability. I've only ever wanted to give you what you wanted. And I thought if things went wrong, that we . . . that you . . ."

"That I'd leave you?" Sal asked, her hackles rising. "Because you lost your job? How dare you, Ed. How dare you think that of me!"

"You always said that it was on your 'to do' list. To marry a financier," Ed said in a strangled voice.

"I married the man I loved," Sal said, putting her arms around Ed's neck and burying her head in his shoulder, knowing that she was speaking the truth, that she loved Ed more deeply than she'd ever realized. "The man I adore. And the man I will continue to love whatever happens. Oh, God, Ed, I wish you'd told me. You don't know what I've been going through. I thought you'd fallen in love with someone else. I thought . . ."

"Never," Ed said, clutching Sal to him. "God, Sal, it's only ever been you. You're my everything. If it wasn't for you, I don't know how I'd have got through this."

"Then trust me, Ed," Sal said, clutching him back. "We're meant to be a team, me and you. We're going to be parents, for God's sake. You have to involve me in things. And I want you to put those investigators in touch with me. I'll prove you didn't know anything. I promise."

Ed nodded, then he pulled away a little and looked at Sal archly.

"Okay," he said, "so if I'm meant to trust you, what's all this about kissing some bloke?"

Sal bit her lip. "He kissed *me*," she said weakly. "For a second . . ."

"I'll have him," Ed said. "Tell me who he is and I'll punch him."

Sal looked at him, worried, but his eyes were twinkling. "No, Ed, this is serious," she said crossly. "I kissed another man and it was wrong. Really wrong."

"And it doesn't matter," Ed said, smoothing her hair.

"It doesn't? But . . . you should hate me."

Ed grinned. "I could never hate you, Sal. I love you more than life itself."

Sal grabbed hold of Ed and buried her head in his neck. "I love you so much, too," she whispered, passionately, clinging to him as if for dear life. "And I've missed you. I've missed *us*. . . . I started to think that our marriage was unromantic and practical and meaning-less. . . ."

"Then the kiss was my fault," Ed said. "And I'm sorry. I'm going to take you out and spoil you and listen to you—whatever you want. Fuck me, Sal, I'm going to be a dad."

Sal raised her eyebrow. "Not in front of Junior," she said sternly, then looked at him closely, a little smile playing across her lips. "Ac-tually, you could, if you wanted," she said, her eyes glinting mischie-vously.

"Could what?" Ed asked, frowning. She leered at him, and slowly a glimmer of recognition appeared on his face. "Are you serious? We can do that? With the . . . with Junior inside you?"

Sal nodded and wrapped her legs around him. "You betcha," she said, grinning. "Apparently pregnant women get very horny. So you need to get in training."

"So you've gone off the idea of being a single mother, I take it?" Ed asked, a playful grin on his face.

"For the time being," Sal said, "but don't think you can rest on your laurels."

"I wouldn't dream of it," Ed said, picking her up and carrying her upstairs.

Lucy stood in the doorway, looking at Tom awkwardly.

"What?" he asked with a sigh. "What's happened?"

Lucy slowly came in.

"She's . . . Well, Mrs. Sandler's just passed away, that's all. I . . . I thought you'd want to know."

Tom looked at her, his eyes searching hers for something that she couldn't give him, and then he nodded curtly.

"Thanks," he said.

"That's it?" Lucy asked.

Tom raised his eyebrows. "Is there more?"

Lucy shook her head and started to walk away. Then she came back, and walked right up to Tom's desk. She put her hand on his shoulder and frowned. "It's alright to be upset, you know. No one will think any less of you."

Tom stared down at his desk. "I'm a doctor. If I got upset about every patient who died I wouldn't be able to do my job properly."

"You liked her, didn't you?"

"She was my patient," Tom said. "And I let her down. That's all."

Lucy nodded. "The thing is, Tom," she said quietly, "people die. That's just what happens here. But she died comfortably, with her family. And all she kept going on about was how wonderful you were, how you'd made her feel like a person, not a patient. How you'd brought her hope. So, you see, you didn't let anyone down."

"I let myself think of her as a person," Tom said. "I let my guard down and put her ahead of my clinical advice. . . ."

Lucy frowned. "She is a person. Was a person, I mean."

Tom looked up at the ceiling and breathed deeply. "It doesn't matter," he said. "Everyone leaves eventually, anyway."

Lucy gave him a questioning look. "What do you mean?"

Tom sighed. "I mean that people form attachments to other people and always end up disappointed when the other leaves, or dies, or falls in love with someone else, but that's just life, isn't it?"

Lucy frowned. "You think life is just full of disappointments? Well, you're wrong."

Tom shook his head. "Lucy, for the past few nights you've been staying at mine to try and make your boyfriend jealous so he'll finally ask you to marry him. If you don't think that you're setting yourself up for disappointment, then you're more stupid than you look."

Lucy stared at him. "Oh, am I?" she said huffily. "Well then, you might be surprised to learn that I don't have a boyfriend anymore."

Tom grimaced. "Sorry. I didn't realize. But you see? I'm right."

"I've got a fiancé," Lucy continued. "Who, incidentally, doesn't know that I was sleeping in the spare room. So don't tell him. You know, if you ever meet him."

"He thinks . . . ?"

"That we had sex? Yes, he does. I told him you were rubbish," Lucy said matter-of-factly.

Tom stared, slightly bemused. Then he broke out in a grin. "Right. Good. Fair judgment, I would say. So, we didn't? Ever, I mean? It's just that when I woke up and you were there in my bed, the night I called you . . ."

Lucy laughed. "In your state? Please. It was all I could do to get you into bed. Didn't dare leave you in case you stopped breathing or something."

Tom nodded. "Well, congratulations. And I hope you're right— about things working out, I mean."

"Of course they will. Connor just needed to realize how good we were together. Men usually don't know what they've got till it's gone," Lucy said. "It's a well-known fact. Now he's got me back, he won't be leaving again. He knows what he wants now."

"I see," Tom said thoughtfully. "And you're not worried what might happen in the future? Several years from now?"

Lucy rolled her eyes. "Yeah, I'm really worried," she said sarcastically. "'Course I'm not. You can't be worried about stuff in the future, otherwise you'd never do anything, would you? You'd just sit around not wanting to go out in case a car knocked you down or something. We love each other now, and that's enough for me."

"What if he stopped loving you, though?" Tom persisted. "What would you do?"

Lucy looked at him incredulously. "I'd punch his lights out," she said. "I'd burn all his clothes, scratch his car, and make him pay."

Tom drummed his fingers on his desk. "Maybe you're right."

"About me and Connor?" Lucy asked. "Of course I am. We're made for each other, we are."

"No," Tom said. "About punching his lights out." He stood up and looked at his watch. "Listen," he said distractedly, "I might need to go somewhere. Can you . . . can you let people know I might be gone for a few hours?"

Lucy shook her head uncertainly. "Whatever," she said. "If I were you, I'd take longer. I think you need a holiday. You're falling apart, you know."

Tom smiled. "Not falling apart, Lucy. For the first time in a very long time I think that maybe I might be able to pull myself together."

Then he picked up his phone and dialed a number.

"Dad?" he said. "Listen, I need you to give me an address."

29

Fight or Flight

There comes a time in almost every person's life when they are faced with the choice of fight or flight. It could be that a love rival is threatening them; it could be parental disapproval of a potential marriage or other important decision; or it could be that something else they have their heart set on is eluding them.

Hopeless romantics, though, know no such choice. For whilst they understand difficulty and are no strangers to potential loss, they also do not give up. Hopeless romantics understand that giving up something that they believe in, means giving away a small part of their soul. Giving up on their desires makes them weak. Once we have given up one thing, it is so easy to give up more, until we have nothing left at all but memories of dreams and ambitions, all of them unfulfilled.

The suffragettes were true hopeless romantics, chaining themselves to railings rather than walk away quietly. All great heroines have also been hopeless romantics—whether they refused to give up on their husbands' ability to change for the better, or refused to lose their men to a rival, pitting themselves against the interloper and not ceasing until the battle was won.

Whatever the battle, consider your strategy carefully. Grand gestures are generally best left to gentlemen, who have the stamina for more physi-

cal demonstration. But that does not mean that a lady cannot make her feelings known. Battles need not be won on the battlefield, or with guns and bombs. Battles can be won at cocktail parties, with a well-considered comment or a twinkling of the eye.

The hopeless romantic who suspects another woman of having eyes for her beau must find a way of showing her up that is generous of spirit and makes her rival look foolish without ever letting anyone guess that this was her aim (see below for some tips, gleaned from fellow hopeless romantics). The hopeless romantic also needs to understand well the art of persuasion, and if her beau, or parents, or some other influential party is determined to prevent her from following a particular dream, she must quickly determine how to bring them round to her view: Perhaps she will prove to them the benefits of her scheme, or maybe she will draw a sober picture of the terrible consequences of saying no. Whichever tack she chooses, her aim must be that the disagreeing party will not only change their mind but will think that the hopeless romantic's scheme was their own idea in the first place.

Be brave, fellow romantics. Face your fear, and step into the breach. For if we care about something deeply and truly, we must not allow it to slip from our fingers without doing everything in our power to stop it.

Gabrielle Price opened the front door with a pout. Then she frowned. "Yes? Can I help you?"

Tom quickly shoved the book in his pocket. He wasn't sure why he'd brought it, except that it reminded him why he was here. And that made it less likely that he'd turn back. Even if it was an absolute crock of shit.

"I don't know," he said matter-of-factly. "But I thought it was worth a shot. I'm Tom, by the way. Your son. The one you left twenty years ago. How are you, incidentally? You're looking well. . . ."

Gabrielle stared. "Tom? Is that really you?"

Tom shrugged. "No, I'm an impostor," he said. "Of course it's me."

"Right," Gabrielle said, looking flustered. "Well, you'd better come in, then. You know, you could have called first. Turning up like this—well, it's quite a surprise."

"Like when you left," Tom said. "That was quite a surprise, too."

"I'll . . . I'll make some tea," Gabrielle said. "Why don't you sit down in the lounge, eh?"

Tom wandered into the sitting room, which was large and cluttered, full of evidence of family life—a large television, squishy sofas with mismatched cushions, DVDs all over the floor. It made him uncomfortable. This was another family's room. Nothing to do with him.

He'd always thought of his mother as living in a pristine house, one where nothing was ever out of place. He'd convinced himself that was one of the reasons she'd left—because he was too messy, because he always left his plate on the side instead of putting it in the sink, no matter how much she shouted at him.

But that wasn't why she left. Otherwise she wouldn't be living here.

"Here you are," Gabrielle said, bustling back in and handing Tom a cup of tea. "I . . . didn't know if you took sugar or not."

"It's fine," Tom said levelly, taking the mug from her—bone china, he noticed. "It doesn't matter." He took a sip of tea, then put it down. "You look different," he said. "Blonder."

Gabrielle shrugged. "Covers the gray better."

Tom nodded. Then he sat back. "I just need to know why," he said, forcing himself to look at her. "I need to know why you went. Why you never even said good-bye. Why there was no warning, no arguments, nothing . . .." He took a deep breath. "You see, I'm having a few problems of my own now. Finding it hard to believe that if I love someone, if I admit even to myself that I might love them, that they won't leave me. It makes no sense, I know. I can see that. But you going didn't make any sense either, and you did. . . ."

Gabrielle nodded. Then she stood up. "Mind if I smoke?" she asked, reaching for her cigarettes.

"Actually, yes," Tom said. "You know they give you cancer?"

Gabrielle raised one eyebrow, and lit a cigarette anyway. She inhaled deeply; then she turned to look at Tom.

"The thing is," she said thoughtfully, "that I just woke up one day and thought, this isn't me. I mean, all of it—your father, you, that little terraced house. I thought he was different when I met him. He had money, took me to smart restaurants. But once we were married, all he wanted to talk about was school fees and savings. You were all he cared about, you and 'the family'—not me, not holidays, or, you know . . . It wasn't me, Tom. I wasn't ready for it. And I just wanted to get out."

"You just wanted to get out?" Tom asked.

Gabrielle nodded. "It wasn't *you*," she said reassuringly. "I mean, not you personally. It was just the package. Being Mrs. Whitson. I realized it wasn't what I wanted."

"And that's it?" Tom asked. "You just went because we weren't what you wanted?"

Gabrielle frowned. "It wasn't easy, you know. Didn't know what I was going to do. But then I met Al at work, and suddenly I realized there was a way out."

"Leaving your son and husband behind?"

"I said it wasn't easy, didn't I?" Gabrielle said. "Al thought a clean break was best. And you were better off with your dad. We both knew that."

Tom stared at her. "You live with Al now?" he asked. "I mean, this house, the children—they're his?"

Gabrielle nodded. "I'm Mrs. Price. And I quite like it now—you know, kids and everything. I just . . . well, I'm older, aren't I? Eldest one's going to be eighteen soon. Funny how quickly time passes, isn't it?"

"Funny," Tom agreed.

"You understand, don't you?" Gabrielle said, stubbing out her cigarette. "I mean, you can see it from my point of view, can't you?"

Tom smiled. "You know, actually I can," he said, standing up.

"And I want to thank you for being so honest. And now I think I'll go, if that's alright."

Gabrielle looked at him, worried. "Already?" She sighed. "Maybe you're right," she said. "But there's no need to thank me. It's nice to see you. You're a good-looking chap, you know. Your father did well with you."

Tom nodded. "He did do well," he said, walking toward the door. Then he stopped.

"You know," he said, "Dad always said that we were better off without you, that you were too tied up with yourself. And I never believed him. I was sure that your leaving was my fault in some way. That I'd ruined his marriage, our family. And I became absolutely convinced that love didn't exist—or, if it did, it could disappear overnight . . ."

He paused, and took a deep breath.

". . . but now—now I know that he was right. You were just selfish. Nothing more, nothing less. You still have no interest in me. Haven't asked what I do, whether I've got any children. You don't care, do you?"

Gabrielle flinched, then looked at Tom curiously. He wore a broad grin. "Don't worry, I'm not going to berate you for it," he said. "I think it's wonderful. Because you never even loved him. Never loved me. I never actually lost you, do you see? Because you were never mine . . ."

Gabrielle looked at him sadly, then she lowered her eyes. "I thought I loved him," she said. "At first, I mean. But I didn't. And you were so like him. . . . I couldn't find myself in you at all. Not one little bit."

Tom nodded. "Thanks, Mum. You know, that's the best piece of news I've had all day."

And with that, he stepped out of his mother's house and walked purposefully toward his car.

◆ ◆ ◆

Sal read and reread the e-mail she'd just composed.

Hi Jim,
Thanks for your message. I'm going to say no, if that's okay. I'd love to have a
drink with you. I really would. But now isn't really a good time. I need to sort a
few things out with Ed. So I hope you'll understand?
Sal

Sighing, she highlighted it and pressed "delete." "I need to sort a few things out with Ed" sounded so trite, so depressing, like someone in a soap opera deciding to work at her marriage. She wanted to write, "I love my husband more than anything in the world and I can't believe I actually kissed you," but she couldn't do that either—Jim was so keen, he'd e-mailed her just a couple of days before to say that he couldn't stop thinking about her, and she was about to break his heart. Sal wasn't accustomed to breaking people's hearts, but she was fairly sure that there was a good and a bad way to do it.

No, if she was going to turn Jim down, she would do it face to face. She wouldn't hide behind platitudes and impenetrable messages. She was not a coward. If she was going to disappoint Jim, if he was going to feel dreadful and lonely because of her, then the least she could do was to tell him face-to-face.

She stood up and slowly made her way to Jim's desk. He was on his own in a bank of four desks—his colleagues in meetings or making coffee.

"Hi," she said awkwardly.

He grinned. "Hi!"

"It's about that drink," Sal began. "I don't think I can make it, I'm afraid."

Jim nodded solemnly. "Okay, not to worry."

Sal frowned. She had expected a bit more than that. "It's Ed," she said. "Our marriage, I mean. You know, I do love my husband, and . . ."

"Yeah, I got it. Husband. Working at it. It's cool."

Sal stared at him. "Actually, it isn't cool," she said hotly. "You kissed me. You turned me into someone who is unfaithful to her husband. And I wanted to say, categorically, that I'm not that kind of person."

"And that's fine. Look, to be honest, I kind of got that idea anyway. And I've sort of started dating Stacey in finance."

Sal boggled at him. "But we only went out a few weeks ago! I thought you said you couldn't stop thinking about me?"

Jim grinned. "I couldn't. But then I got to know Stacey a bit better, and . . ."

Sal shook her head in disbelief and walked back to her desk. She didn't know whether she was relieved or insulted. Probably both.

But mainly relieved. Because she knew *categorically* that no one could love her like Ed did. No one could make her smile, or ache, or laugh like he did, because no one else knew her like he did. And if Jim had helped to remind her of that, then she wished him and Stacey well.

Although she probably wouldn't tell Ed. He had this idea now that she was a femme fatale, and she didn't think it was her place to destroy that particular fantasy.

"Have you seen this? What am I saying, of course you have. But have you read it? Have you seen what a great plug they've given us?"

Magda, who never let her voice betray a hint of enthusiasm unless she absolutely had to, came running into the hospice, grinning ear to ear and clutching the latest issue of *Hot Gossip* magazine.

"Jilted television star Kate Hetherington saves hospice from destruction and says, 'I'm stronger now, and I wish Penny and Joe well,'" she read out. "They mentioned the hospice on the front cover! And that photograph!"

Kate cringed. She still couldn't quite believe that her little interview had been splashed across the front of the magazine like that, but even she had to admit that the photograph looked pretty good. And, far from the hatchet job that she'd fully expected Heather to do on her, she came across amazingly well. Perhaps a little bit more torn up about the whole Joe-Penny thing than was strictly the case, but she could live with that. All day people had been giving her thumbs-up signs in the street. A bus driver grinned at her and told her that she should find a nice British lad, like his son.

The truth was, she was happy. Really, truly happy, and she'd done it herself. No prince had kissed her and no white steed had whisked her away, and the strangest thing was that she wasn't looking for them anymore.

"I've just come off the phone from our editor at Channel Three," Magda continued. "And guess what?"

Kate raised an eyebrow in response.

"They want you to present!"

Kate shook her head. "No way."

"You have to! You're the face of the show now!"

Carole, who'd been watching the conversation with excitement, nodded in agreement. "Oh, you'd be wonderful! Oh, what a super idea!"

Kate shook her head again. "I'm *not* a presenter," she said. "And anyway, I'm too busy working out layouts and color schemes and agreeing fabrics and materials."

"That's the point," Magda said immediately. "You're a new breed of presenter. A presenter who knows what she's talking about and can do as well as tell."

Kate sighed. "I'm not doing it," she said in exasperation. "I don't even like appearing on television."

"That's a shame, because Channel Three says it's a deal breaker," Magda said, shaking her head. "And I'd hate to have to cancel this whole thing. Especially now that Furniture City has said it will provide new beds and sofas for every room."

"A deal breaker?" Kate narrowed her eyes. "Really?"

"And Carpets R Us is giving us carpets and laminate for the bathrooms. . . ."

"There must be someone else," Kate pleaded.

"Brand-new bathroom fittings from Bathrooms Your Way . . ."

Kate sighed. "Fine," she said, defeated. "I'll do it. But when you get letters of complaint, you'll have yourself to blame."

"I'll go and tell them the good news," Magda said happily. "They said they'd want you to appear on *Morning Chat*, too, which I said would be fine. Okay?"

"*Morning Chat?*"

"You'll be great!" Magda grinned, and Kate smiled weakly.

"Now, everything going alright here, is it?" Magda continued as she walked out of the room. "Still ready to start filming on Thursday?"

Kate nodded. Thursday would see them filming the hospice as it was, interviewing some of the residents, and filming Betty in hospital just before she went under the knife to have a lump removed from her breast. It was going to be a long day, but Kate was confident it would all come off okay. She'd been wary about letting the cameras film Betty, but Betty herself had thought it was a wonderful idea and had refused point-blank to even consider saying no.

The residents were very excited, too. Gareth was experimenting with hairpieces, head scarves, and hats, whilst Lysander was exploring fabrics that were soft on sensitive skin, easy to wash, and could adjust to fluctuating weight. Phil had a team of builders working for him, and the whole project was due to be completed in ten weeks. Kate had even ensured that during the major building works, residents would be put up at a local hotel for free, where they would be pampered with beauty treatments for the women and so-called grooming treatments for the men—exactly the same treatments but with a slightly more masculine ring.

"You should be very proud of yourself," Carole said with a little smile as she checked over the plans one final time. "You've done this all yourself, you know."

Kate looked at her and frowned. "Hardly," she said. "I barely did anything."

"Now, that's not true." Carole pursed her lips. "You've done nearly everything. And you've also given the residents hope. Something to get excited about. That's quite an achievement, you know."

Kate smiled and blushed. "It's nice of you to say so," she said. "But I think, actually, I'm the one this whole thing has given hope. I used to think I was just waiting for someone to save me, to make everything okay. But in the past couple of weeks, I've realized that I can do that myself, you know? Be my own hero."

"Of course you can," Carole said, then smiled, her eyes twinkling. "Plus, you're going to be a television star now. And there's no better revenge than success, is there, dear?"

Kate looked at her in amazement. "This isn't about revenge!" she cried, but then giggled conspiratorially. "You're right, though. Penny isn't going to be happy. She isn't going to be happy at all."

Magda saw Penny before Penny saw her. Magda had a sixth sense for that kind of thing; she always knew when there was going to be trouble. She knew when a show was about to fold, knew when the chief exec was about to call her up, and even knew when a check was going to be bad. People said she wasn't much good at trust, but Magda found that her sixth sense was a survival mechanism. At times like this it came in very handy.

Nipping along the hallway to the door of the hospice, she blocked Penny off before she could stride in and start trouble.

"Penny," she said, with the halfhearted enthusiasm she reserved for meetings like this. Like bumping into people at parties who had shafted her or whom she had shafted. They would both smile, share one or two meaningless comments about the wine or the hosts, then move on and bitch about the other for the rest of the evening. "How nice to see you. How have you been?"

Penny stared at her. "Sod how I've been. Just what the hell is this all about? There's no one in the office, and I found this on my desk."

She held up Magda's letter informing her that the current series of *Future: Perfect* had been terminated early owing to production issues and that the jury was still out regarding its medium-to-long-term future. In the meantime, Magda and the directors of Footprint Production thanked her for her contribution and wished her well in the future.

"And I had a bugger of a time finding out where you all were, too," she continued frostily. "If it wasn't for my driver and Kate's puke-inducing interview in *Hot Gossip* I'd probably never have found you."

"Ah, yes," Magda said. "You see, the thing is, with you gone for so long, the show was untenable, so we axed it."

"You axed a program, just like that? Don't be ridiculous. Anyway, you said Channel Three was interested. Interested in me, incidentally. I am the show, Magda, and you know it."

Magda smiled. "Actually, they said they wouldn't go near *Future: Perfect*. Said you didn't fit with their channel's family values. But they loved Kate's hospice idea. Commissioned it for a Saturday-night series."

She watched with some satisfaction as the blood drained from Penny's face, and smiled reassuringly at her. "Now, my boss was a bit upset about your absence and started talking about lawyers and things, but I explained that you had personal issues and that you needed some time off," she continued, "so you're okay on that front. Of course, *Future: Perfect*'s been terminated, but viewing numbers were already low, so we switched to reruns for the rest of the series. They're doing surprisingly well. Bit like Mozart, isn't it? Not famous till you're dead!"

Penny stared at her. "Mozart was very famous," she said haughtily.

"Must have been thinking of van Gogh, then," Magda said, undeterred.

"And this is Kate's little hospice program, is it?" Penny asked, her voice still bitter but without the fight that was there before.

"That's right," Magda said cheerfully.

"On Channel Three?"

"Great, isn't it?"

"And you don't need a presenter? A celebrity with real resonance with the viewing public?"

Magda smiled. "We do, as a matter of fact," she said cruelly, watching Penny's face light up. "And luckily, we've got one. Kate's a natural, you know. Everyone thinks so. And the great thing is that she really knows what she's talking about, too. Anyway, lovely to see you, Penny, but must get back. See you around, eh?" She stood, looking at Penny and making it very clear that her only direction of travel was back the way she'd come.

"We'll see about that," Penny said, her eyes flashing. "Yes, we'll just see."

As soon as she'd gone, Magda dug out her mobile and called the office. "Louis, cancel Penny's driver will you? No, right away. Cheers."

30

Joe was staring at the television when Penny got back to her flat. There, right in front of him on some morning talk show, was Kate, talking about her new show as if she'd been doing it all her life. The diminutive Kate was on a talk show—a talk show that had singularly failed to invite him and Penny on, even though her publicity guy had called them like a million times. And he was sitting on Penny's sofa watching Kate. The world had turned upside down.

He'd thought it was a one-off when he saw her on the front cover of a magazine. He assumed that she'd decided to have her five minutes of glory and had just been relieved that she hadn't made up any horrible stories about him or made out that he was challenged in the bedroom department. That's what girls usually did when they kissed and told.

Penny had had a bit of a fit about it, calling up the magazine and demanding to know why Kate made the front cover while they were relegated to page forty-five, but he figured she'd get over it.

But the galling thing was that in the last week he and Penny had less and less publicity, while Kate seemed to be everywhere. And she didn't even have to pretend to be going out with some straw-haired witch to get attention; she just had to talk about some hospice and cancer patients. Man, why hadn't he thought of that?

For that matter, why the hell had he run off with Penny when

Kate, who he had, after all, actually liked, was slowly but surely eclipsing them both?

"The bastards have terminated my contract," Penny said angrily, before she'd even walked through the door. "Even my driver's gone. I had to take the sodding tube home, can you believe? Bloody Kate stole my Channel Three contract. She screwed me over."

Joe rolled his eyes at her and then ignored her. It had become his default reaction to Penny's outbursts. If he ignored her for long enough, he kind of hoped she might actually cease to exist, like the tree falling in the forest with no one to hear it.

Still, Kate had a contract with Channel 3? That was interesting.

Penny's heels clacked along the wooden floor into the kitchen and Joe could hear her picking up the phone. "It's me. *Future: Perfect*'s been cancelled.... I know.... No, can't sue, they're threatening me.... I know, I know.... Listen, can you get me into *Hot Gossip*? I'll bare my soul about being ousted from a television program that gave so much hope to so many.... Yeah. Call me back."

Again Joe heard the heels *clackety-clack*ing in the familiar routine that he knew so well. *Clack clack* to the drinks cupboard, *clack clack* to the glasses cupboard. Drink poured. *Clack clack* to the kitchen breakfast bar, and right about now Penny would be lighting a cigarette, the ash of which would not be constrained to the ashtray but would fall on the counter and the floor for the cleaner to clean up the following morning. Penny was a slob, Joe thought with disgust. Penny was a nightmare.

A few minutes later, the phone rang again. Penny picked up. "Yeah, it's me. So? You're joking.... They said what? ... What about one of the others? ... Jesus, Michael, what kind of agent are you? Listen to me. I want to be on the front cover of *Hot Gossip*, and I want to trash Kate and her pissy little show, and I want you to sort it for me. Okay?"

There was a pause, and Joe assumed the phone call had ended, but evidently not.

"Seriously?" he heard Penny say. "Look, if it gets me on the cover, then I'll do it. But I want it in writing."

There was another pause, and then the *clack-clack*ing started again, this time coming ominously in his direction.

"We have to get engaged," Penny said flatly, taking a drag from her cigarette. "That's the only way we're going to push Kate bloody Hetherington off the radar and get a cover shot. My agent's going to borrow a ring from Tiffany's. We'll get something suitably big so you don't look like a *total* cheapskate."

Joe stared at her. "You *are* kidding?"

"'Fraid not, sunshine. This is war, and we've got to play dirty."

Joe looked at her, taking in the drawn mouth, etched-in lines from sucking on a cigarette end day-in, day-out, her dry blond hair, and her angular features, and he shuddered.

"We couldn't think of something else?"

Penny rolled her eyes. "Newfound love, weddings, babies, and breakups are the only things that get you attention in this world. So, no, we can't think of something else."

She *clack*ed back toward the kitchen, and Joe frowned. Breakups. Newfound love. He'd thought of something else already.

"Now, your scars are healing beautifully, and I can see your hair growing back. How are you feeling?"

Tom grinned encouragingly at the young woman in front of him. Far too young for cancer, he thought bitterly. Then he shook himself. No more bitterness, he'd promised himself. This woman was lucky. They'd got the tumor in time and she looked like she was making a full recovery. What did that ridiculous book say? *Look for the beauty in all things and point it out to others. Remind yourself of the wonder of nature and life. . . .*

"Fine. I mean, you know. Pretty good, in the circumstances."

Tom nodded and made some notes. "Okay, well the results are looking good so far, so I'm going to let you go now, but I'd like to see you again in a couple of weeks. Sound okay?"

The woman nodded.

"And how's that degree of yours coming along?"

She grinned. "I got a first in my essay last week. And I've completely caught up with my coursework, so looks like I'll be graduating next year after all."

"Fantastic," Tom said. "Good for you."

"Thanks," she said as she got up to go. "I mean . . . Well, really. Thank you."

"Thank me by staying well," Tom said.

She left, and Tom stared after her. He'd never noticed before, but he was surrounded by some of the most amazing people. Nurses and doctors who worked tirelessly to cure people, to help them feel better; patients who battled courageously even when they faced an uphill battle; families who supported them, quietly, diligently, never revealing their own fears or pain. The world was an amazing place. It wasn't gray and bleak; it was bright Technicolor. And until today he'd never seen it.

He shook his head in wonder and looked at his schedule. There was a consultation scheduled in for first thing the following morning with Betty Conway, who was having a mastectomy. But until then, nothing.

He would go and see her, he decided. Check that everything was okay. And then he would go for a walk. Maybe catch a film. Do some shopping. Let the spring sun shine on his face and feel grateful to be alive. To be given a second chance.

Tom strode down the corridor, into the lift, and out onto the third floor, then made his way to her ward, where he found Lucy taking Betty's blood pressure and showing off her ring.

"Ah, Betty," he said jovially, as he pulled back the curtains surrounding her bed. "Looking lovely as ever."

Lucy arched an eyebrow at him.

"Hello, Doctor. I've just been hearing Lucy's exciting news!" Betty said, her eyes twinkling. "So when are you going to get yourself a wife, then? Nice-looking doctor like you—must have the pick of the crop."

Tom smiled and picked up her charts. "So, Betty," he said. "I just wanted to go over a couple of things before your surgery tomorrow. You'll be under for no more than an hour, but you'll probably sleep for a lot longer. The nurses won't give you any supper tonight, but you can sip water if you need to. Nothing tomorrow morning, though, not even a drink. Now, any questions?"

Betty smiled. "I'm going to be on the telly," she said happily. "This afternoon. They're going to film me right here."

Tom gave Lucy a quizzical look.

"The hospice show," Lucy said with a shrug. "Your friend. Thought you'd have known about it. Apparently the press office set it up . . ."

"And they're going to be here this afternoon?" Tom asked.

"That's right," Lucy said.

"They're at the hospice this morning," Betty said authoritatively. "Then they're coming here at four thirty, although Kate says that filming always takes longer than you think, so I shouldn't be worried if they're not here until five. And they're going to ask me about the hospice. I'm going to be one of the stars of the show, you know. One of the 'life stories.' "

"Kate said that, did she?" Tom asked with a little smile.

Betty nodded and smiled back. "And that Gareth, he said I've got a great face for television. Fancy that, at my age. He said it could be my new vocation!"

Tom grinned. "Well, I see you've got this all figured out."

"You've got to have a plan, don't you, Doctor," Betty said. "Got to have something to dream of, something to aim at. Otherwise what's the point?"

Tom nodded thoughtfully. "And you don't ever get worried? You don't ever get scared of failure?"

Betty snorted in derision. "Scared? Young man, the only thing to fear in this world is fear itself. It's paralyzing. Makes you weak and pathetic. No, Doctor, I don't get scared. And if I do, I tell myself to stop being so silly. Isn't that right, Lucy?"

Lucy grinned. "If I was scared of failure I wouldn't be here. Took me three goes to get through my exams."

"There you are!" Betty said triumphantly. "Now, doctor, when was it you said I had to stop eating?"

She frowned. "Doctor?"

But Tom wasn't listening. Instead, he smiled at them vaguely.

"Weak and pathetic, you say," he mused as Lucy and Betty exchanged looks. "Right. Right, well, there isn't much time then, is there?"

He turned and walked out of the ward, leaving Lucy and Betty staring curiously after him.

"Doctors," Lucy said, a few moments later. "Meant to be clever, but they don't half act weird sometimes."

Joe looked up from his vantage point on the sofa to see Penny silhouetted in the doorway. "Okay," she said curtly, "*Hot Gossip* didn't bite, but the *Tittle Tattle* people are going to be here at five to talk to us about our wedding plans." Smoke was curling out of her mouth as she spoke, and her angular bob was as immovable as always. "And they're bringing a photographer, so you might want to get changed."

Joe stared at her insolently. "We've barely discussed this," he said, "and you've already arranged for photographers?"

Penny sighed. "Don't be so dramatic, Joe," she said. "You want publicity, don't you? You want to be a someone."

Joe bit his lip. He didn't want publicity with *her*. Couldn't bear to spend another minute with that woman even if it meant fame and glory. Some prices just weren't worth paying.

"I'm going out," he said, standing up.

Penny frowned. "Where?" she demanded. "The journalist will be here in an hour."

Joe shrugged. "Just out," he said, pushing past her.

As soon as he was out of her flat and walking toward the Kings Road, he called Bob, his agent.

"Hey. Me. Listen, you know you said if I hooked up with a super-model or famous actress that would be the nudge I needed? That I could ditch Penny and this whole crazy charade?"

"Yes . . ." Bob said warily.

"So how about if I get back together with Kate? If I realized the error of my ways and finally got out of the clutches of Penny Pennington, who seduced me and lied to me about her age? You think that would do it?"

"You think she'll take you back?"

"Hey, when I want to charm someone, I know what to do."

"Well, if you can pull that off, Joe, you'll be the hottest property in town."

"That's what I was hoping to hear," Joe said. "Thanks, Bob."

31

Ten Ways of Knowing That You're a Hopeless Romantic

1. You believe in happy endings, and refuse to let others' cynicism or difficult manner deter you.
2. Laughter and tears come easily to you, such is your level of sympathy for, and empathy with, others.
3. When the skies are gray and full of rain, you see the romance of being caught in a downpour; when skies are blue and the sun is shining you are excited by the prospect of a day spent walking in the park. Everything is an opportunity to you; everything brings hope and anticipation.
4. You are not impressed by grand gestures or expensive gifts that are presented as substitutions for thoughtfulness. A single flower that is presented honestly and with love is worth a thousand bouquets of the sweetest smelling roses proffered by a fickle admirer.
5. If something is very important to you, you don't give up. Ever. You chase your dream, refuse (politely, of course) to take no for an answer, and do everything within your power to make your dream come true . . .

Tom put the book down and looked at Sal helplessly. "You have to help me," he begged. "I need a plan. Something dramatic."

Sal frowned and picked up the book. "Kate actually bought this book?" she asked, thumbing through *The Hopeless Romantic's Handbook*. "Anyway, look, it says here that grand gestures and big bouquets of flowers are a substitute for thoughtfulness."

Tom looked worried. "Really? Jesus, why is this so hard?"

Sal shrugged. "I don't think that big bouquets are bad per se. I got the most beautiful bunch of flowers from Ed yesterday and I was chuffed to bits. Look . . ."

She pointed to a vase filled with flowers on the counter and Tom smiled tightly.

"Lovely," he said. "But can we please focus on the task at hand? Kate is going to be at the hospital in an hour and I need to surprise her."

"You and Kate," Sal said, shaking her head. "God, it's just so nice. To think of you both . . ." She wiped a tear away from her eye. "Sorry, don't mind me. Can't stop crying at the moment. You know, you could always turn up on a white steed. That would be grand and thoughtful. I mean, isn't she always saying she wants a knight in shining armor?"

Tom raised an eyebrow. He didn't want to admit it, but he had actually had this little fantasy of turning up in front of Kate on a horse, looking like Brad Pitt in *Gladiator* or something. Or was he thinking of *Troy*? Either way, it wasn't very easy tracking down a horse in Central London. And he couldn't ride. And as for looking like Brad Pitt . . .

He sighed. No, flowers were a much better option. "I think it's probably a little warm for armor," he said. "And I haven't really got the time for riding lessons."

"Fair point," Sal said with a shrug. "Anyway, she told me she's given up on being a romantic. Apparently she's pragmatic and ballsy now. Whereas Ed, well, he's gone quite the other way. Did I tell you that he turned up at work the other day to take me out to lunch? Just out of the blue? The investigation cleared him, and the first thing he wanted to do was celebrate with me. Isn't that romantic?"

Her eyes looked past Tom dreamily, and he cleared his throat. "Yeah. Thanks, Sal. Really useful."

"My point," Sal said, sighing, "is that you don't need flowers necessarily. Just tell her that you're crazy about her and I guarantee she'll swoon. You know, if she likes you back, that is."

Tom looked at her nervously. "What if she doesn't?"

Sal shrugged again. "Then at least you don't have to walk away carrying a huge bouquet of flowers and looking like an idiot. You just . . . walk away, I guess. And come round here for chocolate and sympathy."

"Right," Tom said. "Great. Thanks, Sal."

"You're welcome!" Sal said, beaming. "Now, is that the sun coming out? I rather fancy a walk in the park. . . ."

Kate smiled gently as Betty opened her eyes and looked around her.

"Did I fall asleep?" she asked, as her eyelids fluttered open. "I didn't miss the filming, did I?"

Kate grinned. "As if we'd be able to film without you," she chastised her. "The cameras are just on their way, actually. I just wanted to check that you're okay and that you're feeling up to it. Because we can always reschedule. . . ."

Betty shook her head briskly and pushed herself up to a sitting position. "I wouldn't hear of it," she said, sounding more alert. "I'm the star, and the show must go on, isn't that right?"

Kate laughed.

"And how's the hospice looking?" Betty asked. "Is my en suite bathroom ready yet?"

Kate shook her head. "Right now, I'm afraid that walls are being stripped and electrical points put in, along with a whole new central heating system," she said. "But you'll have an en suite bathroom at the hotel you're going to whilst the renovations are done. Along with a minibar."

Betty's eyes twinkled. "Sounds wonderful. I could do with a quick nip now, actually. Fancy joining me?"

Kate looked at her sternly. "I'm not sure that drinking alcohol is the done thing before an operation, so I'll pass, thank you. But I do have a few loose ends to tie up, so if it's alright with you I'm going to leave you to sleep for another half an hour or so before everyone else gets here. Okay?"

Betty shrugged, then closed her eyes again, and Kate wandered out of the ward and checked her watch. The camera crew would be here any minute, but she'd keep them outside for a while, she decided—Betty might think she was okay, but Kate didn't want the glare of the lights on her until she'd had time to wake up properly.

It was funny, she thought, being here at the hospital and not knowing where Tom was, or even if he was in the building. They hadn't spoken in . . . well, in a long time. She wondered how he was. Wondered if he ever thought about her.

Probably not, she decided. She needed to move on, get on with her life. Like Sal, who now seemed to be on a one-woman mission to create the perfect baby with the perfect environment. Every time Kate spoke to her, she was buying Mozart to develop its brain or eating spirulina to provide it with nutrients; she wouldn't step foot in a smoky joint like the Bush Bar and Grill if you paid her, and even if she would, you'd have to prize her away from Ed, first. The two of them had suddenly become inseparable, spending their weekends shopping for prams and their evenings eating organic food and reading babycare books.

Kate had never seen her happier.

Slowly, she wandered out toward the front of the hospital to wait for the camera crew. But as she got there, she saw a man running toward her, his face partially hidden by a large bouquet of flowers.

He arrived in front of her and prostrated himself on the ground, holding the flowers up to her, a look of absolute contrition on his face.

Kate stared.

"You?" she asked in disbelief. "What are you doing here?"

32

Joe looked up at Kate, his face full of shame.

"I wanted to talk to you before, but Penny wouldn't let me. Wouldn't . . ." He bit his lip. "Kate, I made the most terrible mistake. I don't know what I was thinking. I've been so miserable, and it made me realize . . . I'm in love with you, Kate. I don't expect you to take me back, but I had to tell you—had to beg you to at least hear me out. Maybe over dinner?"

Kate looked at him incredulously. "You want me to have dinner with you? Are you mad?"

Joe sighed. "I know. I've been an idiot. But I was coerced into it. Penny told me that it was the only way to kick-start my career in this country and I believed her. I believed her that you wouldn't want to hang out with some loser who couldn't get past a first audition. But I missed you, Kate. I never stopped thinking about you. God, you have to believe how sorry I am . . ."

Kate took a hesitant step toward him. "You went out with Penny for the publicity?"

Joe nodded. "It was all her idea."

"So you humiliated me just to get your profile enhanced?"

Joe squirmed. "I'm so ashamed," he said morosely. "But you were right. She isn't human. She's like the devil. She was sucking out my soul, every minute I spent with her. Not like you. With you, I was . . . happy."

"So I guess it's been a good lesson, then," Kate said.

"Okay, you're right." Joe nodded. "I've been an asshole. And I know you'll never take me back. But at least let me buy you dinner to make up for it. At least let me say I'm sorry properly."

Kate sighed and looked at Joe. It felt like a million years ago that she'd thought she might be in love with him. A lifetime ago.

"You're right, Joe, I won't take you back," she said gently. "And dinner probably isn't such a great idea either. But thank you for the thought."

"But . . ." A tiny crease appeared between Joe's brows. "Kate, I'm still in love with you. I know I am. All that time with Penny, you were on my mind all the time. I . . ."

"You're not in love with me," Kate said. "And I'm not in love with you. I'm sorry, Joe, but I think it's probably best if we don't see each other again. I've got this program to make, anyway, so I'm really busy right now. . . ."

Joe nodded. "I understand," he said. "But here, these flowers are for you. And if you change your mind, I'll be waiting. I'll be waiting right by my phone."

Kate nodded. "We never said good-bye, did we, Joe?" she asked.

"No," he said. "I guess we didn't."

She took the flowers, put them down, and reached up to give him a kiss on the cheek.

"Now we have closure," she said softly. "Joe, it's time to move on."

Tom stared at the scene in front of him, rooted to the spot. The huge bunch of daffodils he'd eventually decided to buy because they looked so bright and springlike, so full of hope, fell from his hands as he watched Kate putting her arms around Joe's neck.

He wrenched his eyes away and turned, kicking the daffodils out of the way as he raced out toward the Fulham Palace Road.

He was too late. Joe had come back. Kate's knight in shining armor, the one she'd been so in love with, had won her back. With a huge bouquet of flowers, Tom couldn't help noticing. Not some poxy little bunch of daffodils.

What had he been thinking? Had he honestly thought that he had a chance? That Kate was going to throw herself at him and tell him that she loved him, too, that she also thought about him every hour of every day and that she couldn't bear the idea of living without him?

Of course she wouldn't. The one time he'd thought that maybe, possibly there might be something between them had been the night Joe had left her, the night she'd been let down, humiliated. He'd probably seemed quite a good proposition right then. If he hadn't panicked and got the hell out of there, things might have turned out different.

But he *had* panicked. And things were as they were. Which was probably a good thing because even if he'd stayed, even if he'd called her instead of hiding in his flat like a pathetic loser, it wouldn't have lasted. Joe would have come back sooner or later, and he'd have had to see her apologetic face telling him that it wasn't him, it was her; she liked him, but not like that. . . .

No, it was better this way. Hopeless romance was not for him: It made you start hoping for happy endings, and that was dangerous.

Kate wandered back into the hospital in a daze. That had been . . . unexpected. Ridiculous, even. Joe, in love with her? She frowned, and sat down on one of the hard, plastic chairs in the reception area.

She wasn't in love with him, that was the point. She'd thought she was, but she wasn't.

She was in love with Tom. And he didn't love her. Perhaps the three of them should appear in a Greek tragedy or something.

"So is it serious?"

Two nurses were sitting at a table beside her, huddled over their drinks. She frowned, thinking she recognized one of them.

"Totally. I mean, this is it. I'm sure of it."

Oh, God. It was Tom's nurse. Lucy. The one from the supermarket.

Kate looked away, desperate not to be spotted and yet equally desperate to quell her curiosity and take a good look at her. So that was the kind of person Tom fancied, was it? She was short, curvaceous, with a twinkle in her eye. "A good laugh" was no doubt how she was described by her friends.

"No way! So has he met your mum yet?"

"Don't be soft. But look, check this out."

She held out her hand to reveal a platinum ring on which was nestled a small diamond. Kate found herself unable to take her eyes from it. An engagement ring? But she'd thought . . .

She closed her eyes and forced herself to breathe. Tom found having a girlfriend too much commitment, and now he was getting married? Images filled her mind of Tom choosing the ring, of him putting it on Lucy's finger. Her stomach started to constrict.

"No! Wow, it's beautiful. Big, too. Must have cost him a few quid."

"Money doesn't come into it when someone loves you," Lucy said knowingly, with a big smile on her face.

"Wow."

Standing up, Kate walked unsteadily back outside. It was fine, she told herself. She'd known this would happen eventually. She needed to be pragmatic, forget her silly romantic fantasies, and accept that this was the real world.

Taking a few deep breaths, Kate thought for a moment, then took out her phone.

"Joe?" she said hesitantly. "Listen, I've been thinking. Maybe dinner isn't such a bad idea after all."

✦ ✦ ✦

"Joe?" Penny was staring at him. "Joe, Sarah here just asked you a question, love. Can you maybe put your phone away now?"

She had a thin smile fixed to her face, and Joe looked disdainfully into her eyes, watery blue yet cold as steel.

"You know," he said, "actually, I'm going to have to go, I'm afraid. Something's come up."

Penny's eyes narrowed. "Joe, we're in the middle of an interview, love." She smiled apologetically at the journalist and photographer. "Sorry about this," she added, standing up. "Could you maybe give us a minute?"

She walked over to Joe and took his arm, all the time smiling sweetly. "We'll just step out into the corridor, shall we, love?" she asked. Obediently Joe followed her.

"What the fuck is going on?" she hissed as soon as they were out of earshot of the people from *Tittle Tattle*. "You are embarrassing me in there. You're all over the place."

Joe shrugged. "I'm pissed off, that's what's going on. I've had enough, and I'm getting out." He walked over to the coat stand and picked up his jacket.

"But you can't," Penny raged. "You can't just bloody go. What'll I tell the journalist? We're meant to be bloody engaged."

"Tell her I got a better offer," Joe suggested.

Penny grabbed his arm. "If you walk out of this flat, I'll tell them what a small dick you've got. I'll tell everyone what a loser you really are."

"On page seventy-three. I'm scared," Joe said, rolling his eyes.

Penny stared at him, then she smiled tightly. "Tell you what. We'll do this interview, then we'll talk, okay? Just stay until they've left, that's all."

"I'm afraid I can't do that," Joe said, walking toward the door. "I've got a date. With a woman who's actually attractive. And sweet. Qualities you know so little about."

"I'll burn your things," Penny said bitterly.

"Don't worry," Joe said as he made his way to the door. "I intend to buy new ones."

And shooting her a little smile, he left her apartment, slamming the door behind him.

"Is everything okay?" Sarah asked, coming out into the corridor.

Penny grimaced. "It's . . . a family thing. He's sorry he had to go. But I can take the interview from here." She shot a dark look at the closed door. "He'll be back. Don't you worry about that."

33

"Wow, you look amazing." Joe's eyes were shining as he met Kate at the door and led her to the bar. "You want a drink?"

Kate nodded. "Um, gin and tonic. Thanks," she said. A few weeks ago, this would have felt normal, she thought. Exciting, even, to be having dinner with Joe in a glamorous restaurant. She'd have spent hours wondering what to wear instead of pulling the first thing out of her wardrobe and slapping on some lipstick.

Now it felt almost like a letdown. As if Joe was her consolation prize.

Still, that kind of thinking would get her nowhere. That kind of thinking had got her all tied in knots over Tom. She was more sensible now—a "bird in the hand" kind of girl instead of a "grass is always greener" one.

"So, how are things?" she asked, hopping onto a bar stool as the maître d' took her coat.

"All the better for seeing you," Joe said, flashing a smile at her. "I'm so glad you changed your mind. So glad you were prepared to give me a second chance."

Kate blushed. "Well," she said, smiling. "I thought that everyone deserves a second chance. . . ."

"I'm glad to hear it. You're a special girl, Kate. Really special."

He was looking right into her eyes, and she remembered feeling amazed when he used to do that, as if she was the only girl in the room.

"So how's Penny?" she asked lightly.

Joe rolled his eyes. "I don't know, and I don't care. Man, that woman is a nightmare. I mean, a real nightmare, and believe me, I've known a few. I cannot tell you how pleased I was to get away from her."

"Oh, I think I understand," Kate said.

Joe grinned. "And I couldn't stay with her a minute longer when I realized how deep my feelings were for you," he said, taking her hand. "My Kate. My sweet, lovely Kate."

Kate shifted, uncomfortable. "Not yours, Joe," she reminded him. "We're just having dinner."

"Right," Joe said. "For now, that is . . ."

The maître d' appeared at their side and asked if they were ready to eat. Kate nodded, and Joe held out his arm as she got off the bar stool.

"Please, follow me," the maître d' said, and let them through the restaurant to a corner table. "Enjoy."

"You like Daphne's?" Joe asked, picking up the menu.

"Never been here before, actually, but it seems lovely."

"It was recommended to me by a journalist," Joe said. "I didn't want to take you to just any old place."

"Right," Kate said, smiling again, as she looked at the menu. "Well, the food looks great."

"Not as great as you!"

Kate raised her eyebrows. She was beginning to feel a bit embarrassed by all these compliments.

"Seriously," Joe continued. "You look amazing."

"No, I don't," Kate said, then changed the subject. "So, what are you going to order?"

Joe shrugged. "Why don't you choose?" he asked, grinning broadly.

Kate frowned. "Joe, look, I don't want to give you the wrong idea about this. We're having dinner. I'm willing to hear you out. But we're not a couple yet. Things may not even get that far, okay? Because you're making me a bit uncomfortable here with . . ."

Her voice trailed off as her eyes fixed on someone at the other end of the restaurant, a blond girl who had just arrived and was sitting down with a man with curly red hair. It was Lucy, she realized, and the man definitely wasn't Tom. So what was his fiancée playing at?

"God, I'm sorry. I'm so sorry," Joe said quickly. "You're right. I'm coming on too strong. I'm just excited, that's all. Okay? Are we okay?"

Kate nodded, slightly mollified, and continued to stare at Lucy and the unknown man.

"You're the best thing that ever happened to me, Kate," Joe went on, reaching over and taking her hand. "And together I really think we could be a great team. You with your new show, me with some great role. We could be cover stars, Kate, me and you. We could go as far as we wanted."

Kate focused back on Joe, and rolled her eyes. "No thank you," she said. "I mean, frankly I can't think of anything worse than being on the cover of a magazine. I did that interview for the hospice, but never again. All those people looking at me! It's bad enough seeing myself on television without having to see my face in magazines, too."

"You don't mean that," Joe said, shaking his head. "It just takes a bit of getting used to, is all. Kate, you're a someone now. You can't let that go."

Kate shuddered. "I bloody well can. I don't want to be a someone; I want to be me. Just Kate Hetherington. You must feel the same, after that horrible experience with Penny. I mean, talk about someone desperate for publicity. It's so sad."

Joe smiled nervously. "You wouldn't want to do an interview, then? About us finding love again?"

Kate stared at him. "Of course not. And anyway, we haven't found love again, have we? I mean, I wouldn't call dinner 'finding love,' would you?"

Joe looked at her uncertainly, then laughed. "Hey, I'm kidding. I'm kidding! God, you Brits are so serious all the time." He picked up the menu and began to look at it.

Kate saw Lucy stand up and pick up her bag. She was going to the loo. This would be her chance.

"Would you . . . excuse me a moment?" she said, scraping her chair back.

Joe nodded, and she got up and followed Lucy up the staircase in the middle of the restaurant, through a door on the left, and into the ladies'.

"Lucy!" she said, just as Lucy went into one of the cubicles. She came out, a look of surprise on her face, then smiled.

"Oh, hello! You're Tom's friend, aren't you. Well, fancy seeing you here."

"Yes, fancy," Kate said. "You . . . here on a date?"

Lucy grinned. "Yeah. You?"

Kate frowned. "Oh. Yes. Well, kind of. It's just . . ."

Lucy was looking at her curiously.

"I just wondered if Tom knew you were here. I mean, if he'd mind or not?"

"Tom?" Lucy's brow wrinkled. "I don't see why he would."

"Right," Kate said uncertainly. "Well, that's alright, then. I just thought that, you know, when you're marrying someone, you don't usually go out with someone else."

Lucy stared at her, then a look of understanding crossed her face. "You mean the other week?" she asked. "Yeah, that was a bit cheeky. But it was the only way to get Connor to ask me to marry him. I thought if I made him jealous, he'd realize he couldn't live without me, and Tom was nice enough to oblige. Let me crash at his until Connor's jealousy got the better of him. He's lovely, Tom, isn't he? Such a nice bloke. So how did you know me and Connor are getting married?"

Kate stared at Lucy. She could feel herself getting very hot all of a sudden. "Connor? Connor is your fiancé?"

Lucy grinned. "Yeah. He's downstairs."

"Not Tom, then."

"Tom?" Lucy's eyes widened. "I don't think so. I thought he liked you, anyway. Couldn't even talk after we bumped into you like that. Just kept pacing around his flat muttering to himself."

"He was . . . pacing?"

"Yeah. And muttering. He does that at the hospital, too, sometimes, when he's stressed out."

"Well. Okay, then. Thank you," Kate said, her mind racing. "Have a good dinner."

She turned and walked out of the ladies', almost tripping down the stairs as she returned to Joe.

"Waiter came over while you were gone. I ordered you chicken— hope that's okay," Joe said as she sat down.

"Chicken?" she said, distracted. "Yes. Fine."

Tom's not engaged, she kept thinking. Tom was pacing, after we bumped into each other. Pacing and muttering.

"You alright?" Joe asked. "You look kind of hot."

"Hot?" Kate asked, flustered. "Um, right. Yes, I am a bit. It's quite warm in here, isn't it?"

"You wanna get some air?" Joe asked. "We can pop outside if you want. . . ."

Kate nodded gratefully. She felt as if the walls were going to close in on her at any minute. Leaving his jacket on the chair, Joe escorted her out through the bar to the front of the restaurant. She caught Lucy's eye as she walked by and gave her a weak smile.

But stumbling out of the restaurant into the welcome cool night air, she was met by the glare of flashlights as a group of men started to take pictures.

"Joe," one of them called out. "Are you and Kate an item again now?"

"Kate, over here, love. Give us a smile now."

"Is it true you're back together?" another shouted.

Gazing around her, wide-eyed, Kate looked at Joe in incomprehension.

"Ignore them," he said, grinning and putting his arm around her. "These guys have taken to following me around, I'm afraid."

"But . . ." Kate shielded her eyes from the blinding lights. "But how did they know you were here? That I was here?"

A woman rushed up to Joe. "Hi!" she said. "So listen, my editor is very excited by your interview offer. How are you two fixed tomorrow?"

Kate stared at her. "What interview offer?"

The woman smiled. "Sorry. I'm Lucinda Stewart from *Fab!* Joe's agent called me about doing an interview with the two of you this afternoon. And can I just say, you make a great-looking couple. Our readers are going to love you. . . ."

Kate smiled tightly at her and then glared at Joe.

He smiled sheepishly. "Agents," he said. "What do you do with guys like that? I tell him I'm going out to dinner with you, and he does this. I'm sorry."

Lucinda frowned. "But he said that you had asked him to . . ." she began. Joe put his hand up to stop her.

"Thanks," he said, "but Kate is feeling a bit unwell. Can you give her some space here, please?"

He put his arm around Kate protectively, but she shrugged it off. "The only person I need space from is you," she snapped. "Just get the hell away from me, Joe." Then she turned to Lucinda. "And for the record, I am not his girlfriend. I wouldn't be his girlfriend if we were the last two people on earth. And yes, you can quote me on that."

She looked around desperately. "Please, I need a cab," she said to a random photographer. "Have you seen one?"

The Daphne's doorman suddenly appeared beside her. "Please, allow me," he said, hailing her into a passing taxi. "And our apologies—unfortunately we can't stop these people from hanging outside."

Kate arched her eyebrows. "You want to watch out for the people hanging out inside, too," she said with a sigh, then closed the door.

"Shepherd's Bush," she said. "And step on it."

The taxi sped throught the London streets, as Kate tried to figure out what she was going to say. But when she finally got to Tom's flat, when she jumped out excitedly and pressed his doorbell, no one answered. Tom wasn't in. Kate stood for five minutes at the front door, pressing his buzzer and calling up at his window, but even she had to accept eventually that he wasn't home.

She sighed. If she'd been thinking, she'd have kept the cab waiting, but of course she'd let it go. Quickly she dug out her mobile and dialed a number.

"Sal? How's your car these days?" she asked urgently. "I think I might need a lift."

The moment Kate got to Sal's house, the front door opened.

"What happened?" Sal demanded. "What did Tom say?"

Kate stared at her. "Tom didn't say anything," she said. "It was Lucy. You see, I thought he and Lucy were engaged. So I went out with Joe. And then I found out . . . that he wasn't, I mean. And Joe had called all these photographers. . . ." She spat the last word out with revulsion. "And he's not at home," she concluded. "So we have to go to the hospital."

Sal frowned. "Who's not at home? And who's at the hospital?"

Kate looked at her in exasperation. "Tom," she said. "Come on, keep up."

"Right," Sal said. "Sorry. And you haven't seen Tom at all today?"

"No!" Kate said. "Why would I have?"

"Well, it's just that I saw him at fourish, and he was about to declare his undying love for you," Sal said matter-of-factly. "We were debating his choice of flowers."

"What?" Kate was dumbfounded. "But . . . why didn't you tell me?"

Sal sighed. "Hmm. Yes, why didn't I ring you up and say, 'Oh

Kate, just to completely ruin the most romantic moment of your life, I thought I'd clue you in that Tom is on his way to tell you he's in love with you'. God, what was I thinking?"

Kate blanched. "Joe came to see me at about four thirty. Maybe Tom saw him and thought . . ."

"Thought correctly, if you ended up going out to dinner with Joe. Tell me how that happened. I didn't think you liked him anymore."

"I don't," Kate said despondently. "I thought I was being pragmatic. . . ."

"Pragmatic? Kate, listen, I'm sorry to say it but you don't really do pragmatic very well."

Kate frowned. "I do too."

Sal shook her head. "Nope, sorry."

Suddenly there was a ring at the door and they both stared at the other.

"Quick," Kate shouted. "It could be him. It could be Tom. . . ."

She raced to the door and swung it open, then frowned in confusion.

Gareth smiled awkwardly. "Oh, sorry. I was here to see Sal."

"Sal?" Kate asked. "Why?"

Gareth shrugged. "Actually, to talk about you. Listen, Joe's not here, is he? I mean, if you want to get back together, that's your business, but can I say categorically and for the record that I don't approve? I mean, he touched Penny. He's contaminated."

Kate stared at him in complete bafflement. "What?" she asked. "Whyever would you think I'm back with Joe?"

Gareth rolled his eyes impatiently. "*Tittle Tattle* called me up for my thoughts on you two getting back together. You know, as a close friend. I'm sorry, but I said it would never last."

Kate grabbed his arm and dragged him inside. "I'm not with Joe," she said. "I'm going to the hospital to find Tom."

"Ed!" Sal called. "We're going to the hospital."

"Hospital?" Ed came racing down the stairs, a worried expression on his face. "Why? What's wrong?"

"Nothing," Sal said, exasperated. "We're on a romantic mission. At least Kate is; I'm just the chauffeur."

"No you're not," Ed said immediately. "Not in your condition. I'll drive—just let me get my keys."

Sal rolled her eyes at him. "Ed, I'm perfectly capable of driving you know," she called after him, but he emerged, smiling, and kissed her.

"Right," he said. "Which hospital?"

"Yes," Gareth asked, his eyes shining with excitement. "Which hospital? And why are we going?"

"*I* was going to Charing Cross," Kate said, managing a smile. "But now it looks like it's a bit of an expedition."

They all jumped in Ed's car, and he sped to the hospital in record time, avoiding most of the traffic on the Hammersmith roundabout via a nifty shortcut. They pulled into the sprawling 1960s hospital estate and screeched to a halt outside main reception, where Ed parked next to an ambulance.

"Okay, wish me luck!" Kate said apprehensively, jumping out of the car.

Gareth and Sal held up their thumbs and Ed waved, and Kate made her way inside. It was only when she got to the desk that she realized she had no idea what she was going to say.

"Hi!" she said brightly to the receptionist. "I need to speak with Dr. Whitson. Dr. Tom Whitson."

"You are a patient?" the woman asked.

Kate shook her head. "A friend. A good friend."

The woman looked at her. "And this is important?"

"Very," Kate said breathlessly. "Incredibly important."

"Important enough to disturb surgery?" the woman asked.

Kate smiled uncomfortably. "Quite important," she said. "It's quite important."

The woman shot her a suspicious look and picked up the phone. "Hello. I've got someone for Dr. Whitson here. . . . Yes . . . I see. . . . Okay, then."

She put the phone down and looked at Kate blankly. "Sorry," she said with a shrug.

"Sorry he's busy?" Kate asked. "Sorry, I should wait, or come back later? Sorry about what, exactly?"

"Actually, I'm not sorry," the woman said. "I was just being polite. But your Dr. Whitson isn't here. He's not due in till the morning. So you can wait if you want—it's up to you."

"Right," Kate said quietly. "Thanks. I'll . . . I think I'll go, actually."

The woman smiled. "Probably best," she said.

The journey back to Shepherd's Bush was rather more subdued than the one to the hospital.

"He's probably just out with friends," Sal said reassuringly. "Call him in an hour and I'm sure he'll be home."

"*We're* his friends," Kate reminded her. "And what if he isn't?"

"Come and stay with us tonight, then," Sal said, as they turned off the Fulham Palace Road onto the familiar Hammersmith roundabout. "That way you won't obsess about where he is and tomorrow you can see him at the hospital and have your romantic moment."

Kate shook her head. "I want to see him now. What if he did see me with Joe? I can't sleep until I see him."

Sal frowned and nudged Ed.

"Come and stay," he agreed. "I'll make pancakes."

Sal raised an eyebrow and he shrugged. "I will," he said defensively. "I make great pancakes."

"I love pancakes," Gareth said meaningfully, and Sal sighed.

"You can stay, too, if you want," she said. "But you'll have to have the sofa."

"A sleepover!" Gareth exclaimed as they started to drive up the Shepherd's Bush Road. "Can we have a midnight feast? And read each other ghost stories?"

Ed turned a worried look on Sal. "I still have to go to work tomorrow, you know. I mean, pancakes don't take long, but I'm not sure about ghost stories and midnight feasts. . . ."

"Gareth, there will be no midnight feasts," Sal said. "You can have one story, but that's all."

"Fine," Gareth sulked, and Ed grinned.

"See?" he said softly, "you'll be a great mother. You're a natural!"

"Look," Kate said, "this is really nice of you all, but I don't really want pancakes. Or ghost stories, or . . ." She trailed off and swallowed heavily. "I think I'll probably just go home."

"You want me to come with you?" Gareth offered hopefully.

Kate shook her head dolefully, and Ed signaled left to turn in to her road.

"The offer will stay open, Kate," Sal said. "I mean, you know, if you change your mind. If you get lonely or anything . . ."

Kate managed a smile. "Thanks. Really. But I'll be fine. And anyway, I've got a busy day tomorrow."

Ed stopped outside her building, and she gave them each a kiss before getting out of the car.

"Can I still come to stay?" she heard Gareth ask plaintively as she shut the car door and made her way slowly to her door, turning for a brief wave as Ed's car pulled away.

She pulled out her keys to open the door, then stopped as she heard footsteps behind her. Footsteps that were coming from the small paved area outside her flat. That was all she needed—an intruder to attack her. That would make this officially the worst day of her life.

She swung round, and her mouth fell open.

"I wondered what was taking you so long."

Kate stared in amazement as Tom stepped out of the shadows, a slight grin on his face. "You know, it's a lovely evening. I nearly broke into song about an hour ago—that song from *My Fair Lady* about being on the street where you live."

Kate, eyes wide, stared at Tom for a moment, then hurled herself at him. "Tom! I've just been looking for you. I went to your flat, and the hospital, and . . ."

"I thought you might be with Joe," Tom said gently.

Kate shook her head violently. "No way. I mean, I was. For dinner. But only because . . ." She looked down at the ground. "I thought you and Lucy . . . but then I found out you weren't . . . Sal said you came to find me earlier?"

She looked up, hope shining in her eyes, and Tom nodded.

"That's when I saw you with Joe."

Kate looked down again.

"And I ran," Tom continued. "Chickened out. Came back home and listened to a bit of Billie. And read a bit of your book."

"My book?"

"This book." He handed her the old, battered copy of *The Hopeless Romantic's Handbook*, and she gasped.

"I threw that away!" she said in amazement.

"And I rescued it," Tom said lightly. "Ridiculous book it is, too. Full of stupid advice, like being brave and stepping into the breach. Being optimistic and focusing on the positives in life. Never giving up . . ."

"Stupid," Kate agreed, a little smile playing on her lips. "Really silly."

"And so I thought that maybe running away was a bit of a pathetic thing to do. Elizabeth Stallwood would at least have me challenge Joe to a duel or something. Give you a chance to make an informed choice."

"A choice?" Kate said, grinning now.

Tom looked down at the ground, then back at her. "Kate, I . . . I like you. I always have. No, that's not even it. I love you, Kate. I love everything about you. I've even grown to love this book—this dangerous book with its really quite disastrous fashion tips. I want to be your romantic hero, Kate. I want to be the one who sweeps you off your feet and rides off into the sunset with you slung over the back of my horse. And if I can't be that, then at least let me be the person on your reserve list. In case the hero gets waylaid. Held up—"

Kate kissed him. "How about you just be the love of my life?" she whispered hoarsely. "The one I can't wait to get home to. The one I would really like to hold me right now?"

"Like this?" Tom said, leaning down and embracing her.

"Exactly like that," Kate breathed, pressing her head into his neck.

"At least let me wear a jaunty hat." Tom laughed, kissing her lips, her nose, her forehead, and then her lips again.

"The thing is, Tom, I'm not a hopeless romantic anymore," Kate said seriously.

"But you have to be," Tom said, a hurt expression on his face. "You've converted me completely, and you've hooked Sal in, too, by the looks of things. You can't turn pragmatic on us now. Please."

Kate shook her head. "I'm sorry, Tom. I'm just not."

Then she grinned mischievously. "I'm a hope*ful* romantic, instead." She reached up to kiss Tom again. "After all, what's this if not a happy ending?"

TITTLE-TATTLE MAGAZINE
YOU'LL HEAR IT FIRST HERE!
MARCH 19, 2006

CHANTELLE says she shan't tell about latest love intrigue, *page 5*

Makeover queen **BETTY CONWAY** tells all about her new career in front of the camera and why cancer was the best thing that ever happened to her, *page 11*

DOCTOR LOVE: exclusive photographs of **KATE HETHERINGTON** enjoying a break with new man Dr. Tom Whitson in Barbados, *page 13*

Ex–television presenter Penny Pennington announces engagement to Kate Hetherington's ex, Joe Rogers, and the couple reveals plans for their new reality show, **PENNY AND JOE**, a 24/7 look at their happy life together, *page 78*

HOT GOSSIP!
★ WE KNOW CELEBS ★
JULY 2006

BIG BROTHER brouhaha on live television—we have all the gory details, *page 7*

Kate Hetherington on her directorial debut, a documentary following her boyfriend Dr. Tom Whitson and **MEDECINS SANS FRONTIERS** on a journey into Kabul's forgotten suburbs, *page 12*

Penny Pennington and Joe Rogers on being **DROPPED BY THEIR CABLE CHANNEL**, Joe's fight with **ALCOHOLISM**, and their hopes for their new singing careers, *page 92*

FAB!

THE NEW ESSENTIAL WEEKLY

OCTOBER 2006

Why **JAMES HOFFMAN,** star of **OVER HERE, OVER THERE,** is desperate to put his gorilla days behind him, *page 7*

KATE HETHERINGTON seen shopping with best friend and godson. **FAB!** asks: Is she getting broody herself? *Page 11*

PENNY PENNINGTON reveals why she didn't want to be on **CELEBRITY BIG BROTHER** anyway and is relieved that they turned her down, *page 99*

CHAT!

YOU KNOW YOU WANT TO . . .

DECEMBER 2006

GOLDEN COUPLE TO TIE THE KNOT? Kate Hetherington and beau spotted in Tiffany's—we have the photos to prove it, *page 9*

Betty Conway and gorilla-man-turned-heartthrob-actor James Hoffman hit LA with their new show, **MAKING DREAMS COME TRUE**—we have the low-down plus exclusive behind-the-scenes pics, *page 15*

Former celebs Penny Pennington and Joe Rogers are hoping to reignite their failing careers by signing up to **CAST-OFF,** a new reality television program that pits ex–celebrity couples against each other, living on a desert island off the coast of Australia with no amenities and nothing but what they can catch to eat. Read all about it on *page 103*

◆ ◆

THE HOPELESS ROMANTIC'S HANDBOOK

Condition: Used

Description: Are you a hopeless romantic? Do you long for love and passion, and feel disappointed and let down by the reality of dating? Don't despair. The Hopeless Romantic's Handbook will save you. The Hopeless Romantic's Handbook is a handbook for life. Romance is yours for the taking; you just have to find it. The Hopeless Romantic's Handbook won't just tell you where to look; it will help you every step of the way. This book will change your life—satisfaction is guaranteed—if you don't find true love, get your money back.

Seller: C*P1D25 (kate.whitson@hotmail.co.uk)

◆ ◆

PHOTO: © MILLIE PILKINGTON

GEMMA TOWNLEY is the author of *When in Rome, Little White Lies*, and *Learning Curves*. She lives in London with her husband, Mark.